THE FIRST

WISH OF

MR. MURRAY

McBRIDE

Also by Joe Siple

The Five Wishes of Mr. Murray McBride

The Final Wish of Mr. Murray McBride

Charlie Fightmaster and the Search for Perfect Harmony

The Town with No Roads

The Last Dogs

THE FIRST

WISH OF

MR. MURRAY

McBRIDE

Joe Siple

**UNION
SQUARE
& CO.**

NEW YORK

UNION
SQUARE
& CO.

NEW YORK

UNION SQUARE & CO. and the distinctive Union Square & Co. logo
are trademarks of Sterling Publishing Co., Inc.

Union Square & Co., LLC, is a subsidiary of Sterling Publishing Co., Inc.

ISBN 978-1-4549-6114-7

For information about custom editions, special sales, and premium purchases,
please contact specialsales@unionsquareandco.com.

Printed in Canada

2 4 6 8 10 9 7 5 3

unionsquareandco.com

Cover design and art by Patrick Sullivan
Cover images: Classic Picture Library/Alamy (couple reference);
Packaging Monster (road pattern)/Shutterstock.com
Interior design by Rich Hazelton

This book is dedicated to everyone living with dementia, and to those who care for them.

PROLOGUE

30 Miles Outside Waukegan, Illinois
1864

In a matter of minutes, Sean Brennan would be an orphan. His father lay under the hot sun, nearly hidden beneath the tall alfalfa that swayed in the breeze. Blood continued to flow from a deep gash in his upper leg. A scythe lay menacingly nearby.

Sean hadn't seen the accident, but he'd come running when he heard his father's cry. Now, there was nothing to do but hold his father's hand and watch as the face he knew so well slowly turned pale, then ashen.

"It's too soon," his father whispered, and Sean thought, *Of course it's too soon. What will I do without a father?*

Sean considered running to find help. But his ten-year-old legs were as paralyzed as his ten-year-old mind. Besides, if these were to be his father's final minutes, Sean knew he needed to stay.

"I never told you," his father said. "I was only waiting for you to be old enough. But I waited too long."

"You'll be okay," Sean said. Although the futility of his attempt to provide comfort was obvious, it was all he could think to say. Just a few minutes before, he and his father had been harvesting alfalfa under a clear Midwestern sky, not a care in the world. How could this be happening?

"Listen to me, Sean."

It didn't make any sense. How could the world shift so completely, so quickly? "You'll be okay," he said again.

"Listen to me!" The desperation in his father's voice snapped Sean from his thoughts. "I buried it."

Sean had no idea what his father was talking about. He buried it? Buried what? What could be so important that his father would use his dying breath to utter those words?

His father's voice was barely a whisper and fading fast. "To keep it safe. From fire. An old church. The beautiful . . . a dirt floor . . . a graveyard . . . the hillside." His eyes widened, and he struggled to swallow. "From your mother."

Vertigo threatened to overtake Sean. His mother had died just days after giving birth to him. He had no memories of her.

With his free hand, Sean's father reached into the pocket of his overalls, his fingers searching.

"I don't understand," Sean said. The sun beat down on them, so hot Sean could feel his skin burn, and yet the alfalfa smelled sweet. "What's buried? What church? I don't know what you're saying."

His father licked his leather-dry lips and tried to swallow again. His eyelids drooped heavily, and his pupils rolled back before finding Sean's gaze again. "Your mother."

Sean knew the moment was upon him. His father couldn't keep his eyes open. His hold on Sean's hand was weakening. Then, with one last gathering of strength, his father put his other hand on Sean's and looked him straight in the eye.

"A treasure . . . worth more . . . than . . . gold."

And then his eyes closed and his hand slipped to the ground.

In the palm of his hand, now open to the scorching heat of the sun, lay something Sean hadn't noticed before. He tilted his head to get a better look. All at once, he realized what he was seeing. Despite everything, he felt a flutter in his chest.

It was a small brass key, glinting in the sunlight between his father's motionless fingers.

CHAPTER 1

Lemon Grove, Illinois
1996

I smile at my wife as the brass band plays "The Wedding March," just like it did eighty long years ago. Most people don't even live for eighty years, and here I am, ninety-eight years old and married to the love of my life for longer than most people get to spend on God's green earth. It's quite a day. A day for celebration, and that's a fact.

It's an extraordinary accomplishment, according to the people who dutifully walk through the greeting line to shake our hands as they try to think of a compliment appropriate for the situation. People have their typical compliments for twenty-five-year anniversaries and fifty-year anniversaries, for milestone birthdays like twenty-one and forty. But I have the feeling, as person after person I barely recognize shakes my hand and tells me how impressed they are, that both Jenny and I are a novelty more than a loved family member or close friend. Get to be our age, and most of those have passed on. Now we're like something out of a zoo rather than loved ones. But at least we're in the zoo together.

With Jenny sitting quietly at my side, I accept the awkward congratulations. What else am I supposed to do? My grandson, Chance, arranged this whole event out of little more than obligation, most likely. Maybe a way to draw attention to himself, through my unique "accomplishment" with Jenny. I barely recognize anyone in the crowd. Don't have a clue who most of them are. Something tells me the details of this little shindig were handled by Chance's second wife, Olivia, who's currently pressing her soft hands into my cheeks and crying.

Doesn't make any sense to me, why this lady I barely know is squishing up my cheeks, and that's the God's honest truth of the matter. But I smile because that's what zoo animals are for— the enjoyment of the customers. It's not about the animals—not about their beauty, their interesting histories, or unique aspects that make them special; no, it's all about the people who've come to see them. The paying customers, as it were.

When Olivia moves on from me and turns her attention to Jenny, I squeeze my wife in tight to my side. Spend a whole bunch of decades with the same person as your partner in life and you get a little protective, and I'm fully willing to admit I might be a bit overprotective of Jenny at this point. Just stands to reason, I figure. I'll protect this woman until my dying day. Or hers, if she goes first.

"You look so beautiful," Olivia says, and she squeezes Jenny's cheeks up just the way she did to me. "Thank God for you two, and thank God for your marriage."

She moves her hands down to Jenny's hands and pats them like she's trying to figure out if they're real. Or maybe she just wants to know what ninety-nine-year-old skin feels like. People are strange like that.

Sandpaper, by the way. But sandpaper that tears like a wet Kleenex. Pretty amazing stuff. Couldn't grow it in a lab, far as I know.

One of the last people to come through the line is a man with a camera. From the local newspaper, he says. I've been reading the *Lemon Grove Gazette* for decades, so I perk right up when

I hear that. The man asks if he could take our picture, and I say sure he can. "Just give us a moment."

I lean over and whisper into Jenny's ear. Then I press my cracking lips against her wrinkled cheek. I'm pleasantly surprised when she beams from ear to ear just as the photographer snaps a photograph of the two of us.

You're beautiful.

That's what I said into her ear. And I meant it too, just like I did when I was twelve, and twenty-two, and ninety-two. A stunner, that's what she is. Always has been. And her looks have never even been her best quality.

"Speech!" someone yells from the crowd.

It looked for a bit like I was going to get out of this here obligation. Several people have already wandered toward their cars, ready to head back to their lives with a little story to tell about the ancient couple they once saw. Can you believe it? She was ninety-nine, and he was ninety-eight. Married eighty years!

I don't particularly care, to tell the truth. Let them have their story. That's what zoo animals are for. But a speech? That's something else entirely.

Still, the voice—which I realize now belongs to my grandson, Chance—has caught everyone's attention. And, it seems, their imagination. What could a man as old as the carburetor come up with to say at his eightieth anniversary? They probably think I won't even be able to get to my feet. Well, if for no other reason than to prove them wrong, I stand and accept the microphone from Chance's second wife.

I guess I should have planned for this, but I didn't. I have absolutely no idea what I should say. But I smile warmly at this woman sitting next to me, who's been such an integral part of my life ever since I can remember. The mother of our children. My partner through thick and thin. And we've had both, believe me.

I stand and gaze down at her with all my love. I'll rely on her presence and those stunning ocean-green eyes to be my muse.

"Well," I say into the microphone, and a surge of feedback screeches through the speakers, causing several people to cover their ears with their hands. Some start to a speech.

"Apologies," I say. "All this technology . . . we didn't have microphones back when I was a lad."

This gets a few chuckles, but the strained look on their faces tells me they're just humoring me. Well, that's just fine. I'm not here for them anyway. Whoever they are. I'm here for Jenny. So instead of talking to all those strangers out there, I decide to just forget them. I'm talking to Jenny, and that's that. I turn my undivided attention to her beautiful face.

"I've known you my whole life," I say. "Sure, there might have been a few years of breathing before we met, but it wasn't life. Not for me, anyhow. The day I met you is the day I started living. And the day I lose you will be the day that living stops for me, no matter who goes first."

A lady wearing satin-looking pants and a tight, low-cut shirt takes a tissue from her pocket and taps at her eyes. The priest next to her smiles his approval, but it's not Father Paul. Everyone out there seems fully engaged in what I'm saying, but they're just a distraction. I turn my attention back to Jenny.

"Now, we've had some hard times, sure, like any married couple. But we've always been a team. No matter how hard things got, I always knew that. You were in my corner and I was in yours. No matter what."

I use my left thumb to spin my wedding ring around my finger. The gold is scratched and beaten, but it's still there. Hasn't been above my knuckle in decades, to tell the truth. At this point, I'm not sure I could get it off if I wanted to. But that's just fine with me, because why would I want to?

"And now they tell us it's been eighty years. Well, I for one don't have a clue where all those years went, but I know that I'm forever grateful I got to spend them with you."

I look deep into her ocean-greens, trying to see them anew, these eyes I've looked into an infinite number of times. Sure enough, they still knock the wind out of me.

"I love you, Jenny McBride. I've loved you since the day I first met you." I pause, feel a crooked smile on my old, wrinkly face, and say, "Well, maybe the second or third day. You terrified me at first."

Another round of chuckles emerges from the guests. But I plow on, focused only on Jenny. "I'll love you until the day I die, sweetheart. After that, my soul will love you for all eternity. For the last eighty years, you have made me the luckiest man in the history of the world."

I lean over and gently kiss her forehead. When I straighten back up, I can't read the expression on her face. "I love you, Jenny. I love you more than life."

I lower the microphone, and the entire crowd explodes in a thunderous applause. The teary woman doesn't bother wiping her face with her tissue anymore. The priest next to her is clapping so hard it hurts my hands to watch. Everyone around them joins in, celebrating the old man's love for his wife.

But as loud as they clap and cheer and shout, it's not quite loud enough to cover Jenny's soft voice, magnified by the microphone, which I've left dangling just close enough to pick up every one of her words as she looks up at me and says:

"Who are you?"

* * *

It was May 2, 1994. Two years, four months, and five days ago. We'd been living in our little house in Lemon Grove for round about seventy-eight years, Jenny and me. That's when she first forgot where the house was.

She'd gone out to get a few groceries from the supermarket. It was something we both took pride in, our independence. The fact that our old age—some even called it "extreme old age"—didn't stop us from living our lives. Most people hit ninety and stop doing things. Now, it's no fault of their own, mind you. The Good Lord created us to grow old, to slow down, to age. On one hand we get the wisdom that comes with that. On the other, we get bodies that slowly stop working. It's all part of the deal.

But Jenny and I, for reasons I'll never know, we were given some sort of gift. A few more years of health and vitality than most people get. And we've been able to do it together. If anyone tries to tell me that either one of us would have had that extra vitality without the presence and support and love of the other, I'd tell that person to stick his ear in a jar of raspberry jam. If it weren't for Jenny, I'd have followed my boys right after their lives came to an end. But I didn't. Because of Jenny.

Maybe that's why it scared me as much as it scared her when she forgot who I was at the anniversary gathering. That's never happened before, and the fact that we knew the time would come did nothing for the shock and helplessness I felt, just as much as she felt in that moment.

Actually, that's not true. That moment was terrifying for me, sure. But I can't imagine the disorientation, then the confusion, and finally, the fear Jenny must have felt.

Now the sun comes up on the following morning while I watch her sleeping calmly in our bed, hoping she'll be better today. And I try to figure out what on God's green earth I'm supposed to do if she's not.

At eight o'clock, having finished my breakfast and taken my pill, our full-time nurse, Deb, who also happens to be our neighbor, taps on the door right on time. Same thing, every morning. Deb taps lightly on the door, smiles wordlessly so we don't wake Jenny, and I make my way—walking on my own, mind you—to St. Joseph's Catholic Church and back.

Deb really is a saint. But unfortunately, she's also hanging up the spikes, so to speak. I guess it all worked out—just as Jenny was showing signs that she needed another level of care beyond what Deb and I could give, Deb was trying to find a way to retire. We all decided the two things could happen at the same time. So when Chance and Olivia offered to host an anniversary party for us, we had them schedule it as our final little shindig, and Jenny was able to get a room at the new memory care center Doc Keaton says is so top-notch. Yesterday, the party. Tomorrow, we move into Aspen Leaves.

Technically, Jenny moves in. But I put up enough of a fuss that they finally relented and agreed to put two beds in the room, so I can basically live there, too. We'll still have the house, of course, but I'll be damned if I'm going to abandon my wife. Where she goes, I go. Simple as that. It's that protector in me again, I suppose.

As I approach the end of the block, my grandson Chance leans his head out the driver's side window of a small moving truck. He must see the shocked look on my face because he's talking before the truck even comes to a stop.

"Don't worry, Granddad," he says before I can get a word in. "It's not as much stuff as it looks like."

"I should hope not," I yell back into the road. "I thought we had an agreement, you and me."

"We do, Granddad, but it's just a few things. I'm sure Grandma won't mind. She seemed happy about Olivia and me staying at the house. And it's not even for the whole remodel. Just until they get the kitchen wall taken out."

"The agreement was you wouldn't move anything into the house until we got your grandmother moved into Aspen Leaves. That's tomorrow, not today."

"It was Grandma's idea, remember? She wanted us to stay at the house during the remodel. She was the one who said that staying in a hotel was ridiculous, remember?"

Of course I remember. The question is, does Jenny? What'll probably happen here is Chance will show up at our house with a truckload of his things and Jenny won't have any recollection as to why. She'll get confused, then scared, and all because Chance decided that breaking our agreement was no big deal. Well, of course he thinks that. He won't be around for the fallout.

"I have to get these things dropped off so I can get back to work," Chance says. "Don't worry, I'll make sure to stay out of Grandma's way."

And with that, the truck's engine roars and Chance's hand waves out the window as he pulls down the road and into my driveway.

Part of me—the protector—wants to make my way back to the house and help Jenny understand what's happening. But Deb is there for that and besides, by the time I'd be able to get all the way back to the house, whatever's going to happen will already have happened.

So I put my trust in Deb, turn away from the house, and make my way around the block. Not long after, I lift my feet one at a time up the stone steps of St. Joseph's, amazed at how hard it's become to climb these stairs.

Back in my youth, back when I was playing professional baseball for the Chicago Cubs, my feet danced around with the slightest effort. I could jump, spin, sprint, and twirl, and not even break a sweat.

Now, just climbing the twelve stone steps to the church pushes my heart rate to frightening levels. And lately, this right knee's been giving me fits. Nothing unusual, mind. Pain is pain is pain once you reach ninety-five, in my experience at least. But the knee pain isn't just knee pain anymore. It shoots up and down my leg at the smallest misstep.

Welcome to "extreme old age," I guess.

But I make it up the stairs. I always make it. I might be slow, I might have to put up with discomfort that's becoming all-out pain, but I always make it. I just keep going. Sometimes I wonder if the Good Lord ever plans to take me. If he wants my input on the matter, I'd point out that it would be awful convenient to take me at the same time he takes Jenny. Simplify the logistics and all, see?

A bright sliver of sunlight slices into the church as I open the large, wooden door. Dust motes fill the sunbeams, but they disappear with the closing of the door behind me. I limp my way to the first pew I come to—the last row of the church—and ease myself onto the hard hickory bench.

As my eyes adjust to the relative darkness, the man in the priest get-up I saw in the crowd at the anniversary party sweeps a broomstick back and forth up near the altar. When he notices me sit, he puts his broom down and makes his way to the back of the church. When he arrives, he sits directly next to me.

I scowl and slide back several inches. I like some time and space when it comes to new people. If I don't know someone well, I don't get all touchy-feely. The priest seems to get the hint at least, and slides in the other direction a good foot, putting a reasonable amount of space between us.

"Where's Father Paul?" I say, which isn't much of a greeting, I know.

The man has dark eyes, dark hair, and a dark beard. Still, he somehow seems to resonate light, which is a pretty neat trick. "He was moved to a parish on the south side of Chicago. I guess the Lord decided he was needed there."

I grunt. "You mean the diocese decided." I've never been a fan of how the church lets a priest stay in one place just long enough to build a relationship with his congregation, only to rip up all those roots and send him off somewhere else.

"I'm Father James Gonzalez," the man says, and he reaches his hand toward me. I don't like the fact that a new priest has been brought in, and I especially don't like that they did it just before our anniversary party. Father Paul didn't even make it to the festivities. Instead, this stranger showed up, as if anyone in a collar was the same as all the rest. Still, I was brought up right, so I give the new priest's hand a firm shake.

"Mr. Murray McBride," I say. "You can call me Murray, since you're a man of God and all."

The corners of the priest's mouth turn up slightly. "And you can call me Father James, if you're okay with that."

"Why wouldn't I be okay with that? A man should be called what he wants to be called."

Father James's smile grows, and I get the feeling the priest likes me, for some odd reason. Well, he better. With Jenny's condition, I have a feeling I might soon be spending a lot of time in this church.

"It was a beautiful party you had," he says. "And a touching speech. In all my life, I don't think I've ever met a couple who have been married for eighty years, and I've met a lot of married couples. It's truly remarkable."

I'm not sure what to say to that. Should I point out that I didn't, in fact, invite him to the party? Actually, I didn't invite anyone. Chance's second wife took care of the details. But even she didn't send a personal invitation to this man. It was addressed specifically to Father Paul. And yet, the one who'd shown up was this young fellow.

Or should I explain that eighty years isn't some sort of accomplishment, like everyone insists, because each and every one of those years was a privilege? After all, it's a rare man lucky enough to spend his entire life with the woman he loves. In the end, I mumble a "Thank you," because that seems most likely to be what Father James is looking for.

"And how is Jenny?" Father James asks. He leans in a little, but he does it in a nonthreatening manner—just tipping his forehead toward me—so I don't mind his proximity too much this time. His voice is pretty comforting, it turns out. Actually, his presence isn't too annoying either, now that he's given me some space. "I heard she was having some health issues," he says.

He was there. He heard what she said through the microphone. Everyone did. I guess he's trying to be gentle or sympathetic or something. But I'm no child, so there's no reason to treat me like one.

"Alzheimer's," I say defiantly. I hate the very sound of the word. Poor chap, that Alzheimer. Discover a disease, do a bit of good for science, and what do you get? People hate the sound of your name for the rest of eternity, that's what.

"I'm sorry, Murray. That must be hard. Terribly hard."

I nod. "Can't say I know what to do about it. Some days she's almost like normal, but those don't happen as much anymore. Not for a good while now, to tell the truth. But forgetting who I am? Me? The man she's been married to for so long?" I shake my head, trying to clear the pain and confusion. "It's never been that bad before."

I shift in the pew. They don't make these things comfortable for an old man, and that's the truth. "I keep thinking she might get better," I say. "But Doc Keaton says I should let that hope go and just focus on giving her all the love I can." I wipe at the corner of my eye. "Good man, Doc Keaton. Smart man."

"I'm sure he is," Father James says.

"We're moving her into Aspen Leaves tomorrow morning, eight a.m. sharp. Apparently we were lucky to get a room, but it doesn't feel like luck. It'll be hard, I think. For both of us."

We sit in silence for several moments after that, but for some reason it isn't awkward. I can't explain it; I spoke my first word to Father James just a few minutes ago, and here I am spilling my guts to him like I've known him all my life. Well, he is a man of God, after all.

I hear a small whooshing sound from the bank of candles flickering in a far corner of the church. "What is it you came here for, Murray?" Father James finally asks. "What are you seeking?"

"I don't rightly know," I say, and I think on the question. "I guess I'm trying to figure out what to do, now that I can't be sure if my own wife will even recognize me anymore."

"And if she doesn't?" Father James says.

"What's that?"

"I said, what if she doesn't know who you are anymore? What if you go home from here and your wife doesn't recognize you? What if that's how it is now?"

I shift uncomfortably and feel my teeth clench. Father James doesn't seem to notice, so he keeps at it.

"What if she never recognizes you again?" he asks. "What will you do, Murray, if she turns into someone different from the woman you've always known?"

He's poking at me, although I don't know why, and sure enough a flare of anger jumps into my gut. I don't know what Father James is trying to accomplish here, but I came here for help and comfort, not so some priest I've never met can point out all the terrible things likely to happen.

"What are you trying to say?" I ask, and I don't try to mask the defiance in my voice. "You think I can't handle it? You think I can't take care of my own wife?" My teeth are clenched tight now, and my fists are following suit.

"That's not what I'm saying at all." Father James's voice is soft, calming. "You said you're trying to figure out what to do. I'm simply asking you to think it through. What will you do if Jenny never recognizes you again? What will that do to your love for her? Will it go away? Disappear into thin air? Right along with her ability to recognize you?"

"My love for her?" I realize I'm standing over Father James without having decided to stand. I shake my fist at him. "How dare you question my love for her. My wife means everything to me, always has. There's nothing she could do or say—nothing that could happen—that could change my love for her. Nothing, you hear me?"

Father James slowly stands from the pew, until he's drawn up right next to me. His smile is soft and understanding. His black eyes sparkle. He touches my wrist and looks straight at me, making sure I'm listening.

"Good," he says. "No matter what happens, Murray. Remember that."

＊   ＊   ＊

I'm a little ruffled when I leave the church. No one's been able to get me riled up like Father James just did for a good long time. Everyone's always so tentative around someone as old as me. It's like they see how physically fragile I am and assume I'm just as unable to handle anything emotionally challenging. But I understand what he was up to now, and I'm grateful.

He's a good man, Father James. I can tell you that already.

The church is only a block and a half from the house, just down to the end of Maple and then along the sidewalk of Fifth Street. But at my speed, it gives me plenty of time to think on things. Lately, there's been a lot to think on, like what's going on in Jenny's brain right now.

I don't know much about the brain. Sure, I've spent some time down at the public library, where a friendly librarian named Helen helps me check out books with titles that include phrases like "emerging neuroscience" and "cognitive decline" and even "miracle cure." But I still don't understand how an entire life could up and disappear on someone, along with all the people they've ever loved.

And the way the disease has played out makes no sense either. How can Jenny remember what she'd been wearing the day her little sister was diagnosed with polio as an eight-year-old child, but she can't remember what she ate for breakfast a half hour before, even though the house still smells like bacon?

In a strange way, I guess I'm lucky. Since Jenny and I met so early in our lives, I'm included in most of those long-ago memories that remain miraculously untouched. It's a very different version of me, of course, but it's better than my wife confusing me for some other man. Say, Ernie Wells, for example.

Jenny's memories can be almost therapeutic sometimes, even though she seems to think things from the past are happening now. Lately, she'll talk as if she thinks it's 1910, or 1940, or 1985. As hard as it is to see her confused and unable to be present in this current time, there's an element of comfort in joining her in the past, because it's our past. Sure, her life is fading before her very eyes, but the parts that remain are little shelters for the two of us.

But when she didn't recognize me at the anniversary party, I knew Doc Keaton was right. It's time for Jenny to get the help she needs. The help I'm not able to give her. It'll be hard, moving into that home. But I'll be with her every step of the way. They'd have to pry me away from her, and I dare them to try. I can be a mean old rooster when it comes down to it, I can tell you that much.

"I'm home, love," I announce as I cross the threshold of the front door. Several of Chance and Olivia's things are stacked in the corner, but I try not to let that bother me. I'm happy they'll be using our house while theirs is being remodeled, but he could have waited to move things in until tomorrow, like we'd agreed.

I catch Deb's eye and raise my eyebrows questioningly, the flicker of hope in my chest aching to jump into a full flame. Thankfully, mercifully, Deb doesn't even get an answer out before Jenny's twinkle of a voice drifts in from the bedroom, saying, "My Murray!" in that same old way.

Deb pats my hand as she walks past on her way to the kitchen. "She just woke up ten minutes ago. By the looks of it, she's having a good day." She leans in and whispers, "Make sure you enjoy it, now."

Deb makes herself some breakfast—we let her do that for free—and I make my way into the bedroom to find Jenny. She's sitting up against the headboard, leaning against a pile of pillows with a sheepish look on her face. Like she just stole a cookie from the cookie jar.

"I'm sorry, Murray. Deb told me about yesterday. At the party."

"What are you talking about?" I say, and I sit right next to her on the bed. I take her hand in mine and hold it for all it's worth. "You have nothing to be sorry for."

"But it was supposed to be such a happy time. Deb wouldn't say it, of course, but I can read between the lines. I know I ruined everything."

"You didn't ruin anything, you hear? Not a thing. It was a wonderful party, everybody says so."

"Like who?" she says. When I hesitate, she shakes her head sadly. "Deb told me what I said, Murray, and that the microphone picked it up. I don't even remember saying it, or why in the world I ever would. Asking who you are. You, of all people. My Murray, and I couldn't even remember you."

"You remember me now, don't you?"

"Of course I do," Jenny says, and she plants a kiss on my cheek just for good measure. "But it scares me, Murray, and I know it scares you, too. No use pretending. Before too long, not remembering is going to be more normal than remembering. A while after that . . . poof." She flicks her hands into the air like a bursting bubble.

It's so beautiful, the way she talks about it. Of course, we both know the hard times that lay in front of us, or at least we can imagine them. But to see Jenny now, eyes sparkling, talking about her disease and her brain and this whole terrible situation as if it's nothing more than a fluff of dandelion seeds floating through the air. "Poof," she says! In this moment, I couldn't love her more.

Part of me wants to disagree with her. Tell her that I'll make sure that doesn't happen. I'll take care of her. I'm her protector, after all. I'll make things right. Or, short of that, it won't be so bad. For-getting will be peaceful and comfortable, nothing to worry about.

But I love her too much to lie to her like that, and she wouldn't believe me if I did. So instead, I wrap my arm around her and squeeze. That says all I need to say.

"Is there anything I can do for you, love? Anything at all?"

I think she understands what I'm saying. Tomorrow morning, we're off to Aspen Leaves. So today's our last chance, in a way. Our last little bit of freedom.

Jenny rotates her body a bit so she can look right in my eyes. Her neck doesn't bend quite as much as it did once upon a time. "I've been thinking a lot this morning," she says. "Remembering things. Maybe because I understand that my memories are leav-ing me, I want to spend a bit more time with them. Does that make any sense?"

"All the sense in the world," I say. "What have you been remembering?"

"Oh, all sorts of things. Good things and bad things . . . a per-son gets both in a life, as you know. But I've lived a lucky life, haven't I? You and I both. Together."

"That's the truth if I've ever heard it," I say. "The God's hon-est truth."

"Just think of the adventures we've shared," she says, nuzzling in a little closer. She must have put on a bit of her favorite perfume while I was away this morning because I can smell it—jasmine and peach and something deeper, more raw. She's been wearing the same perfume since she was a young woman and it makes the memories come back in waves.

"Too many to count," I say. "All the trips we've taken, the places we've seen. New York and San Francisco and London."

"Paris," Jenny says, and for the next several minutes we're quiet. A montage of color, romance, and wine flash across my mind. If Jenny's thoughts are anything like mine, she's feeling young again, if only for the moment.

Finally, Jenny breaks the silence. "I was thinking just before you got home about how we met. Do you remember that?"

"Of course I remember. How could I forget?"

"Well, something came to me when I was thinking back on that time. Something I hadn't thought of in many years. Of course, it's so far back now, I can't be sure if it's a real memory or if I invented it. Do you understand that?"

"I do," I say.

There are more than a few "memories" I have that I'm pretty sure aren't actual memories of an actual event. Either they're stories I told myself over and over until they became real in my mind, or they're just snapshots of memory invented from a picture I saw.

Take, for instance, an old photo of Jenny and me in the stands at a Cubs game, after I'd retired. I look at that picture and feel like the memory is so clear, until I try to remember anything about that day other than the exact moment captured in that picture.

Who were the Cubs playing that day? Did we get a hot dog from the concession stand? Was it sunny or cloudy? The truth is, I can't remember a darn thing about that day, other than the moment in the photograph. If it weren't for the picture, I'm pretty sure I would have forgotten it altogether, like most other moments in this long life. So, is that a real memory or just an image I've seen enough times to make me think I remember it?

"What came to you?" I ask Jenny. "What's the memory?"

"Well, I'm not sure if you recall, and maybe it isn't even real. But . . . do you remember a key?"

"A key, you say?"

"Yes. A little, rusted metal key. Esther had it, I believe. She took it from a drawer in our home."

The mention of Esther feels like a little jab to my stomach, even now. But the memory of the key comes back, along with everything that happened so long ago. I shake my head in wonder. "I think about Esther often, but I haven't thought about that key for decades. I guess I blocked it out . . . you know, because of everything."

I'm not sure if Jenny does know, not sure if she can remember. The key was such a big thing in our lives, and it had such enormous consequences. But it was so long ago, and there were good reasons to move on.

But time heals all wounds, as they say. I don't know if I believe that, but it does tend to smooth over the rough edges. And as I think on it now, all I can see in my mind is Jenny's young face. All I can hear is Esther's infectious laugh.

Smooth edges, indeed.

"Do you remember what it was supposed to open?" Jenny asks. "That key. Why we were so excited about it?"

I don't even have to think about it. A phrase I haven't thought of in decades pops into my mind like it never left. Like it has always been sitting just below the surface of my thoughts, waiting for the right moment to bubble back up.

"A treasure worth more than gold," I say. "Esther said that whatever the key opened would reveal a treasure worth more than gold."

Jenny pulls back so she can knock me out with her ocean-greens. "I used to sit up at night wondering what it could possibly be. Emeralds? Sapphires? What could be worth more than gold?" She squints into space, concentrating. "I used to imagine the key would open an ancient trunk, and a trail of mist would come out, like a genie from a lamp. I'd breathe it in, and when it cleared, the treasure would lay before me."

"It was similar for me," I say. "The old trunk, anyway. I didn't imagine a genie, though. Just the treasure. And even though Esther said the contents were worth more than gold, I envisioned gold bars anyhow. That and diamonds."

Jenny takes my hand in hers. "You asked what you can do for me, Murray. That's what you can do. That's what I want. I want to find that treasure. Today."

"Well, now," I say. "I understand why you might want that, but I'm afraid it's not very realistic, love. I'd give you anything I can, but I think that one's a bit beyond my abilities. Besides, you already went looking for it again. After we'd grown up, remember? Back, what, forty years ago? You spent months looking all over for that key and the church where the treasure was supposed to be buried. Drove up to the Fox River over and over, searching. But you never found it, remember? If you couldn't find it when you were younger and the memories were fresher, I just don't see how we'd be able to find it now. Especially in just one day."

Plus, I don't have any interest in digging up the past. Some of the things that would come up with it would be too painful. But I don't say that part since I'm not sure how much Jenny is remembering just now.

"Well," Jenny says. "Maybe to start you could just tell me the story. There's no harm in that, is there?"

"No," I say. "No harm in that, I suppose."

The fact is, I'm relieved. Forty years ago, when Jenny spent all that time searching for the treasure but hadn't been able to find it, she'd practically begged me to go looking with her. I made up excuse after excuse until she finally stopped asking, but the truth was that I simply didn't want to remember everything that had happened way back when.

Because of those things buried in the past, I'm not too keen on telling Jenny the story now either. But I did ask what I could do for her, and telling a story doesn't seem like too much to ask.

"Of course, I only know the story from my perspective," I say. "What you remember could be completely different."

"That's fine," Jenny says, and she squeezes my hand. "That's perfect, actually. So you'll tell me the story of the buried treasure?"

"Of course I will," I say. "Where would you like me to start?"

"Start with how we met. I love that part of the story."

"So do I," I say with a chuckle. My laugh makes us both bounce a little as we lean back against the headboard of the bed, Jenny's cheek resting against my chest. "Okay . . ." After a long pause, I say, "I'm not sure how to start something like this."

"Once upon a time," Jenny says brightly. "You should start with 'Once upon a time.'"

"Sounds good, love." I clear my throat, cover her hand with mine, and begin.

"Once upon a time, there was a boy, twelve years of age, who was picked on by all the other boys at his school . . ."

CHAPTER 2

1910

On a windswept gravel schoolyard, a twelve-year-old boy with mismatched socks cradled a book in his arms as he hurried toward the edge of the playground. Murray McBride knew that if one of the bigger, more popular boys caught sight of him, he would be dragged from his hiding place, surrounded by the group of five, and then shoved from one boy to the next.

It wasn't the physical abuse that bothered Murray. He'd rough-housed with his cousins enough to be comfortable with getting a few bumps and bruises, and before his father left the family, he had given Murray more than a few lashings for misbehaving.

It was the look in the boys' eyes when they shoved him that really hurt. Obviously, they didn't respect him, but more than that, they didn't even disrespect him. No more than they could disrespect a toy. At least disrespect would have been something. But it was like they looked through him entirely. Like he wasn't even there. Nothing more than a plaything.

Murray let out a long exhale as he approached a dip in the ground. He ducked into the ditch that ran along the west side of the gravel field, which the school used as a playground. Once settled in the deepest part of the ditch, among the dandelions and dirt patches and browning early-fall crabgrass, he pulled the book from inside his jacket and leaned back, using the bank of the ditch like a comfortable chair.

He was completely protected there. The wind swept over his head instead of into his face. The boys from school were no longer a threat. The sun even peeked out from behind the thick layer of gray clouds that had been dulling the world all morning. He opened the book to the paper bookmark, grateful for the few moments of peace he had found in the middle of what was sure to be a day full of fear.

Just as he decided he was safe, an unexpected voice came down at him from the top of the ditch. "I definitely wouldn't have pegged you for *Little Women*. Even an abridged version."

Adrenaline flooded Murray's veins, sending his heart racing and his throat tightening. He had been sure no one had followed him. And yet, somehow, some girl had. Before the terror paralyzed him, Murray motioned frantically for the girl to get down into the ditch with him.

"What are you doing?" the girl asked, crinkling her brow at Murray's flailing arms. "Do you need help? Should I call Ms. Carson?"

"No!" Murray yell-whispered. "Just get down here. Quick!"

When the girl stepped to the edge of the ditch, Murray could see her more fully. He'd seen her before, but only from a distance. She was a year older, in the eighth-grade room.

If she didn't get out of sight soon, the boys would see her, wonder why she was staring down into a ditch at the edge of the schoolyard, and find Murray sitting in the dirt with a book. So he scrambled up the steep slope and reached his hands out as if to assist her.

"Can I help you?"

The girl eyed the dirty ground skeptically. Murray watched her ocean-green eyes flicker between the ditch and her clean knee-length skirt. But she must have sensed the degree of Murray's panic, because she finally gave a little shrug.

The girl ignored Murray's outstretched hand and made her way down into the ditch by herself. Once there, she looked around with an exaggerated arc of her head, as if taking in a palace or a castle.

"Well, this is nice," the girl said.

Murray wasn't sure how to respond to her sarcasm. When he settled back into his spot and regained control of his breath—relatively sure the girl hadn't been followed—he finally looked at her properly. The moment he did, his lungs stopped working.

It was the strangest sensation Murray had ever felt. Complete paralysis of his outer body at the same time his insides were exploding. The girl's face enchanted him. The light freckles sprinkled across the bridge of her nose were the perfect complement to the shade of green in her eyes, which was like moss on a sunny day after the rain. And beyond her appearance, she carried herself in a way so foreign, so strange, so confident that it terrified him. He suddenly wished she had never come to his ditch, and he fought the urge to run away.

"No one else knows you're here," she said, misinterpreting his fear. "I promise."

Something about those words—*I promise*—hit Murray hard. In his experience, those words meant something terrible was about to happen. His father had promised to return home, but it turned out the promise was only because he was too much of a coward to admit he was leaving for good.

But somehow the look in the girl's eyes made him trust her. It was as if she controlled the world. If she wasn't worried, Murray needn't be.

The girl sat with her legs crossed and looked to the sky. Murray tentatively followed her gaze. Pillowy white clouds sped through clear blue skies.

They were silent for a long moment, which increased Murray's discomfort. Every time he snuck a glance at her, a flash of terror surged through him and he immediately looked away again. The girl, on the other hand, had a serene expression as she tilted her head to the sun. The rays lit her face so Murray could see that the spray of light freckles also covered her eyelids.

Something deep inside Murray wanted to explain that he wasn't afraid of the boys in class. That he could handle himself if he wanted to. He wanted to impress the girl with that declaration, but the lie wouldn't come.

"I guess I was expecting something like *Sherlock Holmes*," the girl said, as if her thoughts were a world away from Murray's. "Or maybe Jules Verne. Isn't it strange that people think boys only read boy authors and girls only read girl authors? Actually, people think that girls read girl authors and boys can't read at all, which seems mostly true to me. That's why I've been watching you."

Murray stared at her, dumbstruck. She'd been watching him?

"Because you read," she said. "I was intrigued." After a long moment of more silence, she said, "Do you also talk?" She stared at him expectantly.

"Boys can read," Murray finally said, cursing himself for not coming up with something more interesting to say.

The girl shrugged. "So you say. Reality suggests otherwise."

Reality suggests otherwise? Murray thought. *Who is this girl?* Before he could think of anything more to say, her eyes lit up and her posture straightened.

"Since you're the only boy I've met who has shown any scrap of evidence that he can read, you should read to me. It can be our recess tradition. I'm big on traditions."

"Read?" Murray said, cursing his stupidity again. "Read what?" He squeezed his book against his chest, wishing he could hide it. Unfortunately, it was in plain view.

"Your book," the girl said. "*Little Women.*" Despite his best attempts, she eyed the beaten book in his hands, the bookmark halfway through. "But maybe you could start over, at the beginning. I've never read it, I'm embarrassed to say." After a short pause during which Murray could've almost sworn her cheeks turned pink, she said, "Not even the abridged version."

Murray shifted his position in the ditch, terrified of the idea of reading aloud to this girl but knowing he was powerless to say no. As if on autopilot, he removed the bookmark, flipped back to the first page, and swallowed hard. The words suddenly seemed utterly ridiculous, especially coming from him. He had never felt more uncomfortable in his entire life.

He clamped his eyes shut, hoping the words would change by the time he reopened them. But, no, the same words stared up at him from the page. Now completely defeated, he gave up any last hope of salvaging his dignity and began to read.

""Christmas won't be Christmas without any presents," grumbled Jo, lying on the rug.""

Fifteen minutes later, Ms. Carson leaned out of the schoolhouse and called her students back inside. Murray, amazed that he'd read most of the first chapter, finished the sentence he was reading and looked up at the girl for the first time since he had begun.

After a moment in which she seemed to be soaking in his last words, she finally met his eyes. It was as if she returned to the real world. "That was beautiful," she said.

Every fiber of Murray's body froze. He had no idea what to do or say. The girl smiled as if she saw him and understood everything about him. The terror he'd felt earlier increased.

"Of course," she said, "your voice for Jo was atrocious. All squeaky and high-pitched."

Murray felt foolish until the girl reached out and touched his forearm gently. She paired the touch with a smile, and Murray realized he'd happily be the biggest fool in the world for her.

When she removed her hand from his arm, a spell seemed to break, and they looked away from each other. They rose from the ditch and wiped dirt from their clothes. The girl seemed to look at him differently now, but not with the mocking smirk he had expected after he'd read from *Little Women*. If he didn't know better, he would have said it was a look of familiarity. As if the past fifteen minutes had solidified something between them.

"Your name is Murray," she said. "My sister told me."

"Your sister?"

"Esther. She's in your class." When Murray shook his head, the girl said, "The one with crutches."

Of course. Murray had never known her name, but a kid on crutches stood out. Murray had always felt bad for her—she might have been the only person in class who endured more mockery than he did. But he'd never bothered to learn her name. He felt ashamed of that now.

"I think Murray is a really neat name," the girl said. "Do you know mine?"

Murray was amazed to realize he didn't. Shouldn't everyone know the name of the most beautiful girl in the school? Especially considering how kind and confident and friendly she turned out to be? He was saved from his embarrassment when she stuck out her hand as if to make a formal introduction.

"I'm Jenny," she said. "Jenny Brennan."

"I'm Murray. Murray McBride."

Jenny giggled. "I know." She shook his hand firmly, and Murray couldn't believe he was touching her hand. "It's nice to meet you, Murray McBride. I think you and I are going to be friends."

The following morning, Murray had a bounce in his step that he was unable to hide from his mother. He didn't complain about having to go to school. He didn't mope around the house, as if needing to show his displeasure. He even spoke to his mother—unprompted—while eating his bacon and scrambled eggs, asking her what she had planned for the day.

"Work," she said in a long, drawn-out tone, like she was trying to break a code before coming to the end of the word. When Murray nodded thoughtfully, like it was the most interesting thing he had heard in a while, his mother set her fork down and cocked her head to the side. "What's going on with you?"

"Me? What do you mean?"

"Look at you," she said, easing back as if to take in the full view of him. "You haven't been this perky since before your dad left."

Murray turned his eyes back to his breakfast. Any mention of his father still put him in a bad mood, though it had been almost a full year since his dad had packed up and announced that he needed a break. He'd had enough, he'd said. Enough of what, Murray never knew. He never asked, but it only made sense that the answer was him.

"I made a friend," Murray said. Just saying the word *friend* made him fight against a smile. Reading to Jenny in the ditch had been the most enjoyable thing to happen to him in months. He couldn't wait for recess that day.

"A friend," his mom said, and Murray was a bit insulted by the surprise in her voice. "I haven't heard about any friends at school since Leon moved away. I know that was hard for you."

Murray didn't like to think about Leon any more than he liked to think about his father. For all of fifth grade, Leon had been Murray's best friend. His only friend, really. They were outcasts together—Murray because of his small size and high-pitched voice, Leon because of his dark skin. As long as Leon was around, Murray had felt like he could face the world. But when Leon moved to New York, Murray had been left without any friends.

It was a time of hard lessons for Murray, who couldn't understand why people treated Leon differently just because his skin was a different color. Some of the popular kids had blond hair, some brown, some even had red hair, but no one seemed to care. Why was the color of someone's face different than the color of their hair?

But for some reason it was. Murray's mother told him there were actual laws that made it difficult for Black people to live where they wanted to live, go to school where they wanted to go to school, and even vote for who they wanted to represent them.

"But the laws can't be wrong, can they?" Murray remembered asking his mother after Leon had suffered a particularly difficult day at school.

"What's right and what's legal aren't always the same thing," his mother had told him. It was a lesson Murray vowed to never forget.

"What's his name?" his mother asked, bringing him back from his memories.

It took a second for Murray to remember what they were talking about, but as soon as he did, the excitement returned to his voice. "It's not a him," he said. "Every single one of the boys is stupid. They make fun of me because I'm small, even though I'm better than all of them at sports. Or I would be, if I was their size."

"You just haven't hit your growth spurt yet," his mom said for the hundredth time. She sat across the table and grabbed his wrists. "So, tell me about her. What's her name?"

Murray rolled his eyes. He would never admit that he'd hoped she would ask. "Jenny," he said, pretending it was being pried from him.

"Jenny Brennan? Sean and Dottie's oldest?" His mother let go of his wrists and sat back.

Murray shrugged. How was he supposed to know? He'd never heard of Sean and Dottie in his life.

"She's a sweet one," Murray's mother continued. "Her sister, too. Esther, I think her name is? Too bad about the polio, but I hear she still gets around okay. Do you also know Esther?"

"Not really," Murray said. Polio. Crutches. He wondered what it would be like to be defined by something outside his control.

"It was pretty scary for a while, I hear," his mother said. "They weren't sure Esther would make it through." She seemed to finally register the look of annoyance on Murray's face. "Sorry, honey. Tell me about Jenny."

Tell her about Jenny? There was so much he wanted to say— she was beautiful and brave, and she even made fun of him, which was somehow his favorite part. But he couldn't figure out how to say those things. In the end, he shrugged, stabbed some eggs with his fork, and said, "She's nice."

"Well, I'm happy for you." His mother stood abruptly and grabbed her coat. "I have to do a double today, so I won't be home for dinner. You'll be okay by yourself?"

"Yes, Mom," Murray said, dramatizing as much as humanly possible so it sounded like the least important thing in the world. Otherwise she might realize it mattered to him. And she had enough on her plate as it was, dealing with all the bills, the sometimes questionable behavior of her twelve-year-old boy, and the looks of judgment or pity from seemingly everyone in Lemon Grove.

"Good," she said. "Give your mom a kiss."

Murray half-heartedly kissed his mother's cheek and watched her leave through the front door. Turning his attention to the upcoming school day, his heart jumped back into the top of his throat. He focused on the feeling for a moment, curious. He knew the boys at school would mock him for having a crush, but he wasn't sure if that's what this was. He'd never had a crush, so he had nothing to compare the feeling to.

Crush or not, he didn't care. He loved the feeling and understood one part of it perfectly well.

This was what it felt like to have a new best friend.

Murray didn't think life could get any better. Friendship made the leaves of the trees greener and the purple of the wildflowers deeper. It made the scent of the lavender more intense and the song of the robin more peaceful. Friendship changed everything about the experience of living.

As soon as he walked onto school property, his eyes swept the grounds for Jenny. He found her immediately, standing by the door, smiling straight at him as if she'd been waiting for him. The glow in Murray's stomach threatened to burst out of him like rays of sunlight breaking through the clouds.

He waved at exactly the same time she did, which made them both giggle. He wanted to go over and talk to her, or maybe just say hi. But her teacher walked past just then, telling the students it was time to start class. Murray watched Jenny go into the eighth-grade room while he reluctantly entered the one for seventh graders.

The morning dragged on. And on and on and on, as if each minute had somehow become an hour. The pendulum clock on the wall seemed to pause at each side of its swing before slowly, agonizingly, drifting back to the other side. Murray thought the morning might never end.

But then it did, and he sprinted out of the room toward the schoolyard. One of the boys made a comment that included the words *chicken* and *wimp*, which Murray thought was strange because usually he was one or the other but rarely both in the same sentence. It didn't matter in the least.

He continued sprinting until he reached the ditch. He skidded to a stop at the ridge and slid down to the protected bottom, where he waited.

It only took a few minutes before Jenny came running. She appeared at the top of the ditch, then climbed nimbly down next to him in the most beautiful hiding place Murray had ever known.

"Sorry I'm late," she said once they were settled. "Mr. Cash wouldn't stop talking. Did you bring the book?"

Murray never thought he'd be so proud to be holding *Little Women*. "Right here."

"Where were we? The girls had just read the letter from their father, right?"

Murray opened the book and scanned the pages. "That's right. Should I continue where I left off?"

Jenny nodded, her eyes sparkling and her freckles practically glowing. Murray read for several minutes, until he reached the end of the chapter. Then he used his finger as a bookmark and paused to see Jenny's reaction.

"Beautiful," she said. "Just think about them all sitting around together as a family, singing. It's . . . I don't even know the word. *Inspiring* maybe."

"Yes," Murray agreed.

He reopened the book to the start of Chapter Two: A Merry Christmas, and was about to resume reading when a clacking sound from above the ridge of the ditch stopped him. His heart skipped a beat as he envisioned the bullies from his class. But before he could get too worried, the silhouette of a girl appeared.

"You said you'd wait for me," she said. "And show me where you guys hang out."

Murray knew at once who it was. The girl from class who spent all her time drawing in her notepad. Murray knew her by her crutches. But even if she hadn't had them, Murray recognized the way a younger sister talked to an older sister.

"Esther, if you're going to join us, get down here," Jenny said, and Murray also recognized how an older sister talked to a younger sister. "We don't want anyone else seeing where we are."

Murray instinctively jumped to his feet and scampered to the top of the ditch. He took Esther's elbow and helped her down the slope. Once they were settled at the bottom, Esther set her crutches by her side, brushed a strand of hair from her eyes, and pulled a small notepad and pencil from her book bag.

"You don't mind if my sister joins us, do you?" Jenny said.

If Murray was being honest, he did mind. He'd had Jenny to himself for such a small amount of time, and now her little sister was joining them? Sure, she was the same age as him, but it still felt like a little kid crashing his party.

"I can go, if you'd like," Esther said.

Murray jolted from his thoughts. His expression must have given him away. For a moment, he considered taking her up on the offer, but then he saw the look in her eyes and recognized what it meant. It was the look of defeat. As if no matter where she went or who she met, it was always the same. No one wanted the crippled girl around. She was nothing but an annoyance. Murray chastised himself for his initial thoughts. He of all people should know better.

"Of course not," he said. "I'd love to have you join us." He stuck out his hand and smiled at her. "I'm Murray."

"I know. I've seen you in class. I'm Esther, Jenny's sister."

"Great," Jenny said. "Introductions complete. Let's get back to the book."

Murray resettled into his spot and was about to resume reading when Esther surprised him with a question.

"Do you know what treasure would be worth more than gold?" she asked.

"Oh, geez," Jenny said. "Here we go."

"What?" Esther said. "It's just a question."

"I know. It's the same question you ask every single person you meet. And you wonder why you don't have friends."

When Esther's shoulders sagged, Jenny sighed. "I'm sorry. I didn't mean that. It's just . . . you talk about it all the time."

"That's okay," Murray said. "I haven't heard about it yet. A treasure worth more than gold?" he asked.

"Yes. Do you know what it would be?"

"Um, I don't think so." After a moment he said, "I'm not exactly sure what you mean."

Esther's eyes sparkled. "I mean something that's worth more than the most valuable thing you can imagine."

"Oh," Murray said. He scrunched his face in thought. If she was saying it was something beyond what he could imagine, then by definition there would be no way to know what it was. He looked to Jenny for help, but she had turned her attention to the clouds floating through the sky. "No, I don't know what it could be," he said.

"I do," Esther said. "Well, not me exactly, but my family does. Well, I guess not yet. But we hold the secret."

Esther set her notepad and pencil onto the brown grass and reached into the pocket of her jacket. Her movements were slow and dramatic, and Murray barely stifled a laugh. He didn't want to hurt her feelings again.

Esther opened her hand to reveal a small brass key, which she then held up in the sunlight. The key was old and scratched. It looked like it had been buried for two hundred years, then stepped on two hundred times. The shaft bent slightly to the left, and the notches were rounded instead of sharp and jagged. Murray wondered if it could open anything.

He put out his hand when Esther lowered it toward him. She placed it in his open palm and he stared at the key.

"What's it for?"

Esther paused. "I don't know. Not exactly."

"Probably nothing," Jenny said.

"That's not true. And I know you believe it. You told me so."

Murray continued to stare at the key, feeling its weight in his hand. "But you said . . . something worth as much as gold?"

"A treasure worth more than gold," Esther said. "But we don't know what it is yet. We think whatever it is, it's buried in a church, probably somewhere nearby."

"You don't know where, exactly? Or what's buried?"

"No, not for sure," Esther said. "It's been hidden for a long time. My dad doesn't talk about it. The memory is too traumatic, too painful for him, so he tried to forget about it. But my mom told us the story."

"What is it? The story, I mean."

Esther's eyes widened and she adjusted herself in the ditch. Her posture held an intensity that drew Murray in.

"The story goes," she said, and then paused for effect. Jenny smirked at her sister's dramatic voice, but Murray was rapt. "Our grandma and grandpa used to go for long walks. For miles and miles, over the rolling hills, just the two of them, holding hands. My grandma loved looking at old churches all around the country-side, and there were a bunch of them, little ones, all over. But one church was her favorite. The most beautiful of all. But then she died, just after giving birth to our dad."

Esther was quiet for a long moment, but the tension in her shoulders told Murray she wasn't done yet. He waited silently, his eyes never leaving Esther's.

"Somehow, our grandma had a treasure that was supposed to be worth more than gold. Maybe it was passed down to her, maybe she found it herself. No one knows. But when she died, our grandpa realized he needed to keep it safe. The house could burn down. Bandits could come steal it—that was still happening back then. Who knows what might happen? He knew he had to protect it."

Esther nodded slightly and closed her eyes, like she was envisioning what happened next. "So our grandpa went to that church. The one they used to walk to. The one that was our grandma's favorite. And he buried the treasure. Then no one would find it, until he was able to tell his son—our dad—where it was. But before he could tell him, there was an accident on the farm and he died, lying there, bleeding on the field of half-harvested alfalfa."

Jenny burst out laughing, which tore Murray from the spell Esther's story had cast on him.

"It's not funny," Esther snapped. "It's true."

"I'm sorry," Jenny said. "I know it's true. But the way you tell the story . . . I just think you take it a bit too seriously."

Esther gave her sister a dirty look and turned back to Murray.

"I've spent my whole life wondering what it could be. A family heirloom, maybe? No one knows. But," she said, "our grandpa gave our dad some clues, and he gave him that key you're holding. Whatever it opens, it contains a treasure worth more than gold. And I believe it. And so does Jenny."

Jenny just shrugged.

Murray continued moving the key around in the sunlight to get a better look at it. "A family heirloom, you said? So maybe rubies or diamonds?"

Esther shrugged. "I don't know." She looked to the ground for a moment and then all around them, like she was making sure no one could overhear. Her shoulders drooped as she said, "Maybe it's something that can fix someone from being crippled."

Murray swallowed hard and averted his eyes, staring even more intently at the key. Since she hadn't mentioned her handicap, Murray thought it was something she wanted to ignore. And he'd been happy to avoid the awkward silences and uncomfortable conversations that come with acknowledging things like that. But he didn't have a choice now. He was trapped with her in the bottom of a ditch, and she was talking about it.

Murray struggled to find the right words to say next. He almost blurted, *You get around pretty good* or *I didn't even notice you're crippled,* or something else that might close the subject and allow him to get back to reading, which would have been much more comfortable. In the end, he found himself looking straight at her and saying, "I'm sorry."

She smiled like he'd just given her a compliment, and Murray was relieved he hadn't said one of the things he'd almost blurted.

"Thank you," Esther said. "Anyway, I think we should find it. We should go on a quest for buried treasure like the knights of old. The three of us. We'll search every inch of all the churches nearby until we find it. Then we'll unearth it and open it with this key. And then, we'll have a treasure worth more than gold."

Murray had a million questions, and Jenny seemed about to say something, too. But they would both have to wait. At that moment, Ms. Carson's voice carried over the schoolyard, calling her students back inside.

As they gathered their belongings, several things flowed through Murray's mind, but he couldn't decide which one to say. So he didn't say anything as he helped Esther up the slope and they all returned to class.

But his mind was overflowing with possibilities.

CHAPTER 3

1996

Late morning rays of sun slant through our bedroom window. I hold Jenny in my arms, trying to ignore the numbness that's crept into my shoulder where her head lies. If it means making Jenny less comfortable, all the pins and needles in the world couldn't make me move from this position.

"Oh, Murray, what an amazing time that was, wasn't it? We were so young."

"We were," I say. "All of us. You, me, and of course, Esther."

Esther. Both Jenny and I lay in the bed thinking about that amazing young lady, and how important she was in our lives . . . both of our lives.

We spend a couple long moments letting our imaginations run wild. Then Jenny sits up straight in bed and says, "So what do you say, Murray?"

"Say about what, now?"

"About finishing our quest. Finding the treasure."

"Oh, I don't know," I say. For once I was actually hoping she'd forget something. And that's when she goes and remembers? "We've aged a bit," I say. "Not to mention we don't even know where this supposed treasure is. And the logistics of getting there if we did, and Deb is leaving today at noon—"

"Don't think about the details, Murray. Think of the excitement and wonder of it all. Think of what it would feel like to find that key, find whatever it is that it opens, and find a treasure worth more than gold. Aren't you at least curious?"

"Of course I'm curious. Who wouldn't be. But you . . ."

My voice trails off and Jenny turns those ocean-greens on me, which she shouldn't be allowed to do. There's nothing fair about a fight when she does that.

"I understand," she says. "My memory problems. But today I remember. And when you were telling me the story of you and me and Esther in the ditch, it helped me remember even more."

"I'm so happy about that," I say, and I kiss her forehead with all I've got. "But I don't know about this, sweetheart. We're old now. We can't do the things we used to do."

Jenny's voice turns stern, something it rarely does. "That's right, Murray. We're old. Not dead. And tomorrow we go to Aspen Leaves, so today is our last chance. You asked me what you can do for me today. This is it. This is what I want."

Even if I had a good response to that, my wife gives me that look of hers again, and I realize I'll never be able to say no to her, right down to my last breath.

"What if things go wrong?" I say in a last-ditch attempt to insert some reason into this conversation. "What if we get separated or you get lost? Or you forget who I am again, or you get agitated? What happens then? It just doesn't seem very responsible, that's all."

"I know," Jenny says, and the sad look on her face melts my heart. "It's probably not responsible. But Murray, we know my condition is only going in one direction. This could be our last chance. Right now. Today. We have to live while we still can."

I'm hit with a feeling from the past. It takes a moment to place it, but then I do. The idea that we have to live today, right now . . . that it could be our last chance. It makes me think of Esther. Even though Esther's been gone for many years now—like most people I've known—I still miss her all the time.

Jenny might be right. Maybe this is our last chance. Now there's quite a thought. Eighty years together and all along it felt like we would just go on forever. Murray and Jenny. How could that ever change?

But it's a strange thing about our species, isn't it? We always assume things will be pretty much the same as they were the day before. On some level, we understand that things change, but we convince ourselves that nothing tragic will happen on this day. It might happen some other day in our lives, but not this day.

We keep that assumption for every day of our lives, despite the one, undeniable fact that every one of us knows—someday we will die. Every single one of us. Meaning someday, without exception, our assumption will be wrong.

I understand that Jenny will die, and sooner rather than later. A ninety-nine-year-old with advancing Alzheimer's? It's inevitable. And trust me, I could pass on before her. That's just the way it is when you get to our age.

But for today, for right now, in this very moment, she's alive. And she wants to make the most of it. I'm not completely sold on the idea of finding that treasure, but making the most of this last day before going to Aspen Leaves? That much I can do for her.

"Okay," I say, and her eyes sparkle at the words. I put my palm against her cheek and smile. "Let's get you up and dressed. The two of us are going on a quest."

Our conversation makes me want to see Doc Keaton. I want to be there for Jenny and give her this "last day," this quest. But I haven't taken care of her outside our home for a while. Maybe the good doctor can give me some pointers.

So I make Jenny a nice breakfast and tell her I'll be back in less than an hour. I let Deb know I'm leaving for a bit, then I walk the two blocks to Doc Keaton's clinic and stroll on through the door.

"Mr. McBride," the young lass behind the desk says. They all know me here. Jenny too. It's the zoo animal thing all over again, except with these people I don't mind too much. They care about us and want to help. It just so happens we're memorable. When you were born while William McKinley was president, you're not easy to forget.

"Doc Keaton around today?" I ask.

The girl's face freezes in place, like she's trying to hide what she's thinking. "Oh," she says. "Um, I didn't think we had you on the schedule today."

"No, ma'am. I just dropped by."

"Oh," she says again. She busies herself with some papers in front of her, although I don't know what those papers could tell her about whether Doc Keaton is in the office or not. "Well, he has a full schedule today."

"I don't need long. Just got a question for him, see?"

"Um . . ."

The girl seems baffled by the situation, like she's not quite equipped to handle it. I wonder how she ever got this job. She takes a deep breath, like she's about to reluctantly break some bad news, when the good doctor himself turns the corner and smiles at me.

"I thought I heard my favorite ninety-eight-year-old," Doc Keaton says. He extends his hand, and I shake it firmly. Then he turns to the lass behind the desk, who still looks unsure about what to do next.

"It's okay, Samantha. I'll talk to Mr. McBride for a bit."

"But your eight thirty is waiting."

"I understand," Doc Keaton says. "I'll make it quick. Please apologize for my tardiness."

"Okay," Samantha says, but her voice suggests it's not okay at all.

Doc Keaton touches my elbow. "Follow me, Murray. This way." He walks nice and slow through a hallway before he turns into his office. After I make my way in, he closes the door behind us, motions me to an open chair, and sits in his seat across from me.

"What brings you by this morning, Murray?"

"Jenny," I say.

Doc Keaton nods knowingly. "How's she feeling?"

"Up and down," I say. "Good days and bad days. More bad days than good lately, it seems, but a good one so far today."

"We're all set to get her settled in at Aspen Leaves tomorrow morning," Doc Keaton says. "And I know Deb's flying out on her big retirement trip this evening, right?"

"That's right. She's leaving the house for the last time at noon today."

"Do you need to get Jenny moved in tonight since Deb won't be around? We can probably make that happen."

"No, no. I just . . . Is this the right decision, taking Jenny to a home?"

"I feel confident it is. And besides, you'll be there with her, right? After your—let's call it an 'emphatic request'—you got yourself a bed right there in the room with her. I'm still not sure how you pulled that off. It's definitely not their typical protocol."

"What did they expect? That I'd just drop my wife off at some institution and mosey on back to my home alone?"

"It's not just 'some institution,' Murray. Aspen Leaves is the finest memory care center in Illinois. She'll be in good hands."

"Darn right, she will. I'll be there to make sure of it." My bravado falters a bit when I consider the reality of the situation. "How will it work again? When she gets toward the end?"

Doc Keaton gives an understanding nod. "She'll live as independently as possible for as long as possible. With your help, of course. When the time comes, they have a hospice unit right there at the memory care center." Doc looks at me long and hard. "This was Jenny's idea, remember, Murray? She understood she would need more help than you can give her, and with Deb leaving, now's the time. And that's not a reflection on you in any way. It's just the reality of the situation."

"I just can't help thinking Jenny said that for my sake, not hers."

"Well, if you want to know what I think, I think she'll do well there. I really do."

I know Doc has other patients to get to, but he doesn't rush me. "As of tomorrow," I say, "we won't have the freedom to do much, will we? We'll be stuck in that home."

"It's not a prison, Murray. But in a way, you're correct. I know you enjoy having the grocery store and the church and even this office all within walking distance. It's true that when you and Jenny are at Aspen Leaves, most of your time will be spent there. As Jenny's condition progresses, that's going to be the best situation for everyone. And as for you, you always have the option to move back into your house at any time, if you feel that's best."

I know what the good doctor says is true, but the whole situation just makes me so sad. "I'd like to give her one more day," I say. "Just one more day like it used to be. For both of us. Go out with a bang, see? Then she can go to the nursing home. That seems important, somehow. Rather than just . . . fading away. Can you understand that?"

Doc gives me a sideways look, like he thinks I'm backing out of our plan. "It's important that we get Jenny checked in tomorrow. You understand that, right Murray? If we don't, and they give the room to someone else on the wait list, it could be a long time before we can get Jenny admitted. And with Deb leaving today, well, it's important we stay on schedule here."

"I understand, Doc. Don't worry about that. But that's tomorrow. I'm talking about today. I want this last day to be special." I try to organize my thoughts, but they're a big old jumble. "I just don't want this to be another tragic story of someone who loses their mind and gets forgotten by the world. I want better for my Jenny."

Doc smiles at that. "I've always admired the relationship you have with her, Murray. It's truly special."

I know it's special. Always have. I don't need anyone to tell me that. But it's still nice to hear it. "I'm a bit worried about taking care of her today, outside our home," I say.

Doc Keaton turns his attention to his desk and shuffles through some papers. "You've done a good job adjusting. I've seen it. But I was just reading about some new research that came out, and I think it might be helpful."

"How's that?"

"They've found more effective ways of relating to people who are living with dementia. One of the first things they say is that it doesn't have to be a tragedy, just like you said. People living with dementia can lead full lives, even people as far along as Jenny. We just need to change what we do, the things we say, instead of expecting her to change back to how she was before."

"Okay," I say. "I'll change until the cows come home if it'll help Jenny."

"I know you will," Doc says. He hands me a pamphlet, which I take carefully, as if the words might shake loose if I'm not gentle enough. "Read this," he says. "Try some of the tactics. I really think it could help. And remember, Jenny's memory isn't working like it used to, but her feelings are."

I think about that, and it scares me. The thought that Jenny could still be feeling things like normal, even if her thoughts and memories aren't working. But maybe the information on Doc's pamphlet will help.

"She wants to go on a quest," I say.

"A quest?" Doc Keaton smiles like it's funny. That's me, a barrel of laughs.

"That's right," I say. "But we went on this quest long ago, when we were kids. Things happened that I don't think she remembers. Probably doesn't want to remember."

"I don't know, Murray. Sometimes people want to be able to recall their life, the good and the bad."

I grunt a little at that.

"Tell you what," Doc Keaton says. "For this 'last day' as you call it, why don't you start by reminding Jenny of some good times you've had. And just see where it leads you. Listen to your heart. If you do that, I have a feeling it'll work out just fine."

I nod hard and look directly at Doc Keaton. "I appreciate it," I say. "I knew I could count on you."

"Of course you can," he says. "Always. Now, I have to get to my next patient. You go on home to that beautiful wife of yours."

I make my way out of the office and nod at Samantha, behind the desk. She turns to another lady and they giggle and wave back, like they just saw someone famous.

On the way home, I take a gander at the pamphlet Doc Keaton gave me. It has some good advice, I can tell right off. Like don't ask direct questions, that's one I've learned on my own through trial and error. And there's a list of bullet points, too, ordered alphabetically. The first reads:

- Agree, Apologize, Align, Attract.

To some people that might seem like a random list of A-words, but I've been trying every which way to help Jenny through her condition, so it makes sense to me. At the beginning, I'd contradict her if she said something that was wrong. I'd tell her the truth. Figured if I was being honest, what could be wrong with that?

Well, there turned out to be a lot wrong with that. Because the one thing I was trying to do—help Jenny—wasn't getting done by telling her she was wrong. So I've made some adjustments to what I say when that happens, and it's helped smooth over those situations. I fold the pamphlet and tuck it into my pocket, feeling optimistic that the advice within could help Jenny.

As for the quest, I decide the good doctor is right about that, too. I should start by taking Jenny places or showing her things that will remind her of our life together. That'll be our quest—a quest to revisit the happy parts of our past. Instead of digging up traumatic parts by searching for that old treasure.

It'll be calming for Jenny, I reckon. She'll feel like herself, and that's the whole point. I saw how Jenny perked up when I was telling her about that day in the ditch, all those years ago. Something about the past still lives in her.

When I think about how this quest should start, I get a couple ideas. A plan starts to formulate in my old brain. If it all comes together, this could be one heck of a day for my beautiful bride, even without that treasure, without digging up the past.

I enter the house and see Deb by herself at the kitchen table. She says Jenny's doing great—she's in the bedroom right now dressing herself. I thank Deb multiple times, then go out to the

living room and sit on the couch next to the coffee table and telephone. I pull out the phone book, look in a section I've never
searched before, and make a telephone call.

The man who answers is friendly and says he's available all day.
We agree to meet at 1:00 p.m. at Carpenter Park. Then he says he'd
better hang up and go get his hot-air balloon ready.

So there, the quest has begun, although not exactly with a
bang just yet. But I've started. Now, I need to find that old book.
Little Women.

If just telling Jenny about that day back when I was twelve
years old helped clear her mind so much, maybe seeing the actual
book—being able to hold it and flip through its pages—will help
even more.

We only have one bookshelf. Not because we don't love to read.
We've always loved a good story, Jenny and I. We just haven't had
the space to keep all the books we might have liked. As a result, we
don't have many books, but every single one of them is wonderful.

The problem is, when I get myself standing in front of the
bookshelf and look on the top shelf, right in the middle, the book
isn't there. It's been there for years and years. Why wouldn't it be
there now?

I scan the shelves above and below, one by one. With each
shelf that doesn't hold *Little Women*, my heartbeat speeds a little
more. I look on each shelf three times. The book isn't here.

I return to the couch, plop down on the cushion, and think
on it. Where could it have gone? A book like that—one that's so
old and beaten up and used—it stands out from other books. It
should be easy to find.

Then I'm hit with a feeling of dread. I scoot to the end of
the couch, pick up the telephone again, and dial my grandson's
number.

"Hello, this is Chance," a rushed voice says on the other end of the line.

"Chance, this here's your granddad."

"Oh, hi, Granddad," Chance says. "Listen, I'm sorry about bringing that stuff over this morning. Olivia really wanted to get it out of the house today so we don't have to move everything all at once tomorrow. But I should have asked first. I apologize."

"Oh," I say. "Well . . . that's okay. I appreciate the apology. But that's not why I'm calling."

"No? What's going on?"

"Looking for a book, that's what. But it's not where I left it. Just wondering if you've seen it."

"A book? I don't know. Which book?"

"An old one. Called *Little Women*. It was on the top row of the bookshelf here in the house, but now it's not. I know you've been clearing out some of my things. I've noticed that, you know."

"Hold on, Granddad," Chance says. "We've just been getting rid of junk. It's not like I've been taking your things. Trust me, when you and Grandma decide to sell the house, you'll thank me. Elderly people always say that dealing with clutter when they leave the house is very stressful."

"We're not selling our house," I say.

"I know, I know. But you are moving into Aspen Leaves tomorrow, right?"

"Just to get Jenny the help she needs. But we're keeping the house. You know that. Or were you and Olivia planning on staying in our house for good?"

"Of course not. That's just temporary. Olivia would never agree to live in such a small house. But listen, someday maybe you will sell it. And you'll have a lot less clutter to deal with because of what Olivia and I are doing. It'll be a good thing. Trust me."

There's a lot I want to say about a man's independence and minding one's own business. But I have more important things to deal with at the moment. "The book," I say. "Did you take any books from the bookshelf?"

Chance pauses, then says, "I suppose we took a few. But only old, ratty ones. Nothing important, I'm sure. We left anything that looked even remotely new."

I take a deep breath to calm myself. What's with young people's fascination with things being new? It's like they decided the value of a thing has nothing to do with wisdom or experience or history. It's become very simple—if something or someone is new, it has value; if it's old, it doesn't. End of story.

"So you took some old books from my bookshelf?" I'm not able to keep the anger out of my voice, but I don't care. If Chance took anything from my house, it was stealing, near as I can tell. It doesn't matter what he says his reasons were.

"I guess a few," Chance says. "We were just trying to be helpful, you know?"

I grumble under my breath before I force myself into problem-solving mode. Griping about what's already happened isn't going to get me anywhere.

"What'd you do with them?" I ask.

"We donated them," Chance says. "We almost tossed them because they were so old, but Olivia thought someone might want them for their antique shop or something. We didn't know where to go with them, so we just dropped them off at the library."

Chance didn't throw the book away, thank the Good Lord. So maybe it's still out there. "When did you do this?" I ask. And then, because I can't stop myself, I say, "When did you steal my book?"

"Granddad, it wasn't like that. I already told you, when people move out—"

"That's not important," I say. "I just need to know if I'll be able to find it. Was this a few days ago? Or are we talking months or years?"

It's sad to realize I haven't looked at the book in that long. It could have been missing for decades, and I probably wouldn't have noticed. Maybe Chance is right. Maybe having all those books was just clutter. But it was still mine and Jenny's, and we need it now.

"No, no. It was just last week," Chance says. "With the anniversary celebration coming, we were thinking more about those things."

"What branch of the library?"

"East Branch. It was the most convenient since it's near you. If you want, I can see if they still have them."

"No, I'll take care of it," I say. I'm not sure why I decline the help. Chance can get around much easier than I can. But this is part of the quest, I guess, and I want Jenny and I to be the ones to do it.

Of course, there is a part of this quest we can't do on our own. And Deb doesn't drive anymore, even though she's only seventy-five. She's leaving soon, anyway.

"Don't suppose you're free to taxi your grandmother and me around a bit today? We've got a few stops to make, out and about."

"Really? Are you sure Grandma's feeling well enough to do that?"

I'm not sure, to be honest about the matter. But Chance doesn't need to know that. He needs to learn how to keep his nose out of other people's business unless he's invited in.

"She's having a good day," I say. "So, how about it? Can you drive us to a few spots around town today?"

After a long pause, Chance's voice is what I call "forced chipper."

"Sure," he says. "But I have some work things to take care of first. Can I pick you up in about an hour?"

I don't want to waste an hour. If Jenny's doing well, every minute counts. "We'll make our way to the library. East Branch. Meet us there in an hour."

"Okay, I'll be there. Take care, Granddad."

And with that, it's time to make our way to the first destination of this quest—the East Branch of the Lemon Grove Library. To find that old, battered copy of *Little Women*.

I make my way into the kitchen, find my pillbox, and remove a single pill for the day. I pop it into my mouth and swallow it dry. I have work to do—the work of leading Jenny on this quest. I'll need to be at my best for her.

One last time.

Jenny and I say a long, tearful goodbye to Deb, since she'll probably be off on her retirement trip by the time we return home this evening. We'll see her again, of course. This isn't the ultimate goodbye. But when you know things will be completely different the next time you're going to see someone, it can feel awful final.

The sunlight that warms my skin as Jenny and I step slowly and tentatively across the threshold of our home and into the world seems like a good omen. The love of my life is fading before my very eyes, but today is a good day. I'm walking with my girl. She's holding onto my arm for support so she doesn't have to bring her walker with us. Of course, we're supporting each other. I need her for my balance just as much as she needs me for hers. We're . . . I can't quite think of the word . . . *symbiotic*, that's what.

The leaves of the maples are a fiery red today, which mixes perfectly with the yellows and oranges of the birch and hickory. A beautiful birdsong catches our attention at the same time, and without either of us saying a word, we follow the sound. After eighty years together, words are rarely needed. We don't even need to give each other a certain look anymore, like we did after maybe twenty or thirty years. After eighty, we're so attuned with each other's thoughts and emotions that we simply veer toward the sound of the singing bird, each knowing it's what the other wants. The sounds take us to the base of a weeping willow at the edge of our yard. We duck under the drooping branches, into the shaded canopy below.

"It's a wood thrush, Murray," Jenny whispers next to me. And sure enough, I see the spotted white breast with a head the color of rust. Jenny really is on top of things today. The difference between today and yesterday should be encouraging, but it's so stark it scares me. I've seen enough people pass on to know that they sometimes seem at their best, almost cured even, just before the end. After all, if Jenny can improve so much in one day, it would stand to reason she could decline just as much, just as quickly.

We watch for a minute, each feeling a fondness for the bird, its dedication to its song. We stand beneath the protection of the willow, simply listening to the lovely notes, until the pain in my knee overtakes the sound, and I pat Jenny's arm softly. Without having to ask, she knows it's time to continue our journey.

The library isn't within walking distance, at least not for two people with almost two hundred years of life between them. Fortunately, there's a bus stop just a block down the road.

When we get there, a man with long, unkempt hair and ragged clothes is sprawled on the bench, taking up the entire thing. He seems to be sleeping, but there's no way Jenny and I can stand until the bus arrives. Speaking for myself, if I don't get off my feet soon, my legs will give out, and I'll simply fall to the ground. I don't imagine Jenny's faring too much better, although she's always been better at hiding it. She's a tough little hen when she needs to be. Always has been.

Doc Keaton's so impressed by our daily walks. Two of them every day for the past many years. One in the morning, one in the afternoon. They're a chance to keep active and limber, sure. But more than that, it gives me an excuse to hold my bride's hand for a while each and every day.

Of course, we've been missing most days recently, and my body feels it.

"Excuse me there, son," I say, tapping the sleeping man on his back. "I wonder if you might be so kind as to let an old couple have some space on this here bench."

The man turns a craggy face toward me. His expression is sour and tired. I wonder if he sees familiarity in the even craggier face that looks back at him. Of course, something tells me the deep lines in our faces have been created by different things— hard years of drug and alcohol use by the looks of the homeless man, while I earned my deep grooves and liver spots simply by existing for decades.

"We're just looking for a little space to rest, if you don't mind."

The man squints at me, and I wonder if I might have put Jenny and I in danger. We don't have much to steal if the man decides we're an easy target. But we do have shoes, and our light jackets would go a long way for this homeless man, too.

I hold eye contact with him. I'm not naive; I know this man is younger and stronger. But I'd put up a fight, and that's the truth. I'd protect Jenny with everything I have, if push ever came to shove.

Still, I've found over the many years that most people are good, decent people who will treat you like a respectable citizen if you do the same for them.

Sure enough, the man sits up and scoots to the end of the bench, creating room for us to sit, which we do with an immense amount of relief. After our little detour to the willow tree and making our way to the bus stop, we needed a chance to rest for a bit. Recharge the batteries, so to speak.

The man turns his back to us and digs through a green canvas bag on the ground next to the bench. He rummages around for a while before pulling a long-sleeve shirt from the depths. He puts it on directly over his dirty T-shirt that looks like it's been worn for weeks.

Jenny nudges me with her elbow.

"There's a mighty chill in the air today," I say.

My voice startles the man, but I continue. "Can definitely feel fall coming on, and that's a fact." The man grunts. It's not the most polite response, but politeness tends to drop down on the list of priorities pretty quickly when things like comfort, hunger, and warmth come into play, so I don't judge him. "Staying warm can be tricky, I'm sure. Is there anything you need?"

The man's expression changes. It makes me wonder if the look in his eye up to now hadn't been sour like I assumed, but guarded, maybe even fearful. At first, it strikes me as ridiculous that anyone might be afraid of an ultra-elderly frail couple who can barely walk. But now that I think about it, this man could have thought Jenny and I were more of a threat to him than he was to us. We could have been a decoy, or part of a scam. Use the old, innocent-looking couple to get him to drop his defenses, then bring in the thugs to steal his things, maybe rough him up a bit.

I've been around long enough to realize a curveball can come at you no matter how prepared and protected you might think you are.

The man shakes his head. "I'll manage," he says.

As the city bus rumbles around the corner and toward our stop, I feel another nudge from Jenny. I remove my light jacket, fold it neatly until it looks like a small package, and extend it toward the man.

"Take this," I say. When the man starts to protest, I cut him off. "I've got another jacket I can wear. So do an old man a favor and allow him to feel like he's still worth a little something to this world."

I press the jacket into the man's lap, then work myself into a standing position and help Jenny up from the bench. When the bus door swings open and I help Jenny toward the steps, a big smile spreads across her beautiful face, and she gives me one small, quick wink.

The East Branch of the Lemon Grove Library is the oldest branch of the three libraries in town. But that suits me just fine. After all, the phrase "old and wise" didn't come from nowhere. Old people have been accomplishing great things for all of history.

I read in a newspaper article that Noah Webster didn't publish that dictionary of his until he was seventy years old. And it's still the top-selling dictionary in the world. Sometimes I think today's generation thinks *old* means *worthless*. Chance sure seems to think that way.

But I'm determined not to be worthless now. So rather than sitting down and weeping at the sight of the fifteen stone steps leading to the doors of the library, I take Jenny by the elbow and start right up, knee pain be damned.

"Where are we?" Jenny asks, stopping in her tracks as if she's afraid to go any farther.

"The library, sweetheart," I say, and I can tell her question is a result of her condition. I touch her hand gently; sometimes that helps bring her back. "We're going to find that old copy of *Little Women*. The one I read to you and Esther in the ditch, way back when."

Her brow furrows, but she nods. "I remember that."

"We're on a quest now, you and I. To find that treasure worth more than gold. And I think finding the book will be like a clue, see? It might help remind us of something. Point us in the right direction."

I don't actually need a clue, or to be pointed in the right direction. I remember everything about what happened all those years ago. The truth is, I'm skeptical that this so-called treasure exists at all. But if it does, well, I think I know more or less where it would be. I just don't think we should go looking for it.

Jenny squeezes my hand in a way that always pierces my heart a bit. It's tentative but trusting. She does it when she can't quite remember what's happening, but she remembers that she can trust me. When she squeezes my hand like that, I know she's relying on me. It's the greatest obligation I've ever had.

"Okay, Murray," she says. Her soft, vulnerable voice squeezes my insides.

I lead her up the steps and into the stone building. As soon as we enter, I spot the desk with the librarian sitting behind it, and two empty chairs nearby. We head straight to them, and I help Jenny into one before I drop into the other, trying not to let the level of my fatigue show. I don't need to be pampered like a baby. And truth be told, I still want to impress this girl sitting next to me, even after eighty years together.

The librarian at the desk sees us take a seat and perks right up.

"Well, good morning, Mr. McBride," she says. "And this must be the Mrs. McBride I've heard so much about?"

A younger person might be able to stay anonymous while they make all those trips to the library to research Jenny's condition. But get as old as I am and you tend to stand out. Every time I come in, this librarian—Helen is her name—rushes over to check on me, see if there's anything I need. After enough times, we became pretty friendly, this librarian and me. She's a fairly young woman, but she has thick eyeglasses with a chain attached so she can wear them like a necklace. Very library-like, if you ask me.

"That's right," I say. "This is Jenny, my wife of eighty years."

Okay, maybe I do think it's an accomplishment. So sue me.

"It's wonderful to finally meet you," Helen says to Jenny. "I've heard so much about you." She looks to me and back to Jenny, like she's trying to get a full view of us. "How are you two today?"

"Still ticking," I say.

"Lovely, thank you," Jenny says.

She's always been better at that sort of thing.

"Can I help you find something?" Helen asks.

I always have to stifle a sense of annoyance when she asks that. It's insulting that people think we need more help than others. We're people, just like anybody. Sure, we've each been alive for almost a century, but so what if we were teenagers before there was radio? We've come to the library for the same reason everyone does. For books. Not for pity.

Of course, she probably asks everyone that question. It's her job. I'm just a little touchy about people thinking I'm helpless.

"Looking for a book," I say. "Called *Little Women*. You heard of it?"

I have a hard time reading the expression on Helen's face, but it seems like a mixture of shock, humor, and confusion, all in equal parts. It twists her eyebrows up in a funny way, but I don't laugh. Wouldn't be polite.

"You'll have to excuse Murray," Jenny says. "He's not so familiar with books. He only learned to read when he turned ninety-four."

Jenny reaches over and touches my forearm, and I almost weep with joy. Here's a thing about Jenny—she's got spunk. I've known it since the day I met her in that schoolyard ditch. And there's no clearer way she could tell me she loves me than through her gentle ribbing.

Through the years, she's said some things that have made people think she's annoyed with me, exasperated by me, maybe even outright dislikes me. And then, every single time, she reaches out and touches my forearm, just like she did that first day in the schoolyard ditch. It's her way of letting me know she's kidding. That she only kids around like that with people she cares about.

I love when she does that. Makes me laugh out loud sometimes. These days, it lets me know when her mind is working right, too.

Helen seems to catch on and smiles at Jenny. "It's a wonderful book. Is it for your granddaughter?"

When there's a noticeable pause and Jenny still doesn't answer, I glance at her, dreading what I might see. I can tell she's fighting to remember a granddaughter, which we've never had. Only two grandsons—and one married a Japanese woman and moved to the other side of the world, so Chance is the only one we see. But right now, Jenny's wondering if we do have a granddaughter who she can't remember. This is why Doc Keaton's pamphlet said to avoid asking direct questions when someone is having a hard time remembering. Putting Jenny on the spot like this confuses her.

I've watched Jenny so closely over the past couple years, I can recognize what she's feeling just by her expression. Right now, it's that confusion. And it'll go one of two ways. Either something will click back into place, and she'll figure it out—she'll find that piece of information she's searching for—or the confusion will get thicker and thicker until it turns to fear or, worse, panic. That's when she acts like someone I don't know, which is the hardest part of all.

Fortunately, just before I interject, her eyes clear and her expression softens. She must have found the information she was searching her memory bank for. Just like that, she's back with us.

"We don't have a granddaughter," Jenny says. "The book is just for us."

It feels like we dodged a bullet there. But it reminds me that what we're doing here, even just going to the library by ourselves, is a risky endeavor. I look around for Chance, wondering when he'll arrive. No dice just yet.

"It's not just any copy of that book we're looking for," I say. "It's a specific one. One we used to own, way back when, but it was donated when it shouldn't have been. We're hoping we can find it, and maybe it'll remind us about some detail for the quest we're on."

Helen's eyebrows shoot up in response to that. Can't say I blame her. A couple as old as we obviously are talking about a quest? I'm guessing that's a first for this lady. Probably a last, too.

"Well, that's intriguing. What kind of quest?"

"It's a bit of family lore," Jenny says, her mind nice and clear. "When I was a young girl, my mother told me our family knew the location of a treasure worth more than gold, and that it was hidden. Buried in a case of some sort in a church near our homestead. My sister even had the key for it when we were young girls."

Helen stares at her for a moment, then moves on to me. It's like she's trying to decide if Jenny might still be joking around.

No prank here. Just a couple half-crazy birds on a treasure hunt.

"We think our grandson might've donated the book we're looking for when he shouldn't have," I say. "It was just within the last few days. Have you seen it?"

"Oh," Helen says. It's like she's startled back into the moment. I don't have any idea if she believes we're on a quest or not, but I don't suppose it matters much. She puts her eyeglasses on, as if seeing straight helps her think straight. "Actually, I think I might have," she says. "We get a lot of donations that we can't put on the shelves, for a variety of reasons. We sell those at the Friends of the Library book sale and use the proceeds to help fund things around here. When I saw an old copy of *Little Women* last week, I just had to grab it. It's the story I used to read to my daughter when she was young. So I left a little donation and took it home to her." Helen rolls her eyes dramatically. "She couldn't believe I would buy it for her. It's so uncool, apparently. But she accepted it—against her will, of course. Then again, everything is against her will right now. She's at that age."

"I understand that," Jenny says, giving Helen one of her winks.

"I wonder if we might be able to get that copy back," I say. "We'd buy you a new copy, of course."

"Oh, don't be silly," Helen says. "I'll just check out a copy from the library, in case my daughter actually is reading it, by some miracle. Then I'll run home and get your copy for you."

Just then, Chance bounds through the front doors and practically jogs toward us. He has a bead of sweat on his forehead, like he's been jogging everywhere he's gone today. Young folks are in such a rush all the time, it seems. It's like they think the world is going to leave them behind if they don't hurry everywhere and stress about everything. I think they could all do with a good book, a wood-burning fireplace, and some time with nothing to do but read or stare at the flames. Course, that's not something he'd ever do. He'd see it as a waste of time. Unproductive, that's what.

"Granddad, Grandma," he says, half out of breath. "I was worried I might have missed you."

"I said we'd be here," I say.

Jenny accepts Chance's hug and says with the most beautiful smile, "Did Denise come with you?"

Now, it's sweet of my bride to ask about Chance's wife. Only problem is, Denise was his first wife. His current wife is Olivia. The one who squished our cheeks at the anniversary party yesterday.

It's hard enough for me to keep them straight, so I can't imagine how difficult it is for Jenny. But at the moment, she doesn't seem confused at all. She seems fully confident that Chance is still married to Denise. I remember the first word listed on Doc Keaton's pamphlet: Agree.

"I'm sure Denise had things to do," I say. "You know how busy she is. I know she would have come if she'd been able."

Chance looks at me like I've lost my mind. "You mean Olivia? You know, you should really keep that straight, Granddad. Olivia wouldn't take kindly to you two calling her 'Denise,' I can tell you that for sure."

I'm hoping we can just move on, but Jenny's eyes squint tight. "Who's Olivia? What happened to Denise?"

"Grandma, Denise and I got a divorce, remember?"

"Oh my, when did that happen? Why didn't you tell us about it?"

I want to jump in and smooth this situation over, but I can't think of how to do it. The right words won't come. If Chance wasn't here, maybe. If I had more time to consider what might be most helpful to Jenny. But Chance seems unable to let this slide. He's still playing this game like I used to, assuming the right thing to do is to make sure Jenny knows what's real. I know now that's not the best play. But Chance doesn't, so he plows forward while Helen and I watch helplessly.

"Denise and I have been divorced for three years, Grandma. I've been married to Olivia for almost a full year. You came to the wedding, remember?"

"What?" Jenny says, and the panic in her voice is painful to hear. "No. I remember your wedding. Denise wore that beautiful dress, and we talked about how it was okay that it wasn't white. Remember that, Murray," she says, clinging to my arm for help.

"Of course," I say. "It was a lovely wedding."

"Yeah, and my wedding to Denise was five years ago," Chance says. "I'm talking about Olivia. You seriously don't remember that? You were there, Grandma, just last year."

I pull Jenny close to me and glare at Chance, trying with all my telepathic might to holler at him with my stare. He raises his eyebrows and shrugs his shoulders, as if to say he has no idea what he's done wrong. When Jenny nestles her face into my shoulder and starts crying, I whisper in her ear. "You're right, it was a lovely service. But I can't seem to remember what church that was at."

"St. Joseph's, right here in town," Jenny says through a sniffle.

"Ah! That's right. It was St. Joseph's, wasn't it? Thank you for reminding me. I remember it clearly now. A beautiful service, indeed."

Chance is looking at us like we're aliens when some contraption on his belt starts beeping something fierce. He pulls a little device from the waistline of his trousers and squints at the face of it.

"Shoot," he says. "Look, Granddad, I know I said I could drive you two around today, but something just came up. Work stuff, you know? I don't think I can get out of it. I'm really sorry."

I hide my disappointment, both in losing our transportation and in my grandson. "We'll find another way. Don't know what it'll be, but we'll figure something out."

"Thanks, Granddad." He looks at Jenny with pity, which makes my temper flare. "I'm sorry to upset you, Grandma. It was really nice seeing you."

"It was nice seeing you too, sweetie," Jenny says, wiping a tear from her cheek. It appears our whispered conversation was enough to calm her, thank the Good Lord. "Come by the house more often, will you?"

I don't point out the fact that Chance and his wife will be staying in our house for a few weeks, or that as of tomorrow morning, we'll be in Aspen Leaves.

Chance gives Jenny a quick kiss on her cheek and pats my shoulder firmly. Then he strides out of the library as quickly as he entered, leaving an uncertain silence in his wake.

I told Chance we'd figure out another way to get around, but the truth is, I have no idea how this could work out. We don't have the stamina to take the city bus all day and, besides, it wouldn't go where we need it to. I bet the old Chevy in the garage at home would still run, but Jenny's been clear on her desire to never again get into a car I'm driving. All because of an episode with a stop sign that I still say was never there before.

Just as I'm becoming discouraged, Helen, who's been watching our little drama all along, leans forward like she has a secret to tell. She takes her eyeglasses off so they dangle around her neck, then puts them right back on.

"I didn't mean to eavesdrop," she says. Of course, there was no way she could have avoided it. It's not her fault if something takes place right in front of her. Still, she looks a little embarrassed as she says, "But I might be able to help."

"How's that?" I ask.

"It sounds like you need a way to get around."

"Sure do. Our grandson there was supposed to be our ride. I have an old Chevy in the garage at home, and she'd probably start right up. But it's been a few years since I drove a car."

Helen nods knowingly. "I might have a solution that could help us both out," she says. "Let me check out a copy of *Little Women* real quick, and then I'll take you to my house, if you'd like.

My daughter's been having a hard time recently, and I think it would do her some good to get out of the house, maybe be a help to someone. It'll get her out of her own head, you know? And she can drive you where you need to go. What do you think?"

"That's so thoughtful of you," Jenny says, back to herself now. "We'd be so very grateful."

"We have a busy day planned, though," I say. "A few stops. Probably take most of the day."

The last thing we need is to get a ride somewhere and then be stranded by some teenage girl. But Helen says, "I'm sure Brooke can drive you wherever you need to go. She's completely free all day."

"That sure is thoughtful," I say. Then, because I can't help myself, I add, "I can drive just fine, even if I haven't had the chance to prove it for a while. It's just that Jenny prefers to catch a ride these days."

"I understand," Helen says. Out of the corner of my eye, I can see Jenny shaking her head and rolling her eyes. But that's okay. We've been married for eighty years, and she's rolled her eyes at me the entire time. Sure, I'm ridiculous. I know it, and she knows it. But it's something she's accepted about me, which makes me feel like the luckiest man in the world.

Helen says she's just going to tell her coworker she'll be gone for a few minutes. She speeds off toward a back room, leaving me and Jenny to ourselves.

Truth is, I'm glad I'm here, right where I am. Anytime Jenny seems to forget things, I want to be there. Sometimes it feels like if I can just witness her disorientation, just that simple witnessing, my simple presence, might help diminish it. At least a little bit. And I'm learning how to help her better, too, thanks to Doc Keaton's pamphlet.

But I know she doesn't have much time left. What I don't know is what I'll do when my love is gone. I just hope I don't have to stick around for long without her. There's nothing for me in this world without Jenny.

"All set," Helen says as she rounds a corner with a book tucked under her arm.

I lift my elbow toward her. "Shall we?"

Helen wraps her arm through mine, and I stride out of the library like the king of the world, a beautiful dame on each arm.

In the parking lot, Helen helps Jenny and me into the back seat of her car. I take Doc Keaton's pamphlet out of my back pocket so I don't squish it, and toss it onto the passenger seat where it'll be safe.

Helen apologizes over and over for the state of the car. And she's not wrong—it's about the worst-looking vehicle I've seen outside the confines of a junkyard. The windshield has a spider-web crack that makes it almost impossible to see the road. The passenger-side window is stuck a quarter of the way down. And it turns out second gear no longer works, meaning she has to rev first gear all the way up, then skip to third gear as quick as she can.

On top of that, the light on her dashboard says she needs gas. The gauge is all the way past the E. I don't know how far away she lives, but I'd put her chances of making it a mile at no better than fifty-fifty.

"Looks like you're running a little low there," I say, hoping she'll catch my drift.

"Oh, my," she says. She squints at the gas gauge like the squinting might make the needle move up. When it doesn't, she says, "There's a gas station just around the corner. Do you mind if we swing through?"

"Seems like a good idea."

She keeps one eye on the road as she rifles through her purse. She removes a billfold and looks inside, then mutters under her breath.

"Murray," Jenny says, "if we're going to get a ride from these nice people, we should at least pay for their gas."

"Of course," I say, wondering why Jenny picked up on that before me. I pull my own billfold from my back pocket, remove a twenty-dollar bill, and extend my hand between the front seats.

Helen sighs deeply, as if she regrets needing the money. "I'll pay you back," she says. "As soon as I can. I promise."

"You'll do no such thing," I say firmly. "We'd like a ride, and I'll be damned if I'm not going to pay a fair rate for it. Just because your car isn't yellow doesn't mean you shouldn't get paid for being our taxi."

"Thank you," she says, but she still avoids eye contact. No reason for any shame, of course. Not in my mind. I've never understood the idea that having money makes someone a better person, and not having it is something to be ashamed of. The way I see it, some of those folks making the millions are the ones who ought to feel shame. A least when they get those millions off the backs of those going without.

We make it to the gas station on the fumes that remain. As we pull in, my eyes are drawn like a beacon to the most beautiful vehicle I've ever seen. I nearly bump my head on the top of the car as I bounce in my seat and point out the window.

"Look, Jenny, look!"

Helen is startled by my outburst and looks out the window where I'm pointing. "What's wrong? Is everything okay?"

"Everything is fine," Jenny says, and it sounds like she's having her patience tested. "Murray just saw a minivan."

Helen freezes for a moment, like she's trying to figure out an equation. "A minivan?"

"Murray loves minivans," Jenny says through an eye roll. "He thinks they're the greatest invention since sliced bread."

"A minivan?" Helen repeats.

"Look at that shape," I say. "It looks like a new model. And it's a Chevy!"

Not everyone understands my love of minivans, I've learned. Some people actually seem to think they're no better than any other vehicle. But I know better. They're sleek and trim and attractive, to say nothing of their practicality and usefulness. If I ever find out who invented the minivan, I'm going to send him a letter. Fan mail, that's what it'll be.

I gaze at the beautiful marvel of automotive engineering while Helen fills her tank with unleaded. When her Ford's all filled to the brim, she opens the creaking door and hops back into the car.

"Now, let's go get your book."

I watch the minivan as it turns out of the gas station and disappears from view. What a species it was! I'm not sure how this day could get any better. I squeeze Jenny's hand, happy as a clam.

Helen puts the car into first gear, revs it all the way to the max, and slips it into third, quick as can be. It's pretty impressive, actually. I'm not sure I could drive this old hunk of junk as well as this lady can.

Jenny smirks at me as if she can read my mind, which of course she can after all our years together. Then she turns her attention to Helen.

"How old is your daughter?" she asks.

Helen gives an exasperated sigh. "Sixteen," she says. "And acting every bit of it."

"How's that?" I ask.

Helen pauses, as if considering how much to say. She must decide old people aren't prone to gossip, because she ends up saying quite a bit.

"She had her first boyfriend recently, a boy from school, and it didn't end well. She fell head over heels for him, like teenagers do. And he seemed like a nice enough guy. But then one day he came to the house and, well, the timing wasn't great."

"What was wrong with the timing?" I ask.

"I've been having some financial difficulties," Helen says. "I have student loans and credit card debt from a little health scare last year, and I'm still paying on this car, if you can believe that." She motions to the air around her, as if to display the entire wreckage of the car. "Apparently my ex-husband didn't get a fixed-rate mortgage, so when that adjusted up, well . . ."

Her voice trails off. I'm not sure what this has to do with her daughter's boyfriend, but after a few seconds, she shakes her head and continues.

"When Brooke's boyfriend showed up at the house and saw an eviction notice stuck to the front door, he turned around and walked away. Broke up with Brooke the very next day at school and started dating another girl. One whose family has money.

"Brooke couldn't understand how someone could do that. She thought he loved her. I've never emphasized money as something that's important. But that was obviously a mistake. It turns out, you actually need enough to pay the bills."

"Seems to me your daughter just got mixed up with the wrong kind of fella," I say.

"Yes, well, she's been a bit of a wreck ever since. She's pretty jaded right now, so prepare yourselves."

"Oh, don't worry about us," Jenny says. "We've been around the block a time or two. Our boys weren't always angels. Murray can attest to that."

Helen pulls the car into a cracked driveway in front of a small, sagging house. Jenny and I wait for her to make her way around the hood. As much as I'd like to get out of the car unassisted, it sure would be easier to have some help, considering how low the car is to the ground.

I think about my old batting stance, back in my ball-playing days. I always liked to crouch low, make the pitcher think he really had to squeeze it into a tiny little strike zone . . . and then I'd launch out of my crouch, rotate my body in one fluid motion, and whack the ball all over the yard.

Now, I can't even stand from a car. It makes a little dent in my ego when Helen takes my hands and pulls me out. I hate for Jenny to see me needing help like that.

"Much obliged," I say through my embarrassment. Even with her help, it's a struggle. Jenny seems to make her way out more easily.

We pass a drooping maple tree just off the sidewalk, and when we get to the front door there's a red piece of paper taped to it, just like what Helen described when Brooke's boyfriend came by. Apparently, the problem hasn't been resolved just yet.

Helen snags the paper and shoves it into her purse. I consider asking what it's about, but I figure it's not my business.

Jenny and I follow her inside where, sitting in a recliner in front of the television set is a blond girl in sweatpants and a hooded sweatshirt. She definitely has the look of a teenager. Although these days, anyone between fifteen and forty-five looks the same age to me.

"The school called, saying you weren't there today," Helen said.

"I tried to go," the girl says, "but then I thought about seeing Jacob in first period, and I just couldn't do it. So I took another mental health day."

Helen's eyebrows stretch high on her forehead. "That's three in a row now. Are you going to be able to keep up? Even with trig?"

"I'll be fine."

"I'm starting to worry about you, you know."

"I'm fine, Mom. Seriously."

"If you were fine, you'd be in school right now, wouldn't you?"

The girl has nothing to say to that. When Helen introduces the girl as her daughter, Brooke, and tells her we're "a nice couple I met at the library," Brooke gives me and Jenny a little wave and says, "Nice to meet you. Now that you know all the intimate details of my personal life." She gives her mother a stern look and continues. "Why are you even here, Mom? You're all over me about not being at school, but aren't you supposed to work until noon today?"

"The library wasn't busy this morning. Mr. and Mrs. McBride came in looking for that copy of *Little Women* I gave you."

"You mean we can get rid of it?" Brooke says. "Rad."

I'm not sure what *rad* means, but it seems to be some sign of approval.

"I made sure to get another copy from the library, in case you're reading it," Helen says, and she tosses the library copy to Brooke, who catches it with a pout. Then Helen turns to me and Jenny. "My hope was to read the story to Brooke in the evenings, before bed. She doesn't think it would be cool to have her mother read her bedtime stories, but I think it would be a nice way for us to connect. A way to show her I love her."

"Yeah well," Brooke says. "Experience has brought me to the irrefutable conclusion that love is complete BS."

"How's that?" I say.

Brooke leans toward me, like she's making sure I understand. "Love is something Hollywood made up to sell movie tickets. It's the biggest fraud ever perpetrated on the human race."

"Oh?" Now, this is a take I don't think I've ever heard before. But Brooke's not shy about educating me.

"Seriously," she says. "I mean, think about it. Up until a couple hundred years ago, people married for money and status, and most marriages were arranged, all over the world. It worked just fine, for literally thousands of years. Then Jane Austen went and wrote *Pride and Prejudice*, and all of a sudden this image of romance is everywhere. Everyone thinks they should marry for love, whatever that means. But it's all a mirage. It's a farce. If you'll excuse my French, it's bullshit."

"Oh, I don't know," I say, surprised by how adamant she is. I could point out that she attributed the invention of love to both Hollywood and Jane Austen, but I don't think that would be constructive. "I've been in love with this knockout for a good eighty-six years now," I say instead.

I squeeze Jenny's hand, and she smiles sheepishly. "And I've loved him, too, for at least twenty."

Brooke actually laughs at that. Can you imagine? A teenager so depressed she can't even get herself to school, so jaded she thinks love is a farce, and my bride makes her laugh, quick as a whistle. Then Jenny squeezes my arm just in case I might have thought she was serious. As if I don't know, after all these years.

"Well, I'm glad you guys believe in love," Brooke says. "Ignorance is bliss. Indulge in it. I remain unconvinced."

The words are still harsh, but at least she has a small smile now, thanks to Jenny.

"Well," Helen says, puffing her cheeks as she lets out a big exhale. "On that happy note . . . Mr. and Mrs. McBride are actually going on a quest today."

Brooke sticks out her bottom lip and nods approvingly at us. She seems more comfortable showing affection for Jenny than for her mother. But I guess that's probably not uncommon with teenagers. "What kind of quest. Like, the Holy Grail or something?"

"Not quite," Jenny says. "According to the story my mother used to tell me, there's something buried in a church near my family's old homestead, a little ways north of here."

"How far north?" Brooke asks.

"Well, a lot has changed," Jenny says, "but somewhere in the Fox River Forest Preserve, most likely."

"No kidding," Brooke says. "Jacob and I used to go up there and wander around. Have little illegal campfires and stuff." She glances at her mother, as if realizing what she just said. "We spent a lot of time in those woods. It's cool. There's, like, new hiking signs mixed with old, fallen-down cabins and stuff. What do you think is buried up there?"

"We're searching for a 'treasure worth more than gold,'" Jenny says.

"And I told Mr. and Mrs. McBride you'd drive them wherever they need to go today," Helen says.

"What? Mom!" Brooke's body slouches and she pouts like the teenager she is. "I don't want to drive old people around all day. No offense," she says to Jenny. "You guys seem super cool for old people. But I can't do it. I was just about to start a movie."

Her mother gives her a scolding look. "I'm not asking, Brooke. You've been moping around for three days now. It's time you get

out and do something. You can either come help me at the library
or you can drive Mr. and Mrs. McBride around."

Brooke's shoulders droop dramatically. "Fine. Whatever. But
you know I can't stand driving that stupid car. I don't see why
we can't just get it fixed. No one else has to drive a piece of junk
like that."

"Yes, well, other bills need to take priority right now," her
mother says.

"Oh, that's right. So let's see if I can recap, for anyone keeping
score out there. We have a car that's an unaesthetic compilation
of trash basically held together with duct tape, we're going to get
kicked out of our house any day now, and I'm a sixteen-year-old
whose mom wants to read to her at bedtime. No wonder Jacob
dumped me. I'd dump me, too."

Strange as it may sound, I'm getting a kick out of this kid.
Sure, she's jaded and seems to have a pretty pessimistic take on
the world right now, but underneath it all, it's not hard to see her
true personality shine through. I mean, *Unaesthetic compilation of
trash held together with duct tape? Ignorance is bliss . . . indulge in
it?* How could anyone not see straight through her rough exterior
when she says things like that?

Brooke's mother leans over and kisses her cheek. She has to
be quick about it too because Brooke pulls away as quick as a cat.
"Things will turn out," Helen says, and she ignores Brooke's giant
huff of a response. "I'll walk back to work. Make sure you get the
book for Mr. and Mrs. McBride, okay? And drive safely. You have
passengers."

"I know, Mom. You don't have to remind me every single time I
drive somewhere. The assumption of immaturity is condescending."

And there the kid goes again, showing her hand. Jenny's little
smile tells me she sees through the kid as well.

Helen purses her lips, says goodbye to Jenny and me, and exits through the front door. That leaves the three of us, with Jenny and I standing over Brooke as she lounges in the recliner.

"Mind if we take a few minutes to rest before we go?" I say.

"Fine with me," Brooke says. "Take all day if you want."

I take Jenny's hand, shuffle over to a couch, and help her sit. With a bit of effort, I plop down right next to her.

"So, do you guys have kids and stuff?" Brooke asks, rocking her chair back and forth.

The question seems out of the blue, considering the pouting teenager Brooke was around her mother. Now, with her mother gone, it's like her angst has dissolved.

It's a strange phenomenon that kids can sometimes be at their worst around their parents, but someone once told me that it can be healthy. It shows they know they're loved. They can be obnoxious and rude and inconsiderate because they know their parents love them enough not to leave them. Helen must do a pretty good job of making sure Brooke knows she's loved, whether Brooke likes it or not.

"Two," Jenny says, answering Brooke's question. It takes everything I have not to point out that our two boys have passed on, but I'm not sure if Jenny remembers that right now, so I let it go. Jenny smiles as she says, "It was a few months after our second son was born that Murray finally figured out what was causing it."

She reaches out and touches my forearm, sending warmth throughout my body. Brooke, after a moment of confusion, bursts out in laughter. That's the thing about Jenny's little jokes about me—not only do they tell me she loves me, but other people tend to get a kick out of them as well.

My wife really is quite the woman.

"Oh," Brooke says. "I'll go grab that book for you."

"Thank you kindly," I say.

After she disappears into the hallway, I touch Jenny's cheek and look at her ocean-greens closely. They look clear enough to understand what's happening, even if she did forget that our boys have passed on. So I decide she'll be all right alone for a minute, then I kiss her cheek and say, "I need to visit the restroom. I'll be right back."

I make my way down the hall, but instead of going into the lavatory I knock on the slightly ajar door of Brooke's room. She shows up at the entrance holding the old copy of *Little Women*. Sure enough, it's my old copy, in the flesh.

"I wonder if I could have a word," I say.

She hands the book to me. "Sure. What's up?"

"This quest," I say. "To tell the truth of the matter, the plan isn't to go on the quest at all. Least, not the one Jenny's expecting."

"Really?" Brooke says, and even though she tries to hide it, I notice her shoulders deflate a bit. "Why not?"

"First off, I don't think the treasure exists. Second, if there is something buried, I don't think it contains 'a treasure worth more than gold.' And third, we went on this quest before, Jenny and I, along with her sister, Esther."

Brooke must see the tears building in my eyes, threatening to break free. Her voice softens. "What happened?"

"Well," I say, stammering about for the right words. "Things didn't work out. And see, Jenny has Alzheimer's. Do you know what that is?"

"Yeah," Brooke says, looking out the bedroom door like she's trying to see Jenny, trying to see if she can recognize the disease in her.

"Well, I don't think Jenny's remembering what happened. If she remembered, I don't think she'd want to go on the quest either."

After a long moment of taking it all in, Brooke says, "Then what are we doing? Why do you need me to drive you around if you're not looking for the treasure?"

"I've decided to take Jenny around town, to places we went when we were young. Places where we had good experiences, good memories. She's having a good day today, and I want to use it to remind her of a few wonderful times we had. I figure that'll be a nice gift to her. I want to do that for her because I love her more than anything in the world. Do you understand that?"

Brooke's smile is small, sad, and a bit confused. "Not really," she says. She looks at me real close, like she's searching for an indicator that's present when a man truly loves a woman. Her lips turn down a little, like she's dissatisfied with what she sees. Well, welcome to the club. I'm almost a hundred years old. Everyone who looks at me is dissatisfied with what they see.

"Anyway," I say. "Jenny's dead set on this quest, so I want to keep her thinking we're looking for the treasure, see? And we'll search all right, it's just that the search won't lead us to a treasure. It'll take us to places that'll remind her of our life together. Do you think you can keep that secret for me?"

Brooke shrugs. "Sure. Whatever."

"Much obliged," I say. I reach out to seal it with a handshake. Brooke tilts her head like she's not sure what's happening, but eventually she figures it out.

And just like that, Brook and I have a deal. Me and my new coconspirator.

After I answer nature's call, I return to the living room and find Jenny and Brooke deep in conversation.

"I was just telling Brooke our story, Murray. The one you started telling me this morning, about when we were young."

Jenny pats the spot on the couch next to her. "You should tell more of it, since Brooke will be joining us. If she's interested, that is."

"I'm definitely interested," she says. "It sounds like it was, like, a completely different world back then."

"You have no idea," I say. "But don't we want to go on our quest?"

"Oh, we should definitely go on the quest," Brooke says, and she gives me a conspiratorial look. "But maybe you could tell me the story really quick before we go?"

It's not necessarily a quick story, but both of these ladies stare at me like they expect me to tell it. So I make my way down onto the couch while Jenny recounts with perfect clarity everything I've told so far—about the two of us meeting in the ditch, me reading to her, meeting Esther, and learning about the key and what it might open. Then they both look to me, ready for more. I think about where I left off and gather my thoughts for a few moments.

"Well, I didn't know if there really was buried treasure worth more than gold or not," I say. "But I knew one thing—I couldn't stop thinking about it."

CHAPTER 4

1910

That night, Murray couldn't sleep. He lay awake, wondering what could possibly be buried in a church that contained a treasure worth more than gold. What could that mean?

Esther had said it might be a family heirloom, but that was just a guess. The possibilities seemed endless. Murray tossed and turned in bed, imagining what it would be like to open the treasure and peer into it.

In the morning, Murray couldn't wait to get to school and tell Esther and Jenny about his plan. They would search all over the countryside together, they would find this church built into a hillside, and they would dig up the treasure. Together, they would open it with her old, brass key . . . and they would discover a treasure worth more than gold.

Murray felt so emboldened by the thought of seeing Esther in class and telling her about his plan that he didn't wait to enter the classroom until everyone else was seated, the way he normally did. Instead, he was one of the first to sit at his desk. Esther's desk was on the other side of the room, near the windows, and one row behind his. He tried not to be obvious, but he couldn't stop himself from tilting his neck just far enough to see if she had taken her seat. Recess couldn't come fast enough. He couldn't wait to see Jenny.

When five minutes before the start of class turned into three, and then one, Murray felt a lump forming in his throat. When

Ms. Carson strode to the front of the class and told them to get out their math homework, Murray's stomach began to ache.

Where was Esther?

He wondered the same thing the entire morning, but she never showed up. When the class dismissed for lunch, Murray wasn't sure if he should run to the ditch and wait for Jenny or not. First, he dodged a few of the bigger boys and made his way to the teacher's desk at the front of the classroom.

"Ms. Carson?" he said, still unsure how exactly he was going to ask. Ms. Carson's eyes flicked up to him, then immediately back to the papers she was shuffling through.

"Yes Murray? Is there something I can help you with?"

"Where's Esther today?"

Ms. Carson's hands stopped mid-shuffle, which Murray thought was a strange reaction to a pretty simple question. "She's ill," the teacher said. She said it in a way that made it clear further questions were unwelcome.

"She seemed fine yesterday," Murray said.

"Well, she's not today."

Murray felt a spark of defiance in his chest, but before it could spread, he took a deep breath—something his mother taught him when he'd started having nervous episodes after his father left. Instead of saying something he would regret, he dropped his head and turned to walk away.

After a few steps, he heard a deep sigh and a stack of papers drop to the desktop. "I didn't realize you two were friends," Ms. Carson said.

"We weren't," he said. "Until recently."

"Murray," Ms. Carson said. Her voice was different now. As if she had given up in some way. "Esther may not be in school for quite some time."

What she said next became a blur in Murray's mind, as if her words were overcome by static. He stared at his teacher, trying to comprehend her meaning. But it was like his brain had suddenly put up a barrier, one that blocked everything from getting through, not allowing him to hear or think or feel. Despite his mind's best attempts at self-preservation, however, one word did make it through, unabated and crystal clear. The scariest word Murray had ever heard.

Consumption.

Murray ran to the ditch. When he saw Jenny sitting on the grass at the bottom of the slope, an enormous weight eased from his shoulders.

"You're here," he said.

Her eyes were red around the rims. She smiled at him, but there was a sadness behind it. "I wanted to stay home with Esther, but my father said I had to go to school. He's worried I'll catch it, too."

"Consumption?"

Jenny's eyes flared, and Murray thought she might be angry with him. But then she looked at her hands, folded in her lap, and nodded.

"Will she be okay?"

"No one knows," Jenny said. "She's been sick before. She gets sick a lot. But not like this. They won't even let me see her."

"That must be hard." Murray sat next to her, forcing himself to keep a few inches between their elbows.

They sat in silence for a long time, with Murray wondering what Jenny was thinking, and whether his new friend was okay. Was Esther in pain? Was the consumption severe?

He knew all about consumption, of course. The illness had struck fear in the heart of every single family he knew, but Esther had already contracted polio and would never walk unassisted again. How could someone who had already been through so much also get consumption?

As far as Murray could tell, both sicknesses were pure evil. Polio was painful, caused permanent paralysis, and most cruel of all, it seemed to take a particular liking to children. And while polio seemed to revel in disabling children, consumption tended to finish them off. Both diseases had put the fear of God into Americans.

Despite all the panicking adults and the sensational newspaper articles, Murray had never seen either disease firsthand. But he heard about them so much he'd started wondering each time something felt strange in his body if he'd caught polio and was on the path to paralysis; each time he coughed, he wondered if consumption had finally found him and he would be dead in two days.

Everyone understood, no child was safe.

Murray knew he should be scared. He knew he should put as much distance between him and the Brennan girls as he possibly could. But he also knew that Jenny and Esther were the only ones at school who had shown him any kindness. Murray had just two friends, and he had only met them the day before. He wasn't about to abandon one of them now.

"Can I come see her?" he asked Jenny. "After school? Esther might like me to keep reading the story to her. In fact, I'm sure she would."

"I'm sure she would too, Murray, but our father won't let you in. He's already said no visitors while Esther is sick."

Murray felt a flame inside his chest. "I'm coming anyway," he said.

"Suit yourself, but he won't let you see her."

Murray kept his word. As soon as school let out, he didn't race home like he normally did. Instead, he joined Jenny. Together, silently, they walked a mile down dirt roads until they made their way up the Brennans' winding driveway.

The corn was tall and turning golden. It swayed in the early fall breeze on either side of the gravel drive. A large stone farmhouse came into view as they rounded the final twist in the road.

"Give me a minute," Jenny said when they arrived.

Murray could hear voices inside and strained to understand what they were saying. But it was no use. A few moments later, Jenny opened the door, but only a crack. She gave Murray an apologetic look.

"My father says you can't come in now. Not while Esther's still unwell. I'm sorry. I'll see you tomorrow."

She closed the door, leaving Murray to stare at the wood fibers. He wasn't surprised that Mr. Brennan wouldn't let him in. After all, if Esther's story was correct, this was the man who was given the key to a treasure but had never tried to find it. *Who does that?* Murray wondered.

He stood just outside the farmhouse for a long time, unable to decide what to do next. He knew he should go home. But he couldn't stand the idea of doing nothing.

He scanned the area around the farmhouse. In the distance, cornfields stretched as far as the eye could see. But nearer the house, a ring of maple and oak trees provided a wind barrier for the farmhouse . . . and a perfect place for Murray to shelter. He walked toward the grove, scanning the windows of the house for any sign as to which might be Esther's room, where she surely lay sick in bed.

From the oak grove, he could see several windows. Most had the curtains pulled open, but one had the curtains drawn. He sat where he could be seen if someone opened those curtains and looked out that window, then leaned against a giant burr oak.

He looked toward the curtained window, wondering if Esther or Jenny would ever look out and see him. For a moment, he wondered if he was trespassing, or otherwise poking his nose where he shouldn't. He decided he didn't care. Not if he could help Esther, even in the smallest of ways.

Murray wasn't sure what he was hoping would happen. Did he think Esther would see him, throw open the window, and wave to him? Call out to him? Did he think she could somehow convince her father to let him come inside, or let her come outside? Or was he hoping to see Jenny?

Murray wasn't sure. The only thing he knew was that he needed to be there for his new friend. And since her father wouldn't let him in the house, this was the best he could do. Maybe it was ridiculous. Maybe it was a waste of time. To Murray, it didn't matter. He was doing what he could, and that was all he could do. So he settled into his newfound reading nook and opened the book.

The next day, school passed by without Murray even noticing. Not only was Esther absent again, but Jenny wasn't there either. Murray spent the entire day imagining all the terrible reasons why his new friends weren't at school.

As soon as the bell announced the end of the school day, Murray gathered his books, stuffed them into his bag, and half walked, half jogged to the Brennan farmhouse.

Everything looked exactly the same, as if not a moment had passed from the prior afternoon. But as Murray made his way around the farmhouse—not bothering this time to knock on the door—he saw something in the oak grove where he had read yesterday.

Jenny.

She was sitting cross-legged against a burr oak, looking toward the farmhouse just as Murray had done the day before. Murray made his way toward her and tentatively approached, fearful of what she might say.

"Hi," Jenny said when he reached her.

Murray wanted desperately to know about Esther's condition, but asking felt like too big of a risk. So he stood there stupidly, silently.

"Want to sit?" Jenny asked. She patted the ground near her, and Murray immediately obeyed. "I saw you out here yesterday."

"Is that okay?" Murray asked. "It probably seems weird, but I just wanted to be close. It felt like where I was supposed to be. I'm sorry."

Jenny's laugh was light and unexpected, considering all that was going on. "There's nothing to be sorry for. I think it's sweet."

For the first time since he saw her in the grove, Murray found his breath. "How is she?" he asked.

"Better, actually," Jenny said, and Murray felt a relaxing of muscles he hadn't realized he'd been tensing. "Last night started bad, but then she fell asleep sometime in the middle of the night. When she woke up, she seemed almost like it had never happened. It sounds like she might even be back at school on Monday. And there's a hot-air balloon festival next month that she's been dying to go to. Have you heard about it?"

"I don't think so."

"Esther's been saving her money all year so she can take a ride in one. I hear there will be dozens of them. Can you imagine?"

"I'm so happy Esther's feeling better," Murray said. It was the only thing he could think about. He breathed another sigh of relief, suddenly feeling light, as if he could fly, just like one of those hot-air balloons Jenny talked about.

Jenny stood then and looked down at him. "I have to go. My parents have been busy caring for Esther, so I have to do most of the chores. I just wanted to say thank you for coming. Thank you for caring."

She stared into his eyes for a long moment, freezing Murray in place, helpless. But then she looked down at her hands.

"I'll see you Monday," she finally said. "Don't forget the book."

Murray struggled to find his voice. "I won't," he eventually said. But Jenny was too far away to hear him.

Murray barely slept that weekend. When Monday finally came, he jumped out of bed, dressed for the day, and nearly sprinted out of the house, giving his mother a quick hug on the way out.

The sun was bright when he took his seat in class. And it brightened even more when he heard Esther's crutches click and clack against the wooden floor, the sound growing louder until she finally entered the room. She came directly to Murray's desk, a smile illuminating her entire face.

"I hear you came to the house," she said.

"I hope that's okay with you."

"Of course. I'm happy you did. I'm sorry my dad wouldn't let you in. I get sick a lot, and he's pretty protective. I think he was trying to prevent you from getting sick, too."

"That's fine," Murray said.

"Jenny says you brought your book and read in the oak grove."

"That's right," Murray said, and he couldn't explain why he didn't feel embarrassed. Somehow he knew Esther would understand. Her smile verified his hunch.

"You didn't finish it, did you?" she asked. "I was hoping you could read more at recess, maybe start where we left off?"

"Sure," Murray said.

"Great. Then I'll see you at recess."

"See you at recess."

With that, she hobbled over to her desk just as Ms. Carson began roll call.

The morning took twice as long as forever, but eventually Ms. Carson announced that it was time for lunch. Murray scarfed down his sandwich and made a beeline for the ditch at the edge of the playground.

He didn't have to wait long before the silhouettes of Jenny and Esther appeared at the top of the ditch. He leapt to his feet and helped Esther down. He chanced a quick glance at Jenny, whose cheeks were a bit red as she said hello.

When they were all seated in the bottom of the ditch, Murray opened the copy of *Little Women*.

"Do you remember where we were?" he asked.

"Chapter three," Esther said. "Laurie and Jo just met."

Murray skipped back to chapter three and began reading. Esther pulled out her notepad and pencil and began drawing scenes from the book. Ten minutes passed peaceably before they were interrupted. When shadows appeared at the ridge of the ditch, Murray felt his breath catch as he realized who it was: the popular boys.

"What's going on down here?" one of them said, his voice menacing and, for some reason, angry.

Murray didn't even know their names. Not that it mattered. He didn't think they were there to converse.

"We're reading, obviously," Jenny said. Murray felt grateful for her presence, her confidence. If her effect on these boys was anything like her effect on him, she could simply order them to do something—like leave them alone—and they would obey without hesitation. But their response seemed to indicate her spell wouldn't work on them.

"Let's see the book," another of them said.

The very last thing Murray wanted was to show these boys the book, but he didn't see any alternative. Besides, down in the bottom of the ditch he was at a disadvantage. The boys had unknowingly invited him to escape from his vulnerable position. Murray scrambled up the side of the ditch and handed the book to the much taller boy. They were all carrying sticks, he noticed, and holding them as if they were weapons. Murray heard Esther's crutches behind him and saw Jenny help her out of the ditch.

"Are you serious?" the boy said, gawking at the book. "*Little Women?*" He turned his incredulous expression toward Murray. "You're reading a book called *Little Women?*"

Murray didn't know how to respond, so he tried to remove all expression from his face and stand stoically as the group of boys fell into hysterics.

"What's so funny?" Jenny said.

The boys stopped laughing immediately, which seemed like a bad omen. One of them, the one who had spoken first, stepped close enough to Jenny that Murray's heart started pounding.

"What's so funny is that this loser is reading a girl's book to a couple girls. In a ditch."

"He's not a loser," Esther said, and for a moment all tension released from Murray's body as he felt a fondness for his friend.

But it didn't last because the boy then turned to Esther. "What do you know about it?" he said, and he swung his stick casually in her direction. It wasn't an attack exactly, but intentionally or not, the stick connected with one of Esther's crutches, knocking it out from under her. She lurched forward, trying to maintain her balance with one crutch. But the removal of the first crutch was unexpected, and she swayed slightly before losing her balance entirely and falling to the dusty ground.

Rage flared in Murray's chest, a searing heat that emanated from the core of his being. The thought that anyone would pick on someone as innocent and vulnerable as Esther ignited an explosive, visceral response that Murray hadn't known lay dormant inside him.

He lunged at the boy who had done it, his fists flailing wildly. Murray had never been in a fight. He had no idea *how* to fight. But he didn't care. He threw his fists at every part of the boy's body and face that he could reach. He scratched at him and elbowed him. If he'd been close enough to bite him, Murray would have done so without hesitation.

As soon as the other boys recovered from the momentary shock of what was happening, they pounced on Murray like a pack of wolves. It took less than a second for them to pry him off the other boy, throw him onto his back, and start raining blows down on him.

Murray knew all he could do was curl into a ball and try to protect himself as best he could. Some of their kicks connected with his stomach, a few with his legs, and one or two snuck through to hit his face. He felt blood gush from his nose, but because of the adrenaline, he barely felt the pain.

Murray knew the fight wouldn't last long, if he could call such one-sided abuse a fight. These were schoolyard bullies, not gangsters or hardened criminals. He knew he'd take a beating for what he'd done, but at no point during the assault did Murray regret his decision to stand up for Esther. Not that he had made a decision. Instinct had taken over. He'd thrown six punches before he'd even realized what he was doing.

As it turned out, the punishment ended even sooner than Murray expected. As his senses started to return, he not only heard Esther's and Jenny's voices but also the distant voice of Ms. Carson yelling at the boys to stop.

They all stopped at the same time, realizing they were being watched by a teacher and would certainly be sentenced to weeks of detention, based on what the teacher was seeing. Murray inched his eyes open and lifted his head from the protection of his arms. It was a mistake. One of the boys seized the opportunity to kick him once more, flush in the face.

Murray had never experienced a broken nose before, but he recognized the crunching sound and the shifting of cartilage. What had been a little bit of blood dripping from his nose became a flow.

"Follow me. All of you," a furious Ms. Carson said when she arrived.

Murray couldn't see much through the tears that now flowed from his eyes, but he was able to make out the form of his teacher grabbing two of the boys by their sleeves and hauling them away while the others followed. "You two," the teacher said to Esther and Jenny, "help him to the nurse's office. Your classes start in five minutes, and I expect you both to be in attendance."

Murray managed to get onto his hands and knees, but he felt too wobbly to stand. A pair of hands on his shoulder attempted to help him up but lacked the strength to do so. Murray stood, mostly on his own, but then used the steady presence next to him to stay upright and guide him in the right direction.

"I'm so sorry," he heard Jenny's voice say. "Are you okay?"

Murray tried to respond but couldn't. He just focused on walking, one step after another, trusting that Jenny would get him where he needed to go.

When they finally arrived at what Murray assumed was the nurse's office, he was given a bag of ice and guided to a cot, where he sat back and covered as much of his face as he could with the cooling packet. He heard the nurse order Jenny back to class. He felt her hand on his shoulder for a moment, but then her footsteps echoed down the hallway.

The world continued around Murray in the form of nearby movement and distant voices, but for a long time all he could focus on was keeping the ice pack in a relatively pain-free position. The swelling of his nose and the tears that formed every time he opened his eyes made him effectively blind. It surprised him how disorienting it was to lose that one sense.

After what felt like hours, he started to feel close to normal again. The tears had stopped flowing and the ice had apparently helped with the swelling, making it possible to see again. Slowly, he pulled the ice pack off his face and sat up straight.

He was surprised to see Jenny at his side. Her green eyes were soft and slightly sad, enhancing their beauty tenfold. Murray swallowed hard and looked around. Jenny brought her chair directly next to the cot he sat on and reached toward him as if she was going to touch his face. She stopped short, but looked at him gently, with sparkling eyes.

"I don't care what the teachers say, I had to come check on you. Are you okay?"

Murray figured he must be, because he felt no pain. At the moment, he'd forgotten that pain even existed. He tried to speak but all he could manage was a short nod. Jenny breathed a heavy sigh of relief.

"Thank you for what you did out there, standing up for Esther like that."

Murray wasn't sure how to respond. "Didn't have much luck, did I?"

"No. You're really not a very good fighter, are you?"

The momentary hit to his pride quickly dissipated when Jenny laughed a light, twinkling giggle and reached out to touch his forearm. "It was five against one," she said. "It was very brave of you."

When she leaned over, Murray froze, terrified. His heart beat so fast and hard he felt like an animal cornered by its prey. Then Jenny's lips, very lightly and very briefly, pressed against his cheek.

She stood, and they looked at each other in a completely new way. Murray wanted to profess his everlasting love to her, but he didn't know how. Besides, he couldn't have spoken even if he'd known what to say. So he stared after her as she walked away, wondering how it was possible that his body was still attached to the earth.

CHAPTER 5

1996

"That was the day I fell in love with you," Jenny says. She's still sitting on the couch, next to me. At some point, Brooke joined us on the couch, as if to be closer to the story. "I knew you were trustworthy. I knew you had integrity."

I take her hand and kiss it.

"And it was the day I stopped being terrified of you," I say.

Jenny and Brooke laugh at that. An old man using exaggeration to make a joke. But if any part of what I said isn't true, it's not the idea that I was terrified of her, but the idea that the terror ever went away. Truth is, I couldn't be sure I'd remember to take my next breath when Jenny was around. Stupefied me, that's what she did. Still does, even to this day.

"Well," I say. "We're on a quest. Probably better not burn any more daylight."

I wink at Brooke since she knows perfectly well about my plans. Brooke says, "I'm in." And Jenny pats my hand.

So there's our crew. Three of us. Shackleton had twenty-eight, but three of us should be plenty. I start moving my weight back and forth, sliding closer to the edge of the couch cushion. Then, with one big, risky push, I put all my strength into standing from the couch.

And I almost make it, too. But just before I get enough weight over my hips, my momentum stops and gravity catches up with me. I thump back down onto the couch, which is fortunately very soft.

I know what comes next. Brooke will gasp and worry and stand ever so easily on her way to helping me up. And watching her pop up from the couch will make me feel even more miserable about the fact that I can't do that any longer. It's what always happens around well-meaning young people.

But Brooke doesn't do that. Unless I missed it, there was no gasp at all. And instead of bouncing up from the couch to help pull me up, Brooke simply puts a supportive hand on my back and gives just enough of a push to help my shoulders get all the way over my hips the second time around.

It's quite a bit like what I'm trying to do for Jenny, now that I think of it. She's still my Jenny. Still has a bunch of the old memories. She just has a hard time making new ones. She can't do that like she used to. But she doesn't need pity or too much force. She just needs those around her to give her a little support, a little momentum.

"Much obliged," I say once I'm standing. Then I hold my hand out to Jenny and hope Brooke doesn't feel the need to say anything more about it. Sure enough, she's silent as a nightingale as Jenny takes my hand and I help her stand from the couch.

"Where are we going first?" Brooke asks.

"The farmhouse," I say. "The place where Jenny grew up." I feel a little rush of panic, pat my pants pockets and say, "Now where did I put my handkerchief?"

"Is that it in your back pocket?" Brooke says.

It is. I remember moving it to that pocket earlier, and I feel silly for forgetting. It turns out you don't have to have dementia to forget things. You just have to be old. Even though I know that momentarily forgetting something isn't the same thing as having dementia, it still bothers me.

The truth is it scares me, what's happening to Jenny. For her, most of all, but I also worry about my own brain. It's not something young folks probably spend much time thinking about, but when you get to a certain age the idea of losing your mind tends to gnaw at you now and again.

I worry about a time when everything is normal, every day just like the last—and then it's not. Suddenly you can't remember where you parked the car. Well, that might not be too concerning until you realize you left the keys inside. And beyond that, you locked yourself out of your house, which would be a big enough problem if you could remember where you lived, but you suddenly realize you haven't got any idea. Can't even focus on the question of where you live because your mind is simply not working like it used to.

And that's when the real fear sets in. That's when you start wondering how many days you have left before your mind is really and truly gone. And you think about all the things that it'll mean, for you and for everyone around you.

You feel lost because all these things you used to know like the back of your hand are suddenly foreign. You feel scared because, let's face it, if you don't know where your house or car are located, there's not much you can do but stand around looking like a zombie. And you feel confused because you know that you *know* all of these things. It's not that they're gone, that's not it at all. Every bit of information is still there—the location of your car, your house, the name of your spouse. But locating them, that's the problem. They're in there somewhere; you just don't have the foggiest idea where.

At least that's how I envision it. That's what I'm scared of.

"Should we go?" Brooke says, bringing me out of my thoughts.

"Sure, sure," I say, and I take Jenny's hand.

I wish I knew what Jenny was thinking about this whole situation with Brooke. The Jenny I knew back when she had better access to her mind would probably point out how lovely it is that we live in a world where the kindness of strangers makes it possible for an old couple to meet a nice young person and spend a day with her, maybe even become fast friends. That it really is a miraculous thing to be alive.

I give Jenny a moment, hoping she'll say something like that. But she stays silent, and her gaze seems to be fixated on an empty corner of the room.

"Let me help you to the car," Brooke says, and she escorts us out the front door.

Jenny and I ride in the back of Helen's car while Brooke struggles to drive it. Her mother had a handle on the whole first-to-third gear situation, but Brooke's not quite as smooth. She revs first gear all the way to the top all right, but then the car lurches back as the grinding sound of metal on metal fills the car, mixing with the curses under Brooke's breath. Then the car lurches forward with an unnaturally low rumble.

After she kills the engine at the first two stop signs, Brooke starts rolling through them, looking left and right for oncoming cars as she approaches the intersection. My hands are squeezing my thighs something fierce, but I don't say anything. No one likes a back-seat driver.

Brooke sees Doc Keaton's pamphlet sitting on the passenger seat and picks it up. She starts reading, right while she's driving. It makes me uncomfortable, and not just because she might get in a wreck. Part of me still wants to hide Jenny's condition and everything to do with it—hide the pamphlet, refuse to talk about it, pretend it's not real. But I can tell you this much: ignoring hard things doesn't make them go away.

Just as I'm about to tell Brooke it might be a good idea to keep her eyes on the road, she tosses the pamphlet back onto the passenger seat, apparently finished with reading it.

"Where are we going?" Jenny asks, staring out the window.

I'm about to say something like, *To the farmhouse, remember, love? We talked about it just a minute ago.*

But Brooke, apparently having learned a thing or two from Doc Keaton's pamphlet, comes to my rescue before I can put my foot in my mouth.

"I think it would be fun to go on a quest," she says.

Jenny's eyes brighten immediately. "A quest . . . yes, let's do it, Murray. Let's try to find the treasure worth more than gold, just like when we were younger. Shall we?"

"Of course, love," I say, and I kiss her forehead. "We could start by going to the old farmhouse, if you'd like?"

"Oh, yes," Jenny says, and her excitement is both soothing and concerning to me.

"Wonderful. To the old farmhouse it is," I say. It's like a declaration, as if we just made the decision, even though two of us in the car already knew where we were going.

Of course, getting there is another matter. It's been years since Jenny and I have been to her childhood home. I try to think of a time we've been back since her parents passed on, but I can't come up with anything. And that's going on thirty-five years now. So it's no wonder we can't drive straight there. Nothing looks the same anymore.

I direct Brooke the best I can, but it's not long before she realizes I don't know where we are. She asks what city it's in, but I don't think it's in a city. When she asks what direction from

Lemon Grove, I can at least point her to the northwest. Once we get out of town a bit, I'm sure I'll start to recognize things. In the meantime, we pass through neighborhoods I've never seen before.

"This whole area sure has changed," I say.

Brooke nods. "Between gentrification and urban sprawl, it's no wonder our communities are losing their cultural cohesion," she says.

I want to ask what she means, but I can't figure out which of the words she said is most confusing, so I just nod in agreement. Jenny chuckles at my side. I can't begin to comprehend the things she understands and the things she doesn't.

"There we go," I say when I catch a glimpse of the river off to the right a ways. "Follow that river, if you can. It goes right through the homestead."

"Roger that," Brooke says, and she turns the car in the direction of the river. But then, without warning, she pulls the car to the side of the road and stops. "I just want to check the map," she says.

She reaches for the glove compartment, but her movements seem distracted. She touches the handle, but doesn't pull the compartment open. Instead, she just sits still. I'm about to ask what she's doing when I see that she's staring out the passenger side window, entranced.

Jenny and I follow her gaze and see a man in a business suit walking toward the front door of his house, where a woman and two small children wait to greet him with open arms. It looks like he's just returning from a business trip of some sort, if you ask me.

Brooke doesn't blink as she stares at the scene. Then, as if shaken free from a spell, she clears her throat and turns her attention back to the glove compartment, which turns out not to hold a map at all. She closes it and starts down the road without any explanation for her random stop.

"That looked like a nice family back there," I say. And then, although I know I shouldn't, although I know I sound like an old-timer, I can't help myself. "You're still very young. I'm sure you'll find someone better than that last boyfriend of yours."

Brooke's eyes flick to mine in the rearview. "We talk of nothing but lovers and such absurdities," she says. "I don't wish to get raspy, so let's change the subject."

Jenny sits next to me with a little smile on her lips, as if she knows something I don't. And I'm definitely missing something, because what Brooke just said sounds awfully familiar. It's not until a good five minutes later that I finally realize she quoted Jo from *Little Women* directly.

This kid is sure turning out to be more than she first appeared, and that's the truth.

Once we have the river to help navigate, we find our way to the old homestead pretty quickly. At least, we arrive at the spot that's as close as you can get these days. It's still here, the farmhouse, which is amazing in itself. It's just far enough out of town that the sprawl hasn't caught up with it yet. The two-lane highway cuts through the land not a half mile from where the barn still stands, and the smaller gravel road, where Brooke pulls the car off to the side and parks, is only about a hundred yards away from the stone farmhouse.

The three of us walk like a line of soldiers headed to battle. Jenny holds one of my elbows for support, and Brooke holds the other, as if I'm supporting her, too. It's a little silly, I know. I should be holding onto Brooke, not the other way around. But I still get stability from her this way, and something about the posture makes me feel able-bodied. Like I can still assist a young lady, even if all of earth and creation knows I'm the one in need of assistance.

It's amazing how strong young people are. Brooke is stable as can be and has no problem keeping Jenny and I steady as we slowly make our way toward the old homestead.

The first building we come upon is the old hayloft. It's one of the hundreds of old buildings you can see these days along the side of the road—neglected wooden structures leaning so far that one more good gust of wind will knock it clean over, the red paint so chipped and faded you can hardly tell it was ever there. All the windows of the hayloft are long gone, with only scarred and empty windowpanes remaining. It's a ruin. A relic. If I hadn't seen it back in the day, I wouldn't believe it had ever been a sturdy structure that held several tons of hay for the livestock on the farm.

It breaks my heart to realize that every one of those decaying buildings throughout the middle of the country has a lively history. Babies were born within the now-tumbling walls. Men worked the fields from sunup to sundown, hauling their planting and harvesting tools into the barn at the end of a long day's work. Kids threw balls against the large, red face of the barn and picked raspberries from the patch around the side of the house.

But you'd never know it by looking at them now. The structures that remain are old and rotting, not even safe to enter because they might fall right on top of you.

It was a simpler time back then, when people lived real lives in the real world. These days, everyone's cooped up inside. No one sees the sky anymore, smells the long grass, feels the sun poke around a puff of cloud. It's bittersweet to see these buildings—the hayloft, the big barn nearby. The memories are still fresh, even if the structures are sagging.

We make our way past the barn, which used to contain the family's farming equipment, and turn toward where the old farmhouse is situated. After seeing the state of the other buildings, I expect the house to be in a similar state. But as it comes into view it seems, from a distance anyway, to be standing tall. The closer we get, the sturdier it looks. Much of the exterior is dilapidated and cracking, and the windows are nothing but broken shards of glass. And I don't even want to imagine what the inside might look like. But the structure stands.

Most of the house was built with stone, which is the reason this farmhouse is still standing while all the wood-framed houses in the area have collapsed.

We walk right up to the front door, and Jenny puts her hand on the stone around the doorframe. She's taken back in time, I can see. Her mind is clear as can be.

"Oh, Murray," she says. "Can you believe it? I grew up in this house. This was my home." She turns in a slow circle, as if remembering the property from each angle. She stops when she's facing the old oak grove. "And that's where you read when Esther was sick."

"That's right," I say. It's amazing how much she can remember, despite her condition.

"She had tuberculosis," Jenny says, a small crinkle forming in her brow. "We called it 'consumption' back then."

"Yes," I say.

Then Jenny looks at me with an aching helplessness in her eyes. She looks all around the property once more, ending back on the stone farmhouse.

"Esther," she says sadly.

When my beautiful bride starts to weep silently into her hands, I know it's time to leave.

Maybe taking Jenny back to the old homestead was a mistake. Why dredge up all that pain? Didn't I decide to try to avoid that today? Why not let the past stay in the past? It's so much easier to suppress our difficult memories, the bad times in our lives, and pretend they never happened. It's so much better to focus only on the good times.

Except, that's not true. Pretending isn't authentic, nor is it honest. And I've found that sometimes suppressing things can take more energy than facing them.

Brooke watches Jenny cautiously, like she's trying to figure out what to say or whether to say anything at all. I see it all the time with well-intentioned people around my bride. They want to be helpful and show they care, but they're worried they'll do more harm than good if they stick their foot in their mouth, maybe say something that'll set Jenny off. So they decide to play it safe.

The problem is, playing it safe means not doing or saying anything at all. When Jenny's surrounded day after day by people so darned well-meaning that they don't do or say anything at all, she loses. She loses conversations; she loses experiences. She loses friends.

Life is nothing but a series of risks. Some you take, some you allow to pass by. Choosing the right risks to take can be tricky. It can also be the difference between a rewarding life, full of close relationships and wondrous experiences, and one that's safe, secure, and slowly sucks the energy out of you.

I need to let Brooke know that this risk—talking to Jenny and risking setting her off—is a risk worth taking.

"That was beautiful," I say as we return to the beat-up car. I hold Jenny's hand and smile into the sunlight. "Sad, to be sure. Hard memories. But beautiful. Thank you for joining us, Brooke."

"Sure," she says, and I can tell she's tempted by that instinct to suppress and pretend, but to the kid's credit, she looks square at Jenny when she says, "Thanks for letting me tag along."

Jenny smiles that sweet smile of hers, but focuses on making her way into the car rather than saying anything in reply. I know there's a whirlwind of memories going through her mind.

"So, are we going to the park you talked about before?" Brooke asks me. "Is that the next stop?"

"That's the plan," I say. "But we'll need one more thing before we go there."

"What's that?"

"A couple chairs of some sort. Something to sit on. Should have packed some earlier, but I guess I didn't think of it until just now."

"My mom has a couple camp chairs," Brooke says. "I'm sure we could use them. And my house isn't that far out of the way. Want to swing by there on the way to the park?"

"That sure is thoughtful of you," I say. And the plan is set.

Some of the roads are a bit on the bumpy side, and in this little Ford we can feel every crack and pothole. Jenny nuzzles into my shoulder, as if for protection from the bouncing. So I feel like all is right with the world.

But that changes in a heartbeat when we approach Brooke's house. She slows the car and leans forward, like she's trying to see the address numbers on the houses, even though it's her own neighborhood and she's been here a thousand times. As we get closer, I understand why.

In the front yard of one of the houses, someone has put a bunch of things in the yard. The closer we get, the more stuff we see. Couches, beds, clothes, lamps. You name it, it's there in the yard. It's like someone decided to put every one of their worldly possessions on their front lawn.

And then it hits us all at the same time, what we're seeing. Brooke's shoulders slouch and her head leans to the side, like the effort of holding it straight has suddenly become too much. "Shit," she says under her breath.

But here's the thing—I can't blame her for cursing. Not in this situation. Because it's her house we're looking at, and those things thrown all over the yard? Those are her things. Hers and her mother's.

She parks the car across the road and hops out. I watch her cross the street with barely contained energy threatening to break loose with every step. Jenny pats my hand softly and says, "You should go, too, Murray. See if there's anything you can do to help her."

I don't know what I could possibly do to help in any way, but that's Jenny for you. You can't help if you're not there, she likes to say. And if you're there, you never know how you might be able to help.

It takes several minutes to get out of the car, make my way across the street, and pick my way past a large wooden dresser on one side and one of those new tape players—a boombox, they call it—on the other. When I walk through the open front door, I hear Brooke pleading.

"You can't do this. It's our house. It's our stuff!"

"The house belongs to the bank now," a level voice answers. It's the kind of voice that has practice in removing all feeling, all compassion. It's a voice meant to give bad news without escalating a situation.

When I turn the corner and see them, Brooke is facing a man in a black suit, the kind I imagine an old coroner would wear. His eyes dart to me when I arrive, but then turn back to Brooke.

"Unfortunately, that means you're trespassing. And your 'stuff' as you call it, is outside. You have twenty-four hours to remove it, or it will be donated or taken to the dump."

"You can't do this!" Brooke says.

"I'm afraid I don't have a choice. You can't keep your house without paying your mortgage," the man says. "You had several warnings."

"We've been trying."

"The mortgage should always come first," the man says, a little heartlessly, if you ask me. "I'm sorry you're learning that lesson the hard way."

Brooke seems to look right where the couch used to be. The one I sat on not two hours ago, telling a story to Brooke and Jenny. It's surreal to see it removed.

"You say pay the mortgage first," Brooke says. "The collection agency said we had to pay our medical bills first. What are we supposed to do when we don't have enough money for both?"

The man looks flustered for the first time, anxious to leave. "I'm sorry. There's nothing more I can do. You need to leave the house now so I can administer the new lock."

For the first time, Brooke looks defeated. "Does my mom know?" she asks.

"A notice left on the front door this morning listed the time of eviction. So if she read that, then yes, she knows. If not . . . well, she should have read it."

The man motions toward the open front door, and we all shuffle out of the house. For Brooke, it's her last time leaving her home, I realize. Once we're outside, she looks back through the open door as if trying to catch a final glimpse of where she grew up.

Then the man closes the door and hangs a lock on the handle. He says nothing and avoids eye contact as he strides toward a large sedan parked at the curb and drives away. Brooke and I are alone on her lawn. Well, what used to be her lawn.

"I can't believe this is happening," she says. "I don't know what we're going to do."

Jenny and I had some lean times, and that's the truth. I remember eating bread and crackers for long stretches after that crash back in the twenties. But I was fortunate to have my baseball career, which insulated us from the depression that followed. Even though we didn't have much, we always had a roof over our heads and food in our bellies.

But as Brooke stands in the yard, looking at every one of the worldly possessions she and her mother own, I see realization hit her hard. She no longer has a home. No protection from the elements at all, other than a beat-up car with no second gear.

Just then, Brooke's mother, Helen, comes walking down the sidewalk on her way home from work. She stops several houses down, moves her eyeglasses from her neck to her eyes, then hurries straight to her daughter and tries to give her a hug. Before she can get too close, Brooke pushes her mother away.

"Why didn't you pay the mortgage?" she demands.

I don't feel like this is something they'd want me around for, and besides, my knee is acting up again. So while Brooke and her mother argue, I hobble to the car and make my way into the back seat next to Jenny.

My wife looks at me hopefully, but I just shake my head. "There was nothing I could do," I say.

"They lost the house?"

"Sure looks that way."

Jenny's eyes glisten as she looks past me to where Brooke and her mother are no longer arguing, and have begun rummaging through their things. Trying to decide what to sell and how to go about it, I guess. Or what to try to keep in their car. I don't know how it works when someone loses their home so abruptly.

"What will they do now?" Jenny asks.

"I don't know," I say, and saying it makes me feel worthless, incompetent.

"They should stay at our house, Murray. No one will be using it once we move out tomorrow."

It's always difficult to know what Jenny does and doesn't remember at any given time. Right now, she seems to remember that we're moving into Aspen Leaves tomorrow, but not that Chance and Olivia are moving into our house while they remodel their mansion. "I don't think that could work with Chance and Olivia staying there," I say.

Before Jenny can get too bothered by the fact that she can't remember about Chance and Olivia, I try to move things along. "I'm sure they'll figure something out, but I should let them know we can find another way home, so they don't have to worry about that, at least. Maybe I can call us a cab."

When I get back to the yard, Helen has found the latest newspaper and is scanning the classified ads. She looks to the neighbors' house and says, "Brooke, will you go see if John and Carole will let us use their phone? This apartment complex might still have an opening."

Brooke glares at her mother for a moment, as if infuriated about being asked to help fix a problem she didn't create. But when Helen just raises her eyebrows at her, Brooke huffs loudly and storms over to the next house. She knocks on the door, waits a bit, and knocks some more. But no one answers.

When Brooke gets back to us, I say, "You can use our phone, if you'd like. Mine and Jenny's. Our grandson might be in and out of there today because he's moving in tomorrow—otherwise I'd offer you the house for as long as you need it. But for today anyway, the house is yours."

Helen looks at me in surprise. Then she looks toward the car, as if she's wondering whether Jenny approved this plan. That's another great thing about my wife. If I offered everything we have to someone in need, my Jenny would sign off on it in a heartbeat. That's just how she is.

"That's so kind of you," Helen says. "It would be very helpful. Since, apparently we only have twenty-four hours to move these things, I should really get to work on that right away."

"Of course. Let's get you over there right now."

We start toward the car, but then Helen pulls up short. "Oh," she says. "I forgot all about your quest. Did you find what you were looking for?"

"We've accomplished quite a bit," I say. But then Brooke jumps in.

"We were just about to go to a park," she says bitterly. She gestures in disgust to the things in their yard. "Before this."

"Well, you absolutely must continue your quest," Helen says. She turns to me. "That is, if you're okay with me being in your house without you there?"

I can see her trying to appease her daughter. I wish Brooke would cut her a little slack. Kids sometimes think their parents should be able to control everything, like if something goes wrong and they don't immediately fix it, it must be because they just don't care to. But that's simply not how the world works.

"Think nothing of it," I say. "Think nothing of it."

Helen exhales deeply, like a heavy weight has been removed from her shoulders. "Thank you," she says, and wraps my old bones in a giant hug.

I unlock the front door of our little house and motion Helen forward. It's an old house with small windows, so it's pretty dark inside despite being the middle of the day. I flick on a light switch and see that Chance has been back. Half the living room now looks like a storage area for Chance and Olivia's things. Just a few things, he said. Not as much as it looked like, he said.

I grumble under my breath and point Helen in the direction of the telephone. "The yellow pages should be right there on the counter if you need them," I say.

Helen thanks me about a dozen times as I make my way back to the Ford without a second gear and rejoin my wife and new young friend.

But rather than starting up the old motor, Brooke sits as still as a nun lost in prayer. The moment stretches on and when I lean forward to ask what's the holdup, Brooke has tears streaming down her face.

Jenny is gazing out the window, apparently not recognizing the situation. So I touch Brooke's shoulder. "Are you feeling okay?" I ask.

It's a silly question, and I immediately regret asking it. It's obvious that something is bothering her, otherwise she wouldn't be crying. A better question would have been something like *Would you like to talk about what's bothering you?* Or maybe *Is there anything I can do to help you?* But men of my generation aren't usually the best at that kind of thing. Not that it's an excuse. Just the truth of the matter.

Brooke pulls a sleeve over her hand and wipes at her cheeks. "I'm fine," she says. And that's why my question was the wrong one. It was too superficial. It's the socially expected question that leads to the socially expected answer, which is that whole suppressing and pretending issue again.

But I've learned a thing or two over my eighty years with Jenny. Not as much as I might have, of course, but a thing or two. So I don't let Brooke off so easily.

"There's nothing wrong with being upset," I say. "It's just a feeling, not a weakness. And sometimes it can help to let it all out, if you know what I mean."

Brooke's reddened eyes flick to the rearview mirror as she wipes at them again. She glances at Jenny, but my wife is still looking out the window. I can tell right away that Jenny has slipped back into confusion. She's not agitated, just quiet. It sometimes feels as if she's not really here with me, and that's what's going on now.

But this here's one of the great things about my relationship with Jenny. Normally, she'd be the one to comfort the crying teenage girl. It most definitely wouldn't be me. But there's that old saying, *And two shall become one,* and this is what that means. Jenny's not currently able to do what she would normally do, but a part of her is part of me now. So I'm able to be better than I was before her. Better than I would have been without her. So I sit quietly and don't rush Brooke into anything. Sometimes all someone needs is a bit of space.

Sure enough, Brooke lets out a big sigh, as if her final wall just came down.

"We're losing our house," she says. "I'm going to be homeless."

I can't help but think of the rough-looking gentleman at the bus stop this morning. Being homeless changes everything. When you have to spend all your time figuring out where your next meal will come from or where you'll be able to sleep that night, where you'll be safe from bad weather and bad people, well, there's no room for anything else in a life like that. For this kid, school would take a back seat, just like every other thing would take a back seat. And that's how the cascade starts, and a life really goes off the rails.

Since I know those aren't the things Brooke needs to hear right now, I keep my old mouth shut and let her keep talking.

"I just can't believe it's come to this, you know? I mean, when my dad was around, it's not like we were rich or anything. But money wasn't really an issue." After a moment of reflection, she says, "At least, I never knew about it if it was. But I can't imagine what it's going to be like, you know? It's freezing here in the winter. What do people do?"

I'm not sure, so I don't say anything at all.

"My mom's so naive," Brooke says. "It's her fault this happened."

"Oh, I don't know about that," I say,

"She should have seen that my dad's a deadbeat and he'd leave her the first time things got hard. She should have been smarter when it comes to money. But she's so delusional. She thinks the world is all rainbows and butterflies. She's always saying that everything's going to be okay, but it's not. Life sucks. People you thought loved you just leave you, people lose their houses because they followed their passion instead of getting some soul-crushing corporate job, and nothing's ever okay. I mean, just look at my life."

I wish there was something I could say to make things better, but if such a thing exists, I sure don't know what it is. My boys went through some dark times, too. Times when they were full of angst and anger—usually directed at their father. I didn't know how to fix things then and I don't know how to fix things now. It makes me feel pretty useless, and that's the truth.

Then, as if a switch of some sort goes off in Brooke's mind, she shakes her head a little and says, "I need a distraction. Let's get back to the quest. Which park are we going to again?"

"Carpenter Park," I say, happy to see her snap out of it. "On the double."

Brooke tilts her head like she isn't sure what "on the double" means, but then she nods, turns back to face the front, and starts the old car with a rumble. She manages the transition from first to third a bit more smoothly this time, and we start bumping down the road.

The car's dashboard has a digital clock that reads 12:29 p.m. Normally, Jenny and I would be in the middle of our midday nap at 12:29 p.m. Like clockwork, I'd pull myself out of bed at 5:00 a.m. after a miserable night's sleep, take my pill first thing along with breakfast, spend a bit of time at the church, and then help Deb care for Jenny until noon, when we'd both settle back into bed for a nice nap.

But it turns out going on a quest changes things.

The change to our schedule is a bit disorienting. Only slightly for me, as if there's something on my to-do list that requires attention but I'm not able to figure out what it is. It's like a persistent tapping inside my head, reminding me that something isn't as expected.

Of course, I'm able to recognize that it's the change to our routine. Poor Jenny, she must have the same feelings multiplied a hundred times over but with no ability to reassure herself that everything's okay. That the world actually does still make sense. It's probably why she hasn't said a word since we got back to the car.

Still, sitting next to me in the back seat of the car, even in a ninety-nine-year-old body that barely resembles the person I've known for so long, Jenny exudes pure beauty. And people might think I've truly lost my marbles, but the God's honest truth is Jenny is still sexy. I don't understand it. I've seen all the objective changes her body has gone through over the years. I'm aware. But she's still sexy. Always has been, always will be.

I might not have the ability to do much about it these days, but that's another story.

As Brooke continues toward Carpenter Park, Jenny's eyes have that vacant stare. Beautiful, but vacant. I put a hand gently onto her shoulder. "It's okay," I say, recognizing the disorientation she's feeling. "Everything is okay."

To my relief, the words seem to help with her fear. Not with her confusion, of course. That's something I haven't been able to figure out how to solve.

"Who are you?" Jenny asks in a sweet voice.

It's the second time she's asked me that question, and I can tell already that it'll never get any easier to hear. *I'm the love of your life, don't you remember?* That's what I want to scream. *I'm the father of your children!*

Instead, I pat her shoulder gently. "I'm Murray. And I'm here to take care of you, so don't you worry. You're in good hands."

Jenny heaves a long sigh, as if the words are both enough to calm her and wholly unsatisfying.

Brooke catches my eye in the rearview with an expression that I can tell is intended to be meaningful. "Maybe you could continue your story, Mr. McBride."

She's a smart one, that Brooke. She sees what's happening to Jenny, and she read Doc Keaton's pamphlet. She knows that joining Jenny where she is in her mind is the best thing we can do. And Jenny has clear memories of our childhood. So that's where we'll join her. So I speak loud and clear, as if mostly to Brooke.

"Just before we went to the old farmhouse, I told a story about back when Jenny was a little girl, but I didn't finish it."

I want to ask Jenny if she remembers that, but I trust the good doctor, so I don't ask that direct question. I just go on with my story.

"Murray, Esther, and Jenny had just met. And after the playground fight, the three of them were the best of friends."

CHAPTER 6

1910

It had taken three weeks for Murray's face to return to normal. For the first week, his eyes felt swollen to the size of apples. During the second week, the top part of his face was black and blue, and it changed to a strange green color for the entire third week.

Murray wouldn't have changed it for the world. Each time Jenny and Esther saw his discolored face, they thanked him all over again for his bravery. Part of Murray wished his injuries would never heal. Because of what had happened on the playground, his friendship with the Brennan sisters had become immeasurably deeper. He wasn't sure how life could possibly get better.

For the last few weeks, he had continued reading from his copy of *Little Women* at recess—his favorite chapter recently was when Jo convinced a publisher to run one of her stories. Under a pen name, of course. And Esther would sketch a drawing in her notepad while he read, usually resembling whatever was happening in the story at the time.

But there had always been something Murray wanted to share with his new friends. Something close to his heart, but also embarrassing. After all, how could he take them to watch the local baseball team play when he wasn't even good enough at sports to be invited to join the other boys at recess?

Still, as the three friends grew closer over the course of the weeks following the playground scuffle, Murry's desire to share his passion with his new friends only intensified. When he had finally asked if they'd like to join him for a Lemon Grove Yellow Stockings game, they had been every bit as excited as he had hoped they'd be.

Sitting on a small hill beyond the outfield fence so they wouldn't have to pay for tickets, Murray pointed to the batter now stepping up to home plate and taking a practice swing.

"That's Mr. Schneider," Murray said. "He owns the hardware store in town. He's not a very good hitter, but he can run really fast, so he bunts a lot."

"And that's good?" Jenny asked.

Murray shrugged. "He's no Ty Cobb, but if he gets a bunt single and then steals second base, it's just like he hit a double into the gap."

Jenny nodded as if she understood, but Murray got the impression she was just humoring him, which suited him just fine.

"I think we should find it," Esther said, sitting on the other side of Murray as Mr. Schneider laid down a bunt that slowly rolled foul.

Murray had no idea what she was talking about, but Jenny appeared to understand. She closed her eyes and pursed her lips into a shape that suggested restraint.

"Find what?" Murray asked.

"That stupid buried case," Jenny said, unable to hold back. "And I'm assuming she thinks we'll find a treasure worth more than gold."

"It's not stupid," Esther said. She pulled the old, metal key from a pocket of her pants and held it out before her, like she was hoping it would sparkle in the sunlight between them. Instead, the rusted key failed to impress as it sat dully in her palm. But to see the longing in Esther's eyes, Murray would have thought the key was the buried treasure itself. Of course, if Esther's claims about the key were true, her reverence made perfect sense.

Murray wasn't sure what to say, so he turned his attention to the next pitch, which was a ball high and outside. When the awkward silence between the sisters stretched on, he finally decided on a diplomatic approach. "You said you don't know where the treasure is?" he said as Mr. Schneider hit an easy ground ball to the second baseman. "No," Esther said, her voice dropping in disappointment. "Apparently, all our grandpa was able to do before he died was mutter a few things and pass along the key."

"So you know there's a case or something with a treasure," Murray said. "And you have the key to open it. But you have no idea where it is."

"We have some idea," Esther said. "We know it's nearby because our grandparents homesteaded here. And we know it's at a church with a dirt floor and a cemetery, probably built into a hill. We just don't know which one."

"There are a lot of churches around," Murray said. "Do you think we could actually find it?"

"No," Jenny cut in before Esther could answer. "Not only do we have no idea what church it could be in, we don't even know if it really exists. Our grandpa didn't actually tell our dad very much at all. Esther is filling in the rest of the story with what she wants to be true. And if some treasure does actually exist, buried at some church somewhere we don't know about, we have no idea how something could be worth more than gold. If you ask me, it seems like a fairy tale."

Murray stared at the key, thinking about what Esther had told him. He could understand Jenny's skepticism. What he couldn't understand was why she seemed angry.

"Who's this?" Jenny asked, her voice brighter as she pointed to home plate. Murray could feel the push and pull between the sisters. Esther wanting to dream and make plans to find the treasure, and Jenny wanting to move the conversation onto anything else.

"Tommy Pacelli," Murray said. "He works down at the mill."

"Is he good at baseball?"

Murray shrugged. "He's the only player on the team strong enough to hit home runs, but he has a hole in his swing."

"What's that mean?"

"If a pitcher likes to throw junk, Tommy gets a hit almost every time. But the fastballers can throw it right past him because his swing has a loop in it."

"Is this pitcher a fastballer?" Jenny asked.

Murray loved how she seemed genuinely interested in baseball. He doubted that she really enjoyed the game, but that made it even better. It meant her interest was because of him.

"Yep," Murray said. "And he knows that Tommy tries for a home run every time, and he knows about the hole in his swing. Watch this."

Sure enough, the pitcher threw three fastballs, and three times the batter swung mightily and missed. Jenny looked at Murray with her mouth dropped open.

"It seems to me like you should play baseball," she said.

"Someday I will. Someday I'll play for the Cubs."

"Why don't you play now?"

"The other kids won't let me. I think they would if they could see that I'm actually pretty good. I can hit okay, anyway."

"So you've played before?"

"I used to play with Leon before he moved away."

"I remember him," Jenny said. "He was nice."

Murray felt a stab of regret, although he wasn't sure why. "He was my only friend. We played catch a lot and pitched to each other at the park."

"Why'd he move away?" Jenny asked.

Murray shrugged. He didn't like to think about what his mother had said. But he decided right then and there that he would never treat someone differently because of the way they looked. The whole thing was stupid, as far as he was concerned.

But those thoughts made him feel worse than watching his friends argue, so Murray turned back to Esther. "What makes you so sure there's a treasure to be found?" he asked.

"Mom and Dad told us the story a million times," Esther said.

Jenny heaved a sigh. "If there is something buried in some church—"

"There is," Esther said.

"And if this key could actually open it—"

"It could."

"Then maybe it actually would have a treasure worth more than gold. I don't think Mom and Dad would lie about that, or just make it up."

"They wouldn't. "

"But we'll never find it, Esther. We don't even know where it is. If it—"

"Maybe I do. Or at least, I might have a good idea. I've been thinking about it for a long time."

Jenny gave a short huff, which, in their sister-language, apparently meant she was tired of being interrupted. Esther shrank back, almost like she was retreating into a corner, and Jenny continued. "If it was actually there, of course I'd want to know what's in it, who wouldn't? Buried treasure that's worth more than gold? It sounds amazing. But the fact is, we can't walk all over the countryside searching every church we come across." She gave Esther a meaningful look. "And you know why."

Esther huffed loudly. "I'm so sick of this."

"Yes," Jenny said. "Sick is right."

Murray stared from one sister to the other, trying to figure out what they were talking about. Finally, when there didn't seem to be an end to the silence, he turned to Jenny. "Why? What do you mean she knows why we can't go looking for it?"

Jenny raised her eyebrows to Esther, seemingly looking for permission.

"Fine," Esther said, crossing her arms. "Tell him whatever you want."

Jenny sighed, as if she didn't relish the responsibility of breaking some truth to him. "Esther used to be very strong and healthy. But she got polio when she was eight and ever since then, well, I don't know how to explain it."

"I get sick all the time and Jenny's convinced that if I do the slightest little thing in my life other than sit in a chair or lay in a bed, I'll surely get sick and die." Esther's whole body slumped, and she refused to look her sister in the eye, Murray noticed.

Jenny's shoulders shrugged a little. "It's just that you're my little sister, and I love you."

She said it in such a sweet, honest way that Murray thought for sure Esther would crumble before the argument. If Jenny were to say she loved him—a thought which both elated and terrified him—he would do anything and everything she asked of him, probably until his dying day. But Esther wasn't him. She crossed her arms and glared at Jenny.

"If you really love me, you should want me to be happy."

"I do want you to be happy. What kind of thing is that to say?"

"Then let me live my life," Esther said, and it was the closest thing Murray had heard to a yell from either of them. Then Esther lowered her voice, which seemed to calm them both. "I'd rather live for just a few years—really live, I mean—having adventures with friends and exploring and . . . and *doing* things, rather than live for a hundred years stuck in a bed because I'm afraid of what might happen. What would all those years mean if I didn't put them to any use?"

Esther's eyes shone with determination as she continued. "I'm not afraid, Jenny. I just want to live. I want to go to the hot-air balloon festival next week and ride high up into the sky. And I want to use this key to find the treasure our grandpa buried. Those are the things I want to do. I don't want to sit around waiting to get sick. Can you understand that?"

Jenny turned her ocean-green eyes to Murray, which froze him in place. What was he supposed to do? This seemed like a family argument, and he preferred to keep it that way.

Jenny, sensing his unwillingness to get involved, shook her head and looked to the ground. "If that's really what you want, then fine."

"Really?" The hope in Esther's voice was unmistakable.

"I said it's fine." Jenny glared at her. "But I'm going to be with you every step of the way." Murray could tell she meant it more as a threat than a comfort. "Murray and me both."

Murray got that woozy feeling again as another batter struck out, ending the inning. *Murray and me both,* he thought. He could get used to hearing that.

A week later, the day of the long-awaited hot-air balloon festival dawned clear and calm. Perfect for floating through the skies. Murray couldn't remember being as excited for someone as he currently was for Esther.

She'd been saving her money for years, Jenny said. She'd dreamed of making her way into the wicker basket, feeling the jolt of fear and excitement as the balloon lifted from the earth, and seeing the tall buildings of Chicago in the distance as the balloon drifted higher and higher into the sky.

To Murray, the idea held nothing but sheer terror. But if that's what Esther wanted to do, well, he would sit happily on the ground and watch her enjoyment with pleasure.

Murray left his house quietly so he wouldn't wake his mother. She'd been working a lot of extra shifts recently and needed all the sleep she could get. She knew about Murray's plans and had seemed as relieved as Murray that he wouldn't be the one going up in one of those dangerous-looking contraptions.

Grasshoppers bounced out of his path as he found himself jogging toward the Brennan farmhouse, and several robins chirped at him from the branches of the maples and oaks.

Murray tapped his knuckles against the door when he arrived, unsure if he needed to worry about waking anyone in the house. He needn't have worried. After just a few seconds, the door flew open and Murray was met with a scene of chaos.

Esther was inside the house, arguing with her father and cry-ing. Jenny, who had opened the door, pursed her lips in apology but stepped aside, inviting Murray in. She closed the door behind him, and he followed her into the main room of the farmhouse.

"Sorry," she said. "It's been an interesting morning."

Before Murray could ask what she meant, Esther stomped her foot against the wooden floor. "I've been saving for this day for two years. You told me I could go."

"That was before you got sick," her father said.

"I'm not sick!" Esther screamed, and Murray could tell it was a refrain she'd been repeating all morning, though it continued to fall on deaf ears.

"Everyone heard your coughing last night," her father said. "I can't let you go up into the air like that. Who knows what that might do to you? You've never been up in the air before."

"Exactly," Esther said. "Who knows what it might do. It might heal me. This could be my only chance to be cured."

Her father scowled, obviously not convinced. And Esther, seeing that her reasoning proved no more effective than her screaming had, broke into tears and ran down the hallway, where she entered a room and slammed the door behind her.

Her father heaved a great sigh and looked to Jenny. Murray recognized the pleading in his eyes, as if searching for someone to remove the burden of this terrible choice he'd been forced to make—either protect his daughter or infuriate her.

Jenny gave her father the same pursed-lip look she'd given Murray when he'd opened the door, an acknowledgment of his predicament without the answer he so desperately wanted.

"Will you talk to her?" her father asked.

"I'll try," Jenny said. She touched Murray's elbow, leading him down the hall to the room Esther had entered. Once there, she tapped lightly on the door in a rhythmic pattern.

"Come in," Esther said.

Murray was intrigued. He doubted she would have invited her father in at the moment, meaning she must have recognized the rhythm of Jenny's knock. Murray found the intricacies of sisterhood mystifying.

Murray followed Jenny into the bedroom. He didn't know if he should close the door behind him or leave it open, but Jenny nodded toward the door, so he closed it.

Esther was sprawled on her bed, having just lifted her head from where it had been buried in a pillow. She turned onto her side so Jenny could join her on the bed while Murray remained near the closed door.

"I can't believe he won't let me go," Esther said, tears still streaming down her cheeks.

Murray recognized the tension between them. Esther wanted desperately for her sister to support her, but Murray had a hunch that Jenny took her father's side. She, too, cared deeply about Esther and worried about her health.

"I'm sorry, Esther," Jenny said. "What will you do?"

"What can I do? I'll sit here in my bedroom and dream about how wonderful it would be to sail through the sky in a hot-air balloon."

The sisters sat on the bed quietly. Murray figured they were all imagining the flight, which would never happen now. He'd never heard of a hot-air balloon festival coming to the area before. Surely it was a once-in-a-lifetime opportunity that Esther was missing out on.

But just as Murray was starting to think the girls' father had been too cruel, Esther burst into a deep coughing fit. It grew in intensity, racking her body as she struggled for breath between hacking coughs.

Jenny put her hand on Esther's shoulder, a steady, loving presence. But she didn't move to do anything about it. Apparently, there was nothing to be done but let it run its course.

Eventually, the cough subsided, but it left Esther ashen and disheveled. Her shoulders drooped, and all her energy seemed suddenly gone. The coughing fit convinced Murray that their father had made the right decision in forbidding Esther from going up in that balloon, but Esther's eyes still gleamed with a firm defiance.

Then she heaved another sigh, and Murray thought he saw the beginnings of acceptance in her gaze. She stood from her bed and limped, without crutches Murray noticed, toward her dresser.

It was the first time Murray had seen Esther move anywhere without crutches. The personal nature of watching Esther stumble across the room with nothing to assist her made Murray feel a closeness to her that increased his fondness for her. It was as if he was being welcomed in, past the walls. He was one of them now.

Esther opened the top drawer of her dresser and pulled out a glass jar. She removed several dollar bills from the inside and counted them out. She glanced at Murray briefly, then limped back over to the bed and extended the money toward Jenny.

"You take it," she said.

"What?" Jenny and Murray said at the same time.

"Take it," Esther said again. "It's not doing me any good here. It's for a hot-air balloon ride. So someone should take a hot-air balloon ride." She looked straight at Murray for the first time. "You'll go with her?"

"I don't have any money," Murray said.

"But you'll accompany her there and watch the balloons and take it all in?"

Murray knew what she was asking them to do. She wanted the people she cared for most to get the enjoyment she had long planned for herself. She wanted them to take her place not just physically, but to be the recipients of the joy she had so looked forward to.

"Promise me," Esther said.

Murray met Jenny's eyes. She had heard the meaning behind Esther's request as well. With a somber nod, they agreed.

"We promise," Jenny said.

It was a perfect fall day. Or maybe it was just that Murray was with the girl he liked. And he did, now, admit to himself that he liked Jenny Brennan. More than liked her, if he was being honest. But he didn't know the word for what he felt, so he didn't think too much about it. He just enjoyed the glow of walking beside her. With Jenny, the sunlight was brighter, the air was crisper, and the apples in the nearby orchard were a deeper shade of red than ever before.

Murray was grateful for their slow walking pace. It was as if, rather than trying to get someplace, they were simply spending time together, in no rush to arrive anywhere.

They wandered the countryside, Murray conjuring the courage to walk closer to Jenny—contemplating taking her hand at some point. But he hadn't found that courage by the time they reached the crest of a large hill. Looking over the valley, Jenny's breath caught. "Oh my," she said, and when she touched Murray's sleeve, it sent shivers up his arm. "Look at that."

In the valley below them, dozens of hot-air balloons materialized in various states of preparation. Most were nothing more than colorful cloth spread across the grass field, but a few were fully upright, with intermittent bursts of yellow and blue flame rising into the base of the balloon.

"I've never seen anything like it," Murray said.

Jenny started down the hill, Murray at her side, wondering what it would be like to float away in the basket of one of those balloons. But just being there, just seeing them rise from the ground and sail away with the breeze would be more than enough.

The closer they got, the more amazing it all became. Such colors! Each balloon was different, and as they popped up from the ground, one after another, each one decorated the field with more beauty.

"Which one should we go to?" Murray asked. Jenny had Esther's money, but no plans, no reservations.

Jenny scanned the area, her green eyes bouncing from one balloon to the next. "This way," she said, and she started toward one of the few balloons still lying on the ground. When they arrived, Jenny walked straight up to the barrel-chested man straightening the fabric of the balloon, preparing it to be filled with hot air. "Are you accepting passengers?" she asked.

The man looked up from the material and smiled brightly. "Well, hello. You have an interest in balloons, do you?"

"I'm hoping to ride in one. For my sister."

He responded with a questioning gaze. "That's an interesting favor," he said, then looked at her more closely. "You're Sean Brennan's girl, aren't you?" When Jenny nodded, he asked, "Older or younger?"

"Older. I'm Jenny." She reached out her hand, and the man shook it in formal introduction. "I have money," she said, and she pulled Esther's dollar bills from the pocket of her pants.

The man nodded. "And your friend?"

"My name's Murray, sir. Murray McBride. But I don't have any money. I'll just watch."

"Watch!" The man's barrel chest rolled with deep laughter. "I'll tell you what. Sean Brennan helped me out in a pinch last harvest, and I figure the least I can do is let his daughter's friend keep an eye on her while she's on her first balloon ride." He looked back to Jenny. "It will be your first ride?"

"Yes, sir," Jenny said.

"Then let's get this show on the road. We're already one of the last ones left. Better beat that wind," he said, scanning the horizon as if searching for an invisible breeze.

The man lifted the basket into a standing position by himself and set up a large, metal contraption that began blowing puffs of flame into the balloon. With each blast, the balloon grew until, ten minutes later, it was as big as a house. Soon enough, it was as big as a hayloft. Murray couldn't believe the size of it.

The balloon stretched the ropes that anchored the basket to the ground. "Time for you two to hop in."

Murray and Jenny shared an excited, wide-eyed glance before jumping into the basket. The man pulled a lever and another giant finger of flame lifted into the cavernous balloon. The ropes tightened even more. One side of the basket lifted an inch or two off the grass. Then the man released the ropes. Suddenly, they were airborne.

The world shrunk at the same time it grew. With every second the hot-air balloon sailed higher, Murray's view of the surrounding land expanded. He could see over the hill and into the next valley, and soon all the way to the horizon. But with each expansion, the people below became smaller, the cows in the pasture turned into black-and-white spots, and the land itself took on a softness, a smoothness that Murray had never experienced.

Jenny stood next to him, the two of them poking their heads over the edge of the wicker basket. Jenny's white fingertips squeezed the basket, but fear didn't stop her from leaning forward to take in the entire view.

The barrel-chested man chuckled from the other side of the basket, then blew another plume of fire into the cavernous emptiness above. "First time in the air for you, too?" he asked.

Murray just nodded. There was no way to articulate the impact it was having on him. They were with the birds! Human beings, with no wings with which to fly, were flying. He was astonished.

They floated for about an hour, although it felt like ten minutes to Murray. And then, when the barrel-chested man indicated they were about to start their descent, something unexpected happened. The movement downward startled Jenny and for the first time, she looked toward the ground beneath them.

"Murray," Jenny said, and she put her hand on his forearm.

Murray had decided that one of his favorite things was Jenny's hand on his forearm, usually preceded by a little joke at his expense. But this was different. Her touch wasn't giving reassurance but seeking it. She dug her fingers into the flesh of Murray's arm. He instinctively covered her hand with his.

"It's okay," he said, even though he had no idea if things were, in fact, okay.

But as the basket they rode in dropped closer and closer to the expanding earth, Murray understood perfectly well. It was exhilarating, yes, but equally terrifying. And they had nowhere to go. The balloon dropped more quickly than Murray had expected, and even though the barrel-chested man gave no indication anything was wrong, Murray felt his stomach drop. With nothing below them to break their fall, if something unexpected happened, there would be no hope for survival. Murray considered the safety measures if something were to go wrong. He realized there were none. He suddenly felt claustrophobic.

But Jenny was panicked enough for both of them, so even though he didn't feel it, Murray exuded an air of calm, as if this were nothing more than an everyday jaunt.

"It's beautiful, isn't it?" he said.

"I don't know," Jenny said. Her eyes were closed. She seemed paralyzed. The barrel-chested man continued to allow the balloon to drop, oblivious to their drama.

"I think I'm going to be sick," Jenny said.

Murray searched for any idea of how to help Jenny. Finally, he remembered something he'd seen in a magazine. He put his arm on Jenny's shoulder and spoke as calmly as possible.

"Crouch down with me," he said. When she immediately obeyed, Murray realized just how scared Jenny was, and how much trust she was putting in him. "Have you ever seen a moving picture?"

"A what?" Jenny said, looking at him through squinting eyes. "No, I don't know what you're talking about."

"It's a new invention. You can watch things on a screen, and it looks real, but it's not. You watch it from the safety of your own seat, even though it feels like you're there." The idea seemed to calm Jenny some, so Murray continued. "Imagine it like that. Like you're watching moving pictures on a screen."

As they crouched together in the corner of the basket, Murray found a small space in the wicker webbing. He stuck his finger into it and pushed the wicker away until it revealed a one-inch-square hole. "Look through this," he said.

Jenny lunged toward the hole as if she needed air. She followed Murray's instructions and put one of her eyes against the hole. Immediately, her shoulders released and her entire posture relaxed. Murray also breathed a sigh of relief. And then, in a moment he would look back on with wonder for the rest of his life, he leaned close to Jenny and whispered in her ear.

"I'm going to marry you someday, Jenny Brennan."

When the balloon finally touched down in an open field, it was with the gentlest of thumps. The soft, long grass on the ground caught their wicker basket with ease.

Jenny hopped out, with Murray right behind her. She took a deep breath, as if filling her lungs with ground-level air would put an official end to the flight.

"Wow," she said. "That was intense."

"Yeah," Murray said. He searched for any sign that she had heard what he'd whispered to her, but her eyes betrayed nothing.

With the return to earth came the realization that Esther had missed out on an opportunity she'd been dreaming about for years.

"We should get back," he said.

"Thank you so much, mister," Jenny said to the barrel-chested man.

"My pleasure. I hope you enjoyed your flight."

"We did!" Jenny said, and Murray hoped part of her excitement was a result of what he'd whispered, not in spite of it.

They walked back to the farmhouse at a much quicker pace than before. They talked some about how much they enjoyed the ride, and Jenny thanked Murray multiple times for calming her fears on the way down. But she never mentioned what he had whispered to her. Murray got the feeling Jenny was being pulled back to the farmhouse, her thoughts consumed by hoping Esther was doing okay. When they arrived, they scanned the property for any sign of her.

"There," Jenny said, pointing at the open barn door. "She must be in there."

Murray followed her to the big, red barn, then stepped past the creaking door and inside.

Murray considered himself a "city boy" since he lived in a neighborhood, not on a farm. He'd been in plenty of barns, of course, but never one like the Brennan barn.

It was cavernous. The ground floor was made of dirt but had small bunches of hay spread around randomly. Wooden-handled tools leaned against the slats of the wall and several large, iron pieces of equipment took up most of the space. Chaff cutters, scythes, sickles, hoes . . . everything a family might need to farm the land.

On the far side of the barn, leaning against a ladder that led to a hay loft, Esther scribbled with a pencil into her notebook.

"How are you feeling?" Jenny asked as she and Murray walked over. They approached slowly, trying to gauge her mood, as if she was a wild animal.

"Better physically," Esther said. "I felt fine again shortly after you two left." She looked up at them intensely. "I should have been allowed to go."

Murray and Jenny exchanged a guilty look. It wasn't their fault Esther hadn't been allowed to go to the festival, Murray knew, but the way Esther looked at them sure made it feel like it was.

"What are you doing?" Jenny asked.

"Working on something," Esther said.

"Can we see?"

Murray noticed again how much he liked that he and Jenny were a "we," and he had to remind himself to breathe.

Esther turned the notebook to face them. Murray tried to figure out what, exactly, he was looking at. It seemed to be a drawing of a platform of some sort, with an arm extended out, as if for towing.

"What is it?" he asked.

"A trailer. To be hitched to a bicycle."

"What's it for?"

Murray noticed a small scowl on Jenny's face, but she remained silent.

"For me to ride in," Esther said. "If we're going to find the buried treasure, we're going to need to search all the churches in the area. I obviously can't move as fast as you two," she said, motioning to her crutches, which leaned against the ladder next to her. "So we're going to build this."

"Esther," Jenny started, but Esther cut her off. "Save it, Jenny. I don't want to hear it."

Jenny must have recognized something in her sister's voice because she fell silent. Esther stared at both of them with an intensity that bordered on anger.

"I know it wasn't your fault that I wasn't allowed to go to the festival. And I'm glad I gave you the money to ride. But I'm going to say something, and I want you both to hear me, because I don't want to have to repeat it."

She paused to make sure there was no objection. Murray and Jenny both waited in silence. "This is my life. Not yours, Jenny, not Mom and Dad's, or the doctor's. It's mine. I'm the one who has to live with my legs not working right. I'm the one who has to live with my lungs not working right. I'm the one who has to deal with all these things, and that means I get to decide what I can and can't do. Me. No one else."

"Esther, everyone just wants—"

"I don't care what everyone wants!"

The outburst echoed around the wooden walls of the barn. After a moment of shocked silence, Esther continued. Her voice was calm and measured, but Murray heard the determination in it.

"I know you want what's best for me. I know you love me. I know Mom and Dad love me. But it doesn't give any of you the right to control my life. I get to do that, you understand? It's my life. I get to control it. No one else."

Jenny sighed deeply, but nodded. Murray agreed, his head bobbing vigorously. He wasn't about to get in Esther's way.

"Good," Esther said. She turned her attention back to her notebook, which Murray and Jenny took to be a dismissal. They'd made their way back toward the door when Esther stopped them again.

"One more thing," she said. And she waited until they both turned to look at her. She met their eyes with a steely determination.

"I won't be left behind again," she said. "Never again."

And with that, she resumed her drawing.

CHAPTER 7

1996

B rooke shifts the car into park, which pulls me out of my story. "Are we there?" I ask, still foggy from the memory of Esther. "Carpenter Park?"

"Yep," Brooke says. "And it looks like everything is just like you planned it."

She points to a large, grassy open space. In the middle, all by itself, is a splash of color on the ground. Its bright yellows and deep blues are like an island in the sea of plush green grass.

Right next to the colorful circle is a young man, well, an old man by societal standards. But young compared to Jenny and me. And next to him is a sturdy-looking wicker basket. Plenty of things have changed in the decades since our first hot-air balloon ride, but the wicker basket of this hot-air balloon could be the same one we stood in all those years ago. That's how similar it looks.

"Murray," Jenny says. She squeezes my forearm, as if to verify that I'm here. Or maybe to make sure I don't disappear. For a moment, I'm relieved that she remembers me. But it's short lived. "We need to go to the grocery store," she says. "I forgot the potatoes."

"The potatoes, sweetie?" I try not to let my disappointment show.

Her voice becomes panicked, and she speaks louder, quicker. "We have to go now. The boys and their families will be here in an hour, and I don't have supper on the stove. Please, Murray. We have to go now."

Brooke has a desperate look in her eye. She's new to this type of situation and has handled it admirably so far. But I can tell she wasn't expecting this one. She hasn't been around long enough to understand how it works sometimes.

My heart sinks a bit every time this happens. And it's been happening more and more frequently. But as hard as it is to see Jenny so disoriented, it's a comfort to know that she remembers who I am, at least for the moment. And that I've learned how to handle this type of situation. Like Doc Keaton said, living with dementia doesn't have to be a tragedy.

"Oh, you're right," I say. "I'm sorry. The potatoes."

This here's Doc Keaton's method, and I'm hoping it'll work. I'm supposed to follow those four *A*-words on that pamphlet. *Agree?* Check. *Apologize?* Check. Those two were easy to remember, but the third one I can't seem to come up with. Just because I'm not suffering from the same disease as Jenny doesn't mean I'm as sharp as I used to be, and that's the God's honest truth.

But those first two bits of advice seem to calm Jenny some. It doesn't solve the problem, but at least I didn't make her feel like she's crazy. After all, she's not crazy. I'm sure what she's remembering did happen. She did forget the potatoes. She just didn't forget them today, that's all.

Her moment of calm gives my old brain the opportunity to remember those other two *A*-words. *Align* to her reality and *attract* her to something else. I pat her hand and run my finger over her scuffed wedding ring.

"I forgot to tell you, I bought some extra potatoes, but I left them in the Chevy. I'll make sure to get them out for you."

She nods, seemingly satisfied with my explanation. Then, before she thinks too much about it, I point to the open field.

"Look, love. What do you think that is out there?"

Of course, I know exactly what it is, being that I talked to the man earlier today and arranged for him to meet us out here. But it's great to watch Jenny gaze toward the open space and catch an astonished breath. She puts a hand on her chest as if she loves what she's seeing. And immediately, some mental clarity returns.

"My goodness, Murray. Will you look at that. Why, I think it might be a hot-air balloon." She turns her ocean-greens on me, wide and clear and full of exuberance. I'm going to have to let Doc Keaton know just how grateful I am for his advice. Things looked like they might turn south, but instead Jenny's as alert and excited as she's been all day.

"We'd better go take a look," I say. Jenny's out of the car before I finish the sentence. Didn't even need any help this time.

I can't jog anymore, so I walk as fast as my legs will take me to catch up with Jenny. By the time I reach her, she's halfway to the hot-air balloon, which is still spread out on the grass.

"I've seen these before," I say. "Hot-air balloons that is. Long ago, but I remember."

Jenny doesn't skip a beat. "Me too. We rode in one once, remember, Murray? When we were kids." Her gaze turns inward as she says, "You told me you were going to marry me."

I just about fall over from shock. All these years, I've never known if she heard me say those words. The realization makes me smile as Jenny turns her attention back to our destination. A few moments later, we approach the man and his balloon.

"You must be Murray," the man says, extending his hand. "The one I spoke with on the phone this morning?"

"Sure am. And this here's my wife, Jenny."

"I don't think you told me your plan," he says.

Jenny nods as if this is expected. "He tends to forget things," she says. "To be honest, we're starting to worry about his memory."

She squeezes my forearm, and I laugh out loud. She's quite a woman, my Jenny.

The man looks us over, a skeptical crease between his eyebrows. "Are you planning on riding in the balloon?"

I can tell his thoughts have gone straight to worst-case scenarios and insurance claims. Fortunately for him, there's no way on God's green earth Jenny and I would be able to get into that basket of his.

"No, no," I say, and almost laugh at the man's obvious relief. "But we'd sure like to watch you set it up and take off. That in itself would give us quite a thrill."

"Of course," the man says. He looks around as if searching for something. "I don't have a comfortable place for you to sit. I suppose I could put the tailgate of my truck down, if you want to sit there."

Brooke steps forward. I hadn't realized until then that she had followed us to the balloon. "I put those camp chairs in the trunk," she says. "I'll go grab them."

She takes off to fetch us some seats, and I watch Jenny as she looks at the balloon spread upon the grass. A minute later, Brooke returns and unfolds two little chairs, one each for Jenny and me. They're not the most comfortable things in the world, but it's better than standing on our old legs, that's for sure.

Jenny and I watch as the man tips the wicker basket onto its side and starts a fan that blows air into the bellows of the balloon. It's just like I remember from all those years ago. What starts as a colorful carpet on the ground becomes a small bump, and then a sheath the size of a small house. Before we know it, a cavernous space appears. It looks like it's held up by magic, the fabric of the balloon fluttering like fingers casting a spell.

Inside the ever-expanding balloon, the sun shines through the colorful cloth, lighting the space in shades of orange and blue, yellow and red.

"Look, Murray," Jenny says breathlessly. "It's beautiful."

Her eyes sparkle as the man points a burner toward the opening of the balloon and blasts a spit of fire into it. Slowly, after several pulses of flame, the heated air lifts the balloon from the ground and pulls the wicker basket into an upright position.

"Okay," the man says. "I'm going to take off now."

He blasts another loud burst of yellow-and-blue flame into the balloon, and the ropes stretch tight just like I remember. Soon a corner of the basket lifts ever so slightly off the ground. One more burst and the entire basket is airborne, just a few inches at first and then a few feet. A moment later, the balloon hovers over our heads.

Jenny claps with joy as she watches the balloon rise. I focus on my wife as I lean in and smell her perfume. I get as close to her ear as I can and whisper, "I'm so happy you married me, Jenny Brennan."

She looks at me with pure joy in her eyes. And then my beautiful bride kisses me square on the lips.

When the balloon has drifted out of sight, Jenny and I stand from the chairs. I gather them up and hold Jenny's hand on the way back to the car. She can't stop talking about the feeling in her stomach the moment the balloon lifted from the ground, how amazing it was to see it hover directly above us . . . first just a few feet above the earth, but then slowly fading into the sky. She's as clear-headed as she's been since we left the house this morning.

When we get to the car, Brooke is sitting on the back bumper with the trunk open, waiting for us. I would have thought she'd watch the balloon, too, but she's slouched with her elbows on her knees, staring at the ground.

"Are you thinking about your house, sweetie?" Jenny asks.

"No," Brooke says. "I was just thinking about my stupid ex-boyfriend. Pathetic, huh?"

"No," Jenny says. She's not able to sit on the bumper. Probably hasn't been able to do something like that in fifty years. So I open up one of the camp chairs directly in front of Brooke. Jenny gives me a wink and eases down onto it, then leans toward Brooke. "It's not pathetic. Love is always a risk."

"Love," Brooke says. She makes it sound like a curse word. "What a joke."

I get the feeling this conversation is going to last longer than my legs can hold out, so I unfold the other camp chair and plop down into it.

"How long were you together," Jenny asks. "Going steady, do you call it? Or dating? I can't keep it straight, I'm afraid."

"That's fine," Brooke says. "We just said we were 'together.' And tomorrow would've been our three-month anniversary."

I'm not sure how I keep my guffaw inside, but somehow I manage. Jenny seems to do it more easily, although I know she's thinking the same thing as me. Three months? Might as well have been three minutes.

"Did he treat you well?" Jenny asks.

"I don't know. I guess. But he always pressured me to have sex with him, even though I said I wasn't ready. And sometimes he'd say things that made me feel bad about myself. But he never hit me or anything like that."

I can't help but grunt a little. Not getting hit shouldn't be the bar for any relationship. Or even not saying hurtful things, or not pressuring a gal. But I keep my mouth shut.

After a moment of silence Jenny says, "Have you talked to your mom about how you feel?"

"No. I'm mad at her."

But she doesn't look very mad. The way her bottom lip quivers and her eyebrows turn slightly up, she looks like a wounded animal, not a cornered one. Her shoulders slouch even deeper. "I know none of it is her fault," she says. "Not what happened with Jacob, or the eviction. I know she works hard and everything. She does the best she can. It's just that my mom's annoyingly optimistic, all the time. Even when things are obviously falling apart. It makes me so angry. Sometimes I hate her for it."

Jenny's voice is soft when she says, "I know this might be hard to believe, but someday you might actually admire her for that ability."

Jenny lets that hang in the air for a bit. I can't help but think Helen sounds a lot like my own mother, back when I was a lad. Optimistic to a fault.

Jenny leans toward Brooke. "Do you think it's possible that you're blaming your mother for what Jacob did to you? After all, it sounds like Jacob didn't show you much love, but from what I've seen your mother sure has."

"I guess," Brooke says. "I don't know. I don't even know what love is." She gets that confused look again. "Can you tell me?"

"Tell you what love is?" Jenny says.

"Yeah," Brooke says. She looks desperate, like she's starving and just asked for a loaf of bread.

Jenny scratches her eyebrow, buying time. "Well, now. I don't claim to know everything, of course. But I know that people should love you just like you are, not for how they want you to be."

Brooke nods, but she doesn't seem to think very much of Jenny's answer. Jenny must see that too because she leans farther toward Brooke, takes her hands, and looks right into her eyes. Then, slowly and clearly, my bride drops the real bombshell.

"I'm an old woman," she says. "And I know I'm out of date and old-fashioned. There's a lot I don't know, and I tend to forget things as soon as they happen these days. But there is one thing I know for certain."

"What's that?" Brooke asks.

Jenny leans forward and speaks with perfect clarity.

"As women, we need to let ourselves love ourselves as ourselves."

Her words linger for a moment, working their way into Brooke's brain, I hope. There's no one in the world smarter than my Jenny. "If we can do that," she says, "the rest will take care of itself."

Brooke smiles a little this time, as if Jenny's advice hit its mark. Then she turns to me. "You must be a pretty good husband to have landed this girl," she says.

"He does okay," Jenny says offhandedly, and Brooke bursts out laughing again.

When we're all three back in the "unaesthetic compilation of junk held together with duct tape," Jenny takes my hand and gives me a serious look.

"Let's go find the key, Murray. Remember where it is? In the ditch? We won't be able to open the treasure without it."

The idea of unearthing the so-called treasure still terrifies me, but I figure there's no harm in looking for the key. It's unlikely we'll find it, and it might even be fun. Besides, even if we do somehow find the key, that doesn't mean we have to look for the treasure. By the time we get the key, there's a real chance Jenny won't remember why we retrieved it in the first place.

I pat her hand, appeasing her. "That sounds good, love. Let's go do that. We'll have Brooke drive us there."

"Just point me in the right direction," Brooke says, having overheard us.

"Do you know if Washington Junior High School is still in existence?" I ask.

"Washington Junior High? I think so. I heard they just tore down the old building and built a new one right next to it. Asbestos, I heard. It was really run down, I think. Did you go to school there or something?"

"Sure did," I say. "Jenny and I both. But it's not the building I care about. Do you think you could take us there?"

"To Washington Junior High it is."

Brooke starts driving, but we hit traffic once we're on the main road. The pace is slow and the stop-and-go is so rhythmic is puts Jenny to sleep. It's been a big day for her already. She's been remarkably sharp today, which actually makes me worry. She'll get a span of time where she's pretty on top of things, but it never lasts long. Maybe a little nap will help her continue to do well, but I worry it won't be enough. With her head resting on my shoulder, I clear my throat to get Brooke's attention.

"We'll have to pass pretty near St. Joseph's to get to the school, isn't that right?"

"I don't know," she says.

I know perfectly well where the church is. I was just trying to be polite. "It should be on the right, up a spell. Do you mind stopping by for a few minutes? There's a conversation I'd like to have there while Jenny gets some rest."

"Of course," Brooke says.

A few minutes later, I point out the church. She pulls the little Ford into a parking spot right in front because there's no mass happening now. That suits me just fine.

Brooke jumps out of the car and runs around to help me out. Jenny opens her eyes briefly but then leans against the headrest and falls quickly back to sleep. I thank Brooke for her help and make my way into the church while she climbs back into the car to be with Jenny while she sleeps.

I don't know for a fact that Father James will be here, but it doesn't surprise me to see him near the front of the church preparing for the evening's mass. When he sees me hobble into the back row and sit, it's only a minute or two before he joins me.

"Murray," he says, easing himself into the pew. "It's good to see you. How are you?"

"A bit confused, to tell the truth of the matter."

"It happens to the best of us," Father James says with a smile. "I can't promise I'll have the answers you want, but I'll do my best. What's confusing you?"

"Truth," I say.

I mean to say more but can't quite figure out exactly what it is I'm confused about. I just know something's gnawing at me and that's the word that came out.

"Truth?" Father James repeats.

He gives me a moment to think on it. "I just can't quite figure it. I know the best thing I can do for Jenny is to agree with her when she's mistaken about something. It helps to prevent her from getting more confused, see? But here's the thing, Father. When I'm agreeing with her, I'm lying to her. I was raised to be honest, to tell people the truth. And here I am lying to the love of my life. Something about it feels wrong."

Father James stares up toward the altar for a long time before answering. "The truth is a powerful thing, Murray. They say it will set you free, and that's true. It can. But it can also be a powerful weapon when used with malice."

I wait for him to say more. Just when I think he's done, he takes a sharp intake of breath, like he just thought of something.

"Do you believe in gray areas, Murray?"

"How's that?"

"Gray areas. As opposed to absolutes. Is there absolute right and absolute wrong? Or are things more complicated than that?"

"Seems to me there's right and there's wrong," I say. "Anyone who talks about gray area is probably trying to justify doing something they know is wrong."

"I understand," Father James says. "For example, if you were to hurt someone. That would be wrong, am I correct?"

"Of course. Seems obvious."

"I agree. If someone hurts another person, they did wrong. Should they be punished for it?"

I squirm a bit in the pew. It feels like Father James is setting me up, but I figure I'll just answer honestly and see where it takes me. "People should take responsibility for their actions," I say. "So if they do something wrong, if they hurt someone else, they should be held accountable."

"So, they should be punished. That's what you're saying?"

"Seems right," I say. "It's called justice."

"Okay. So there's absolute right and absolute wrong. No gray area there."

I nod hard, feeling pretty good that Father James agrees with me. Although it doesn't help my feelings about lying to Jenny. I think we're done here and I'm about to thank him and head back to the car when Father James starts up again.

"There was a man at my last congregation," he says. "This man was driving along one night, turned a corner, and hit an elderly woman walking across the street. The woman died from her injuries. The man who hit her was distraught, overcome with grief and regret. He spent years replaying that moment in his mind. Could he have looked more closely? Should he have been driving more slowly? It tore him up inside. He was never the same."

Father James looks directly at me now. "Should that man be punished?"

"I don't know," I say. I consider it for a moment. "The woman is dead. Seems someone needs to be held responsible, and he was the one who did it."

"Fair enough," Father James says. "In the name of justice, as you call it, the man should be punished."

"That's right. It's too bad, but someone needs to take responsibility."

"And do you think he should be punished to the same extent as someone in the same situation who saw the elderly woman and intentionally ran her down?"

"Of course not. That's a terrible thing to do. Much worse than the man in your congregation. A thousand times worse."

"Why?"

The answer is obvious, but I'm not sure it solves my problem. In fact, it complicates it.

"That sounds a lot like gray area, doesn't it?" Father James says. "One person is punished worse than another for committing the same act? That's not very absolute, is it? Not very black and white."

He's got me good and confused now. I sit in the pew, sifting through my thoughts, trying to understand what he's saying.

"You feel guilty lying to Jenny," Father James says. "You feel that it's wrong. It's dishonest. But this isn't about honesty or dishonesty. It's not so black and white. This is about helping Jenny or not helping Jenny, and it seems to me there's gray area there. Do you think you should be perfectly honest with Jenny about everything, even if you know it will hurt her?"

"No," I say. "I'd never hurt Jenny."

"Exactly. I believe right and wrong are less about letters of the law and absolutes, and more about trying to do good, trying to help, even if that means you're acknowledging there's some gray area there. When you're 'lying' to Jenny, as you call it, what you're actually doing is showing her love. And I'm just a humble servant, but if you ask me, I'd say that's a beautiful shade of gray."

I feel lighter as I make my way back to the car. I'm doing right by Jenny, and that's all that matters. It might take a bit of time to adjust my worldview, but like I told Doc Keaton—if it helps Jenny, I'll change until the cows come home.

"Mr. McBride," Brooke says when I'm back in the car. "Do you think we could swing by your house and see how my mom's doing before we try to find the key? I've been thinking about what Jenny said, and I feel bad for leaving her to deal with all our stuff and figure out where we're going to stay and everything."

"Of course," I say, and I'm happy to hear she's considering her mother like that. Doesn't surprise me one bit that my bride had something to do with it. If you were to add up all the good she's put into the world over the course of her ninety-nine years, well, old Wrigley itself wouldn't be able to contain it all.

So we rumble back to the house, and the bumps wake Jenny from her catnap. When we get inside, Jenny seems comfortable, which makes sense considering it's familiar and all. Since Helen is talking on the telephone, Jenny goes straight into the kitchen and comes out moments later with four glasses of lemonade on a tray.

Brooke and I sit on the couch just as Helen hangs up the phone. She's actually smiling. "I found us an apartment," she says, accepting the lemonade from Jenny with a grateful nod. "They really needed to fill this unit, I guess, because the landlord's letting me put down half the first month's rent instead of the entire month. That should leave us enough to rent a truck and get our things moved in. I talked to the moving truck company, and they have one available in the morning. So everything's coming along nicely."

The look she gives Brooke is tentative, like she's expecting her daughter to explode. Must be hard, walking on eggshells like that. But to her surprise, Brooke doesn't have a snide remark for her. Instead, she says, "Thanks, Mom." Although she looks away when she says it. Baby steps, I guess.

Helen's eyebrows furrow a bit, but then her face spreads into a nice smile. "Should we go see it?" she says.

Brooke hesitates. "Well, we were just about to try to find the key Mr. and Mrs. McBride buried when they were young."

"Oh!" Helen says.

I can tell she forgot all about our little quest. It's pretty amazing that people are capable of pushing every single thing aside when something important comes up. I suppose it's a survival instinct.

"We have time," Jenny says. "Murray and I would love to see your new home."

I'm not sure if either of those things is true. Personally, I don't much care to see a random apartment. Their things aren't even in there yet, so what will we look at, the walls? And as for time, it's getting on into the afternoon now. The truth is, the sun's going to set in a matter of hours, and although I don't want to find the treasure, I also don't want the quest to end.

But Jenny didn't say the things she said because they're 100 percent true. She said them because they were the kind things to say. Apparently she doesn't need to have the conversation I just had with Father James; my Jenny already understands about gray area.

So we use valuable daylight to get right back into that hunk of junk and make our way to an old, crumbling apartment complex. As soon as I see it, I understand why the landlord made that exception about the first month's rent. So does everyone else in the car.

The exterior has peeling paint and the swimming pool is drained and somehow rusted. The bottom is coated with empty beer cans. When we make our way to the unit and open the door, we're met with more of the same. At least the hole in the wall is the relative size of a fist. It could have been the size of a frying pan, I suppose.

It's a small studio apartment with cobwebs in the corners and strange-looking blue stains on one of the walls. It smells like stale cigarette smoke. Everyone seems a little shocked by what we're seeing, but then Helen takes Brooke's hand. "It's just temporary," she says. "Only until we find another house."

"Yeah," Brooke says, "because I'm sure the banks are going to be lining up to give us a mortgage."

Her words are still jaded, but her tone is different. More like she's cracking a joke instead of before, when it was like she was throwing out insults. I can tell she's trying, at least.

The silence that follows is broken by distant laughter coming from the direction of the empty swimming pool. We all look out the window and see two teenage boys approach the pool chairs, talking and laughing and generally acting as they would if there were actually water in the pool.

Helen sees her daughter watching the boys, and says, "You should go down there and see if they live here. Maybe you can make some friends before we even move in."

"Perfect," Brooke says. Her sarcasm, like her last comment, seems more good-natured than earlier in the day. "Maybe I'll even find a new boyfriend, and we'll fall deeply in love and get married and have two-point-five kids and a house with a white picket fence."

She's obviously not serious—even I can recognize that—but she still walks out of the apartment and toward the pool area. We watch as she goes straight up to the boys and introduces herself. At least that's what I assume. We can't hear her from here. But she looks to be confident and socially competent in a way that surprises me. It shouldn't, I realize, when I think back on how she's been all day. Whip-smart and full of charisma. And if the looks on the fella's faces are any indication, she's pretty easy on the eyes of teenage boys.

Since there's nowhere to sit in the apartment, Helen leads Jenny and me into the main office area. She goes into a back room and chats with the landlord while Jenny and I take a seat on the only piece of furniture in the place, an uncomfortable green couch. Fifteen minutes later, Brooke bounds into the office with an energy I haven't seen from her.

"Did you have a nice time?" Jenny asks.

"Yep. Their names are Josh and Cory, and they're juniors. They've both lived here for, like, a year. Josh is cuter, but Cory seems nicer."

This kid's a whirlwind. One minute she's quoting books about how love doesn't exist, and the very next she's falling in love all over again. But I know better than to point that out.

Jenny leans in and says, "Most of the time, you'll be happier with the kindest boy than with the cutest boy."

Brooke's cheeks go a little pink. "Yeah, I guess I should have already learned that, huh?" She shakes her head a little. "It just doesn't seem fair. I mean, you found Mr. McBride when you guys were, what, twelve years old? You never had to navigate all of this."

"Oh, I don't know about all that," Jenny says. "A young lad named Ernie Wells caused a bit of drama, way back when."

Just hearing that name makes my blood boil. It takes me right back to high school. Jenny and I had been inseparable since the day on the playground, and then here comes Ernie Wells of all people, trying to make a move. The better man won out in the end, of course, but I still can't hear that fella's name without getting a little worked up.

Jenny knows this. She sees my breathing get a little quicker, a little louder, and she smiles that satisfied smile she gets every time she mentions that fella's name.

"What happened with Ernie?" Brooke says.

Jenny leans in. "He almost stole me away, that's what."

"That's not true," I say. "You were never interested in him. You just needed me to think there was a chance I could lose you so I'd do what I needed to win you over. That's all that was."

Brooke sure seems to be enjoying this, and Jenny's just egging her on. She acts like I didn't even say anything and keeps on talking. "Ernie Wells asked me to go steady," she says.

"Seriously?" Brooke says. "But you said no and went back to Mr. McBride?"

"Oh, no. I said yes to Ernie. If Murray wasn't willing to show me he wanted me to be his girlfriend, Ernie Wells was happy to step up to the plate, as it were."

"A dirty, rotten scoundrel," I say. "That's what Ernie Wells was."

Jenny smiles and leans in toward Brooke like she's telling a secret, but her voice is plenty loud for secrets. "That's how you know if a boy likes you. If he's still threatened by someone who's been dead and buried for thirty-seven years."

"Okay, okay," I say. The woman can't remember the name of her own husband, but she can tell you exactly how many years since Ernie Wells passed on. But then Jenny touches my forearm and smiles at me. I'm the only one who gets to see that smile, so it's hard for me to stay mad at Ernie. Especially considering how long the poor fella's been six feet under.

"Did Esther ever get left behind again?"

It takes me a moment to figure out what Brooke is talking about. Thoughts of Ernie Wells still have me a bit worked up, to be honest. But soon enough, I'm able to put it behind me. For now, anyhow.

"Well, that depends on how you look at it, I suppose," I say. When Brooke gives me a confused look, I realize my answer was inadequate. "A lot happened back then," I say. "But when we started searching for the buried treasure, Esther was right there with us. Actually, she was leading the way."

CHAPTER 8

1910

The next day at school, from the bottom of the ditch during recess, Murray, Jenny, and Esther made their plans. They would search the church closest to the Brennan farm first since it was within walking distance, even for Esther, and they hadn't yet built the trailer.

Esther said she doubted the treasure was buried there because, although there was a cemetery on the grounds, the church itself was relatively new. And since it was the church they'd gone to their entire lives, it seemed strange to think a treasure could be buried somewhere inside. Still, she didn't know enough of the history of the church to rule it out completely and couldn't rationalize overlooking a place that was so easily accessible, no matter how remote the possibility.

When school ended that day, Murray ran to his house with the agreement that he would meet Esther and Jenny at their farmhouse before sunset.

"I'm home," Murray yelled as he burst through the front door.

His mother was sitting in a chair, knitting a blanket and humming a song. It had taken a couple months for his mother to return to her lighthearted self after his father had left them, but lately she showed the occasional burst of joy, usually in the form of singing.

"How was your day?" she asked, barely looking up from her knitting.

"Good. Can I meet Esther and Jenny at their house tonight? We're going to search churches for something their grandfather hid a long time ago."

That made his mother look up. "Is it dangerous?"

"Dangerous?" Murray said. "Of course not. At least, I don't see how it could be."

His mother seemed to consider it. "Your birthday party starts at seven, so you'll need to be home by then. Have Jenny and Esther received invitations?"

The birthday party. If there was anything that could ruin Murray's mood, that was it. He'd never had a birthday party before. It's not that his father had explicitly forbade celebrating his birth, but every year the day would come and go and only his mother would even mention it.

But now his father was gone, and Murray's mom had decided they should start celebrating birthdays for real. Which would have been fine, if Murray had friends who would come to a birthday party. But he didn't. And that wasn't something he was excited to tell his mother.

Against Murray's protests, she had handwritten a small invitation personally addressed to every kid in his class and instructed Murray to give them out at school. Of course, he hadn't. He'd gone into the woods the day after she'd given him the invitations, stacked them in a pile, and burned them. He didn't need the humiliation of inviting every kid in his class to his birthday party only to have nobody show up.

Now he wasn't sure what he would do when no one showed up. Part of him thought if he burned the invitations, the whole idea of the party would go up in flames with them. He realized now it didn't work that way.

"Esther's in my class," Murray said, his shoulders slouching. "Jenny's in eighth grade."

"Great," his mother said. "You can invite Jenny and ask Esther if she's planning on coming." She was obviously assuming Murray had given Esther her invitation rather than taking a match to it. When Murray just looked at the floor, his mother said, "Thirteen is a big one, you know. You don't become a teenager every day."

Murray couldn't believe he was going to say this, but if it meant being able to meet Jenny and Esther at sunset, he would agree to just about anything.

"Fine, I'll invite them. And I'll be back by seven o'clock. But I know no one from school is going to come because they all hate me."

"What about Esther and Jenny? They don't hate you."

"So? Even if they come, what kind of a party will it be if it's me, two girls, and my mom?"

"A birthday party, that's what. Your very first birthday party. And it'll be fun no matter how many people are here, even if it's just me and you."

She stood and kissed Murray on top of his head. "They sound like nice girls," she said. "I'm glad you've found some friends."

The sun had just hit the horizon, throwing rays of purple and red into the clouds, when Murray first saw the church in the distance. He stopped in his tracks, marveling at its beauty. Jenny stopped next to him, and a moment later the clicking of Esther's crutches joined them as well.

"It's beautiful," Murray said.

The girls both stared at it as well. "I don't think I've ever seen it other than on a Sunday morning," Esther said. She wiped a drop of sweat from her brow. "I like it much better this way." She took a moment to catch her breath. "Do you think a treasure worth more than gold could really be inside the same church we've been going to our whole lives?"

Jenny, for her part, was studying Esther closely. "I hope it's in there," she said. "I don't like you walking all around the country-side. Not with how sick you just were."

"I won't be walking, remember? We're going to build that bicycle trailer."

"Esther, I don't know if—"

"Let's go have a closer look," Esther said.

As they approached, Murray realized this actually could be the place they were looking for. Since this was the closest church to where the girls' grandpa lived, it seemed likely. Then a small cemetery came into view, partially hidden behind the wooden structure of the main church. Cemeteries were common with these old churches, so it didn't necessarily mean anything. But it was a good sign.

The three of them walked right up to the door of the church and Jenny reached for the handle.

"Wait," Murray said. "Are you supposed to do that?"

Jenny gripped the handle but didn't pull the door open. "What do you mean? Do what?"

"I don't know. Just . . . go in. It seems weird to just walk in."

Jenny removed her hand from the door and cocked her had at Murray. He felt her ocean-green eyes piercing him again, so he looked at his feet as he said, "I've never been in a church when no one else is around."

Esther nudged her way between them, opened the door, and crossed the threshold. "Yep," she said. "You just go in."

Murray followed Esther, with Jenny close behind him.

It was darker inside than Murray had anticipated. No one seemed to be there, and no candles were burning. Several stained-glass windows lined the walls on either side, but the glass was thick, and the late afternoon light struggled to penetrate it.

"It looks so different," Esther whispered. "On Sunday mornings, it's always so bright and alive. This is kind of creepy."

"I think it's peaceful," Jenny said, and she sat in a pew near the back of the church.

Murray desperately wanted to join her, but Esther pointed one of her crutches toward a dark corner near the front of the church. "If it's here, that's where it would be," she said. "That's the perfect place to bury something if you want to keep it hidden."

Murray and Jenny both followed Esther as she started toward the corner. Her breath was wheezy and short, and Murray decided right then that if they didn't find anything in this church, they'd have to build Esther's bicycle trailer. He couldn't stand the thought of being a part of something that led to her getting sick or injured.

When she reached the dark corner of the church, Esther pulled a small matchbox and candle from her pocket.

"Where'd you get those?" Jenny asked her, but Esther ignored her sister and struck a match. Then she touched the match to the candle, and the light grew to illuminate the corner of the church.

"Let's take a closer look," Esther said. She coughed once and wiped her sleeve against her nose, then set her crutches aside and knelt on the floor. She moved the candle in an arch, lighting the floor in small swatches of light.

Murray looked to Jenny, who seemed as unsure as he did. She gave him a little shrug, and they both joined Esther on the ground.

"It's a wood floor," Jenny said. "I thought you said it would be dirt."

"It should be. But I don't know of any churches around here that have dirt floors. But maybe some did a long time ago. Maybe the wood floor was put down after the treasure was buried. If no one knew it was there, they would have just put the new floor in on top of it." She scanned the wooden planks again. "Look for a loose floorboard or something that looks like it's been disturbed."

The three of them knelt in a row, passing the candle back and forth to illuminate more portions of the floor. A couple times, Esther's breath caught and she leaned forward excitedly. But each time, she ran her hand over the mark in the floor that had caught her eye only to sigh and move the candle again.

They continued looking long after Murray was certain there was nothing buried there. Finally, it was Jenny who sat back on her heels.

"This isn't the church," she said. "It's not here."

Esther shook her head as if ready to argue. But then her shoulders drooped. "I guess I knew it wouldn't be," she said simply.

"What do we do now?" Jenny asked.

"Find the next closest church," Esther said as if it was obvious.

Murray hated what he had to do next. But he had promised his mother, and a promise was a promise.

"Before we do that," he said. "Do either of you have any interest in going to a birthday party?"

The silence that followed could mean one of two things, Murray realized. Either they weren't expecting the abrupt change of subject or, more likely, they weren't sure how to tell him they had no interest in coming to his party.

Jenny was the one who finally broke the silence. "Whose birthday?"

Murray wished he hadn't brought it up. He wished he'd gone home and told his mother he'd invited the girls, but they'd told him they were busy. It was too late for that now, so he swallowed hard and prepared for inevitable rejection.

"Mine," he said. "My mom is making me have a party. I was supposed to invite the whole class, but I knew no one would come."

Esther's crutches dragged against the floor as she moved directly in front of Murray. "Are you telling me it's your birthday?"

Murray shrugged. "It's not a big deal. My mom just—"

"I can't believe you didn't tell us it's your birthday," Esther said, cutting him off.

Murray risked looking up at her and was confused to see a giant smile spread across her face.

"There is absolutely, positively nothing in the world I like more than birthday parties for my friends," she said.

Murray enjoyed the warmth that spread through his chest. It still felt good to hear someone call him a friend.

"We're coming," Jenny said, moving next to Esther. "Of course we're coming. When is it?"

"Tonight. In about an hour, actually."

"Oh, my goodness," Esther said, and Murray was sure she would say they couldn't possibly go to a party on such short notice. But instead, she turned to Jenny and said, "We barely have time to make him a present. We have to go home. Now." She turned back to Murray. "One hour? We can make it. We'll see you there."

She nudged Jenny with her elbow and the two of them quickly strode out of the church. Murray stood in disbelief, watching them leave through the front doors, amazed at his good fortune.

*   *   *

Twenty minutes later, Murray sat in his small living room while his mother arranged four chairs around their dinner table. She spared no expense, at least according to their financial ability. The entire house was perfectly clean, streamers hung from the doorway between the living room and kitchen, and a birthday cake sat in the center of the table.

The only thing missing was the people.

Murray would never understand why his mother had needed to invite the entire seventh grade class. She probably thought half of them would show up, maybe more. It didn't register that Murray had assured her he was the least popular kid at school, that ever since Leon moved away, he hadn't had a single friend. His mother, despite all she had been through growing up in poverty, losing two siblings to polio, and having her husband walk out on her right when she needed him most, still managed to hold the firm belief that "things work out in the end."

Maybe "in the end" people would have shown up for his birthday party, but that wouldn't be possible on this day, since they'd never even received the invitations she'd written for them.

But now he had two friends. Two people who said they would come to his party. Murray watched the hour hand of the wall clock strike seven. He heard its somber tones as it went through the entire dance, culminating in seven deep, ringing vibrations that made him wonder, despite what Esther and Jenny said, if they would show up.

His mother ruffled his hair as she walked by, still doing last-second tidying up. "They'll be here," she said brightly.

Logically, Murray knew she was probably right. The sisters had to go home, which would take a while with how slow Esther was. They said they were going to make him a present. Then they had to walk all the way to his house. Of course it would take them some time to do all that.

But the waiting was driving him crazy. He tried to distract himself with thoughts about the treasure and what they'd find in the case. Part of Murray felt like the thirteen-year-old he had just become, a teenager who didn't talk to his mother about things going on in his life. But the other part of him, the kid whose attachment to his mom grew strong out of necessity after his father left, needed to talk to her. And the subject on his mind was more urgent than the fact that no one from his class would come to his birthday party.

"Mom," he said. "If I told you something was worth more than gold, what do you think it would be?"

His mother stopped in her tracks and looked at him. "That's quite a question. What has you thinking about that?"

Murray looked out the window, searching for any sign of Esther and Jenny. "You know the treasure I told you the Brennans' grandfather buried a long time ago? They have a key that's supposed to open it. That's why we've been looking for it. And Jenny and Esther say that whatever's inside is 'worth more than gold.' But I don't know what that could possibly be."

"Okay," his mom said, sitting in a chair next to him and gazing out the window as well. "It's not always easy to know the value of things. If you're talking about monetary value, anyway."

That made Murray think about the treasure differently. What if the treasure wasn't worth money at all? What if it was something more miraculous? Maybe it was a potion that could make you live forever. Or heal any sickness. Maybe it could make Esther's legs work like they should again. Maybe it could keep her healthy.

"Esther gets sick a lot," Murray said. "And she has her crutches and can't do things other kids can, which is hard for her because Jenny can do all those things. If something could heal Esther, it would be worth more than gold, wouldn't it?"

"I suppose it would," his mother said. "You really like these girls, don't you?"

"I love them," Murray said, without thinking. He snapped his head toward his mother and said, "I mean, not like a girlfriend. Esther's just a friend. But it still counts as love, doesn't it?"

His mother gave him a crooked smile. "I think friendship is one of the best kinds of love there is." She ruffled his hair and stood, then strode toward the kitchen. But over her shoulder, she said, "It's interesting. When you used the phrase 'just a friend' you forgot to mention Jenny."

At 7:07, Murray finally caught sight of two small forms walking along the path toward the house.

The first moved in a flowing way Murray already had memorized. The second bumped and bounced a bit, more stilted yet more eager.

Murray sprinted from his spot at the window. "Esther and Jenny are here," he yelled to his mom.

He didn't even care about the unreasonable exuberance in his voice. He almost collapsed in relief. It took all his strength to hold him in place rather than run out to greet them. When they finally—finally—arrived at the door, Murray opened it before they even finished knocking.

The door flying open mid-knock seemed to startle both girls, but they recovered when they saw it was Murray. They both smiled and said, "Happy birthday," at exactly the same time.

It was the most beautiful sound Murray had ever heard.

Jenny held out a small package wrapped in thin paper, and Murray accepted it, feeling like the world had just flipped over completely.

"Thanks for coming," Murray said. "Come on in."

Even though he had prepared them, Murray worried for a quick moment what his two friends thought about the fact that they were the only ones at his party. The great thing about true friends is that you don't have to pretend, Murray realized. You can be nothing more than who you are, and friends will like you anyway.

As the girls admired the cake on the dining room table, Murray's mother took the gift from him and whispered near his ear, "It all works out in the end." She had a gleam in her eye, and Murray felt a rush of gratitude.

"Well," Murray's mother said, setting the gift on the table near the cake. "I always say a party's not a party until you eat cake. So let's get started, shall we? I'll get the candles."

As she disappeared into the kitchen, Esther sneezed. She rubbed her palm against her forehead and closed her eyes.

"Are you okay?" Murray asked.

"I'm fine," Esther said, but she didn't look fine. Her cheeks were flushed, and Murray saw tiny beads of sweat at her hairline. He thought back on her wheezing at the church. He had chalked it up to the long walk they'd taken—and the same could be true now of their walk to his house—but he couldn't help but wonder if she'd overdone it. Maybe every time she'd caught her breath while they were on their knees searching the floor of the church hadn't been because of excitement, but because she was having difficulty breathing.

Esther wiped her brow with her sleeve and leaned her head toward him conspiratorially. "I have an idea," she said in a hushed voice. When Jenny leaned in as well, they made a tripod of secrecy.

"Elizabeth Pratchett told me her family goes to a church a few miles west of town. She said if you go to the Lemon Grove post office and head straight west for five miles, then south for one, you come right to it. And get this," she said. She looked up from their circle as if checking to see if the coast was clear, then hunched back down. "Elizabeth told me it's built into a hill."

Murray felt chills run up his spine. Jenny's eyes widened for a moment, too. "Six miles?" Jenny said. "There's no way you can walk six miles. And that's each way."

"Tomorrow's Saturday. Let's meet at our house at seven in the morning. Can you do that, Murray?"

"I think so," Murray said.

"Great. Then it's a plan. We'll build the bicycle trailer."

Just then, Murray's mother danced back into the room. She counted aloud as she stuck thirteen candles into the cake, then retrieved a box of matches from the pocket of her apron.

Murray enjoyed his friends' smiles as each candle lit the room a tiny bit more. There was nowhere Murray would rather be. No one he would rather be with. He felt like his entire world was contained in that room. Murray had never felt so much gratitude.

Jenny was the one who touched Murray on the sleeve, bringing him out of his reverie. She looked at him with those ocean-green eyes, which Murray had a feeling he'd be gazing into for a very long time, and said, "Okay, Murray. Make a wish."

Murray closed his eyes. It was his first-ever birthday party. His first time blowing out candles. His very first wish.

He didn't have to think about what it should be. As a smile crept onto his face, Murray closed his eyes, took a deep breath, and made his wish.

CHAPTER 9

1996

"You became a teenager that day," Jenny says to me now.
We're into the mid-afternoon hours, and the sun shines a little lower in the sky. It sends rays through the windows of the apartment complex office where Jenny, Brooke, and I sit.

I remember the joy I felt at making that wish. I'd never made a wish like that before. Sure, there had been things I'd wanted. But I'd never thought to close my eyes, focus on a desire, and wish for it.

It was truly my first wish.

"It was the most important wish I ever made," I say. "That Jenny Brennan might someday love me."

Jenny smiles at this, like it's news to her. And now that I think about it, I'm not sure I ever told her about that wish. It's amazing that after more than eighty years together there are still new things to tell each other. New details we've never shared. "I like that wish," she says.

Brooke has a little smile, which is nice because it wasn't that long ago she was crying about the possibility of being homeless soon, and then disappointed in the state of their short-term apartment. This is a nice break from reality for her, I hope.

"Being a kid back then sounds like so much fun," she says. "Today, everyone spends their time sitting inside watching TV or something. And we're no happier for it. Back then, when you guys were running all around the countryside, going to hot-air balloon festivals . . . I don't know," she says. She gets a little furrow in her brow. "It just seems like it was simpler."

"I suppose it was," I say. "More difficult, too, I should say. Just on a day-to-day basis, see?"

"What do you mean?"

"Well," I say, and I try to choose from a hundred different examples. "We didn't have indoor plumbing at our house until about 1912. So every time you felt nature calling, you had to go to the outhouse."

Brooke is quiet for a moment. I realize she might not know what I mean by "nature's call," or even what an outhouse is. But she seems to put it together, and the look of shock on her face makes me laugh out loud.

"I tell you one thing, I don't miss pulling my boots on at night in the middle of winter to trudge through the snow and sit in the freezing temperatures. Oh, there's always give and take. Take a little bit of convenience, give a little bit of experience. But there's good and bad to both, I'd say."

I check in on Jenny like I often do. She doesn't seem as sharp and comfortable as she has most of the day. It's the way her body tenses as she gazes at our surroundings and tries to put every- thing she's seeing into the correct place. I figure I should help out a little, if I can.

"We're at the apartment complex, love. Our new friend Brooke, here, is moving in with her mother soon. Just temporarily, of course."

Jenny seems to remember Brooke and is pleasantly surprised. "You're moving into a new home?" she says. "How wonderful."

Brooke and I exchange a glance, but there's really nothing to say. Jenny's excited about the news that Brooke will be moving into a new home, so we'll go right along with it.

I won't waver at all. I'll do whatever I can to help Jenny for as long as I'm able. I wasn't kidding about the "till death do us part" thing. But the truth is, it sure is nice to have a partner in this, even if it is a teenage kid.

"We need to make a run to the grocery store, Murray," Jenny says. "We'll need to buy a housewarming gift for our friend."

I ignore the fact that Jenny has already forgotten Brooke's name. That's the least of our worries. Heck, I forget names right away, too. And the idea of giving Helen and Brooke a housewarming gift does sound awfully nice.

Salt, bread, and wine. That's been Jenny's go-to housewarming gift for as long as I can remember. No reason to stop now.

And besides, it feels like our quest is coming to an end. We've found the old book, visited the homestead where Jenny grew up, and even watched a hot-air balloon sail away. Jenny has had a good day, all in all. Sure, I'd love for this day to go on forever, but seeing Jenny struggle to remember things makes me realize how lucky we've been to get this far. The smart move is probably to wrap up this quest and call it a success.

So while Helen continues her negotiations with the apartment manager, the three of us make a run to a nearby grocer with a liquor store next door. I give Brooke a ten-dollar bill from my billfold, and she jogs into the grocery store. When she comes out five minutes later, she has a nice loaf of sourdough under her arm and one of those cylinders full of salt in her hand. I have to be the one to go into the liquor store on account of Brooke being underage, and I pick out a bottle of French wine. I've never heard of it, and it's not the most expensive bottle available, but I figure it's the thought that counts.

Once I'm resettled in the Ford, we make our way back to Helen and Brooke's new apartment. But when we pull the car into a parking spot right near the apartment's main office, we're met with an unexpected and unwelcome sight.

Helen is sitting on the curb. She forces a smile when she sees us, but her eyes are awful red around the edges.

My gut tells me that giving her the housewarming gift might not be the best thing right now, so I set the salt, bread, and wine down by my feet and leave them there for now.

Brooke puts the car into park and is about to jump out and see what's the matter with her mother, but Helen waves her back into the car and comes around to the passenger seat. As soon as she's safely inside, the tears start to flow. It's like she's been holding on by a thread ever since she returned home to see her possessions in her yard, and now something has cut that thread.

"What's wrong?" Brooke asks. Her eyes are wide and her entire body looks tense, like she's not sure what to do about her mother acting like this. I remember what Brooke said about her mom— that she's annoyingly optimistic. It makes her current state even more concerning.

"They said we can't move in," Helen says between sobs.

"What? Why? You just signed the lease, right?"

Helen shakes her head. "It was contingent on an inspection by the state, to make sure it was safe and habitable. The inspector was already here, inspecting another property, so he was able to do it right away. They said they found black mold in the drywall, and it needs to be mitigated before we can move in."

The news hits Brooke hard. She looks like a deer staring down a shotgun. "How long will that take?"

"They have to find a crew to do the work, then schedule it and everything. They said it shouldn't be more than a month."

"A month?" Brooke says. "What are we supposed to do for the next month?"

Next to me, Jenny's been silently watching the drama unfold, but now she taps my shoulder. "We have room, Murray. They could stay with us for a while."

I love my wife. I love her generous spirit and her desire to help. But there are many things wrong with what she said.

She's forgetting that we'll be staying at Aspen Leaves as of tomorrow, not at home. That would open our house for our new friends, but she's forgetting that Chance and Olivia will be staying there while their house gets remodeled, and they've been packing every room of that little house with their ridiculous amount of belongings. And even if neither of those things were true and we were going back to our house to live by ourselves like normal, having people we just met staying there—people Jenny would certainly forget—would surely make things worse for her. Having strangers in what should be a familiar, comfortable space—at the same time our full-time helper, Deb, is no longer with us—would be a recipe for disaster.

As much as I want to help our new friends, and as much as I love Jenny for making the offer, it's simply not possible for them to stay with us.

Helen seems to understand. "It's so kind of you to offer," she says. She looks tentatively at her daughter. With a deep sigh, she says, "But I think we'd better find a homeless shelter for the night."

It turns out, if someone has to be without a home, Lemon Grove is a good place to be. The apartment managers are nice enough to let Helen use their telephone, and it only takes two phone calls for Helen to learn that the city has an overnight homeless shelter for families.

"Should we go there now?" Brooke asks.

"It's just for sleeping," Helen says. "There's nothing there but rows of cots, I'm sure. Besides, I need to figure out how we'll get food, since all our food is locked inside our house. Our old house, I should say."

That's something I didn't think of. Getting kicked out of their house means they're suddenly and completely without anything to eat. "I'm sure we can help with that," I say. But Helen shakes her head.

"I'll call around," Helen says. "See about food kitchens nearby. It's not something you need to worry about."

She turns her attention back to the telephone while Jenny and I follow Brooke to the lobby and find some chairs to sit in.

"I need to get a job," Brooke says. "I should have done that a long time ago, I guess, but I just didn't know. I didn't understand what was happening." She looks toward her mother, but I can't read her expression. "She should have told me what was going on. Maybe we could have prevented all of this. Maybe we could have kept our house."

"I'm sure your mother did her very best," Jenny says. "It can be hard, as parents, to know what the right thing is sometimes."

"I guess," Brooke says. She spends a long moment staring at her hands. "I should drop out of school."

"Well, now," I say. "That doesn't seem like the right thing. Your education is important."

"Yeah, well, so is eating food. And to do that, you need money. And to get money, you need to work. And if I'm at school, I'm not working."

The three of us sit in silence for a long time with Helen's voice drifting in and out as she talks on the telephone. I'm not sure which is worse, seeing Brooke angry and jaded like earlier in the day, or sad and defeated like this. Finally, Brooke bursts out of her chair and stands, as if she's been caged and is breaking free.

"I can't take this anymore. Not right now." She looks to her mom, then back to Jenny and me. "Can we get out of here? Can we just . . . can we go back to the quest? Can we please try to find that buried treasure? I just . . . I need something to do. Somewhere to go. Can we do that?"

Jenny seems to be a little confused, although whether it's confusion about the new people we're with or the new place we're at or something else entirely, I can't be sure. But it's up to me to make the decision. And even though I decided the quest was over not ten minutes ago, if resuming it will help Brooke cope with what's happening, I figure it's the least I can do.

I take Jenny's hand and squeeze it. "Let's see if that old key is still where we left it, shall we?"

Helen decides to go back to our house to make more phone calls to other apartments that have posted vacancies. I offer to help a half dozen times during the drive, but she's determined that we continue our quest. So we drop her off at our house again—I grab a small shovel from our garage while we're there—and I turn my attention back to the quest, and back to Jenny.

Her understanding comes and goes, of course. But that's to be expected. I was never under any illusion that this plan of mine could magically cure her. I just wanted to remind her of some beautiful moments in her life—moments we've shared together—in the hopes that she might remember, and enjoy the remembering. I like to think that she's "living with" dementia, not "suffering from" it. And if that's the case, she should be out there living. So far today, I think I've helped her do that.

But finding the key? Now that would really be something. On one hand, the odds seem long. It's been around eighty-six years since we buried that key. But it's under the ground, so if there hasn't been a large-scale earth-moving project of any kind, it could still be where we left it. After all, I read an article in the Lemon Grove paper not long ago about a high school class that buried some things fifty years ago. Some students from the present class dug it up and looked through it all. A "time capsule" they called it.

When we approach Washington Junior High School, nothing about the area is the same. Of course, Brooke told us they just built a new school, and if you take the old school building away, it's going to look different. But even the open field seems different. Maybe it's just that it's been a while since I was here last. A good long while.

At least it's not a strip mall. If this hadn't been a school for so long, it surely would have been swallowed up by development like everything else around here.

I make sure to grab the handheld shovel and take Jenny's hand as we make our way from the car, across the old schoolyard, and to the top of the ditch. To my pleasant surprise, it's almost the same as I remember. It's overgrown with weeds and not nearly as deep as I remember it—it's barely even a ditch at all—but it's still here.

I'm hit with a wave of memories from so long ago. Twelve years old, hiding alone without a friend in the world, until Jenny Brennan appeared at the top of this very ditch and changed my life forever.

Jenny also seems lost in memory, which is wonderful if it's true. Sure enough, she nods and squeezes my hand. "You read that very book we found today. *Little Women*. Right there," she says. Then she looks at the ground we're standing on. "And right here. This is where you fought those boys for knocking Esther over. This is where I first knew I could trust you."

We all turn our attention to the ditch and come to the same realization all at once—Jenny and I are too old to climb down that slope and dig something out of the ground.

That's something that continues to amaze me—and I'm not new to this "old age" thing. I've been elderly or a senior citizen or just plain old—makes no difference to me what you call it—for a good long time now. You'd think by now I'd recognize my limitations. But no, I still look at a car and think I can drive it. I still look at a sack of potatoes and think I can lift it. And I still look at a ditch and think I can climb down into it.

And the fact of the matter is, I actually do believe I could. It might not be as pretty as it once would have been. Maybe I'd need to sit on my rump and inch down the slope of the ditch like a slide. Might take me twenty minutes when it used to take me five seconds. But I could still do it.

Same for the car and sack of potatoes, if you ask me.

But there's no reason to be proud. We have a young, able-bodied person here with us. So when Brooke offers to do the physical work for us, I hand over the little shovel.

"Just point to where you think it is," Brooke says.

Jenny and I both scan our surroundings, trying to place where, exactly, the school building used to be. Where Ms. Carson's room was, where I would have run each day at the beginning of recess, trying to escape into this ditch before those bullies could see me. Even all these years later, I can still see the path, clear as day.

"Right about there," I say, pointing into the ditch at precisely the spot I used to sit. Close to it, anyhow. After this long, I can't be completely certain. Heck, after this long, the earth could have shifted.

Brooke starts digging right where I pointed. She digs a hole, moves a few inches farther along, and digs another hole. The shovel is small, so it takes a while to dig each hole. This continues until she has a dozen holes in the ground, but no key. It's starting to look like finding this thing is going to be a lot more difficult than I realized.

"How long ago did you bury this?" Brooke asks.

"Too many years to count," I say. "I was knee-high to a grass-hopper at the time. Jenny here was one year older, and she seemed like the epitome of authority to me back then."

"Still am," Jenny says quietly. Then she speaks loud enough for Brooke to hear. "Try a few feet that way," she says, pointing in the opposite direction from where Brooke has been digging each new hole.

Brooke goes back to where she started, moves a few feet away from the first hole, and starts to dig again. Right away, a strangely shaped bit of mud catches my eye as Brooke tosses a shovelful of dirt into the latest pile. She didn't even see it. Must be easier from up here because Jenny gasps a little bit, too, right at the same time I see it.

"Excuse me," I say, calm as I can. "But could you rifle through that last bit of dirt you just tossed. I think we might have seen something up here."

"Oh," Brooke says. She looks around like she's not sure which pile of dirt I'm talking about, then points to the one right in front of her. "This one?"

"That's the one," I say.

"This is exciting," Jenny says next to me.

Brooke uses her hands to sift through the dirt. Sure enough, it takes about five seconds for her to reach down and pick out a clump in the relative shape of a key.

"Oh my gosh," she says. "I think we found it."

She gets all excited then. She wipes frantically at the key with both hands, removing as much dirt as possible and making it more and more into the shape of a key. She wipes it in the grass, then holds it out in front of her.

"Is this it? It must be it. I mean, how could it not be it?"

"That's the one," I say. "That's where we buried it."

Now, this is all very exciting, don't get me wrong. Unearthing a key from a foot underground eighty-six years after burying it is going to get anyone's blood flowing a little bit. But excitement isn't exactly the same as happiness, and when I look at Jenny I expect to see both.

She's excited, sure. How could anyone not be? But there's a sadness in her eyes that makes me think she's remembering why it was we buried this key in the first place.

"Continue your story, Murray," Jenny says.

All day I've been worried that getting too far along in this quest would bring up hard memories. Memories that Jenny may or may not remember, but things that she and I would both rather keep in the past. This is the first time all day I've thought that maybe Jenny does remember what happened way back when. It's just that, for some reason I can't fathom, she actually wants to remember.

CHAPTER 10

1910

The morning after his birthday party, Murray rushed through breakfast and ran over to the Brennan farmhouse. Jenny was waiting for him outside the front door with an expression that cooled Murray's excitement.

"What's wrong?" he asked.

"Esther," Jenny said, but she seemed more angry than worried, which Murray took to be a good sign.

"What's wrong with Esther?"

"She's obviously sick but won't admit it. If our father was here, he wouldn't let her leave the house, but he's in Chicago for the day. I told her we shouldn't do this today, but she's so stubborn. She said—"

"I said I don't need my sister babying me," Esther said. She knocked the screen door with her elbow and hobbled outside, one crutch stretched against the door so it wouldn't slam. She sniffled and seemed to stifle a cough, but Murray was happy to see that her cheeks were back to their normal color.

"Follow me," she said. "I'll show you my idea."

She blew past them and headed toward the barn. Jenny looked at Murray and shrugged, which made Murray's throat feel tight. Anytime something was just between him and Jenny—even just a quick look of exasperation about Esther—Murray felt a little dizzy. Together they quickly caught up with Esther and covered the rest of the distance to the barn.

Murray jogged ahead and opened the door for his friends, so he was the last one inside. Once he closed the barn door behind him, he watched Esther walk straight to an old bicycle leaned against the wall.

"Here it is," she said. "Jenny's transportation."

"Okay," Jenny said, treading carefully. "So what's the plan here? How's this going to work?"

"Murray's going to build us a trailer for me to ride on," Esther said.

"I am?"

"You are. And Jenny's going to pull me behind her bicycle."

"I am?" Jenny said.

"You are."

"If Jenny's riding the bike," Murray said, "and you're sitting on the trailer I'm supposed to build, how will I get around?"

"You'll run."

"I will?"

"You do know how to run, don't you?"

"Well," Murray said, thinking he'd probably never run more than a mile or two at one time in his life. "I guess so."

"Great," Esther said. "Then let's get to it." She pointed around the garage. "There are two tires over there from an old wagon that should work. And plenty of boards over there for the platform. And I don't know what all those metal strips are from, but I'm sure Murray can make a frame using those, right Murray?"

"I guess," Murray said. In truth, he'd never built anything like this in his life, but he wasn't about to admit that now.

"Okay then," Esther said. "Let's start. We're wasting time."

"Wait a minute," Jenny said. "Esther, look at you. You're sick. You need to go back to bed and get some rest until you're better. Then we can do this."

A blackbird flew into the barn and disappeared into the rafters. Murray continued watching even after he couldn't see it anymore, opting not to watch Esther's reaction. But he didn't have to be looking at her to hear the anger in her voice.

"When will you stop treating me like a child? I don't care if you are a year older. This is my life, not yours. I get to decide if I'm well enough, not you. Remember?"

Her confident, assertive argument made Murray nervous. He couldn't imagine confronting Jenny like that. But apparently Esther wasn't as intimidated by Jenny as he was.

"I do understand, Esther," Jenny said, her voice soft and conciliatory. "I just worry about you, because I care for you."

Esther took her sister's hands. "Then support me with this instead of holding me back. Come with me. Because I promise you, I'm doing it either way."

When Murray saw a tiny nod from Jenny, he jumped in, hoping to diffuse the tension.

"Well okay," he said. "It sounds like it's time to build a bicycle trailer."

Considering Murray had never built anything like a bike trailer before, he felt pretty good about the finished product. Sure, it was rickety and it squeaked with each rotation of its tires—it was sure to be a bumpy ride—but it would at least allow Esther to get from one place to another without having to use her crutches.

As Murray was pounding the last nail, Jenny returned with several blankets from the house. They spread one over the wooden planks, bundled another to use as a pillow for extra comfort, and kept the third for Esther to use if she got cold.

"Okay," Esther said. "That should work. Thanks, Murray." She leaned over one of her crutches and gave Murray an awkward hug, which made all the effort worth it.

Then Esther pulled a large piece of folded paper out of her jacket. She unfolded it and spread it out on the trailer Murray had just constructed. He and Jenny leaned in closely and saw that it was a map.

"I couldn't find a map of the village of Lemon Grove alone, so this one will have to do. It covers all of Lake County," Esther said. "It's pretty detailed. See these roads?" She pointed to a couple small lines extending to the edges of the map. "That's the road at the end of our lane. And that one goes past Murray's house, out of town, and into the countryside."

"Where did you get this?" Jenny asked.

Esther smirked. "School's good for something, isn't it?"

Murray was impressed by her work but didn't see how it could help them find the buried treasure. "There aren't any churches listed," he said, "so how does this help us?"

"Look who's mister smarty-pants all of a sudden," Esther said. "Do you think I'm just making this up as I go along? That I just pulled that key out of my pocket, and that was the first time I'd thought about any of this?"

Murray felt silly. Of course Esther had been working on this for . . . how long, he had no idea. But this whole thing—the building of the trailer, knowing where in the churches to search, the map—felt like the culmination of months, or maybe even years, of thinking and planning.

Esther removed a pencil from her pocket. "Our church is here," she said, making a small circle not far from the line she said was the road by her house. "That's the one we checked yesterday, so we know it's not there. I've been able to find five more that are within five or six miles, probably. If the people I spoke with knew what they were talking about. One here, here, here, here, and here," she said, drawing five more circles with a flourish. "We know the church is built into a hill. Since this is where the hills are," she said, drawing a long arch, "that would eliminate these two." She put a big X over two of the circles she'd just drawn. Then she pointed to the three remaining circles. "Since these three churches are closest to the hills, my guess is the buried treasure is in one of these three. From now on, these are our three churches."

"Really," Jenny said. "You think you've got it narrowed down to three?"

"I can't know for sure," Esther said. "But it's my best guess." She pointed to the remaining circle farthest away from the homestead. "This one is neat because it's right by Esther River."

"Wait," Jenny said. "What are you talking about? There's no river nearby called Esther River."

"Then what do you call this?" Esther asked, pointing to a blue line on the map.

"A river, I guess."

"And what's this?" Esther pointed to a spot on the map where the river bent back on itself twice. When Murray and Jenny couldn't come up with an answer, Esther became exasperated. "What shape is it?"

"An S?" Jenny said.

"No, not an S." Esther used her pencil to sharpen the edges of the river and looked at them with a triumphant expression. "It's an E. So obviously, it's called Esther River. Or at least it should be."

"Oh, my gosh," Jenny said, sounding exhausted. "You're actually serious."

"Anyway," Esther said, ignoring her sister. She pointed to the other two circles she had drawn. "These two are close together.

Probably within a mile of here, although I don't know the scale of this map. But we should be able to get to both of those today, if we leave now. The third one is a few miles farther, so hopefully we find it in one of the first two."

After a long moment, Jenny articulated exactly what Murray was thinking. "You've really thought this through, haven't you?"

Esther beamed at her. "What do you think I've been doing every night while you lay around dreaming about Murray McBride?" she said in a teasing voice.

Murray coughed suddenly. He covered his embarrassment by looking closely at the map, but a quick glance at Jenny revealed cheeks as red as his suddenly felt.

Murray had no idea what to say, and Jenny seemed uncharacteristically tongue-tied as well. Fortunately, a smirking Esther bailed them out.

"Anyway," she said. "I think we should grab some apples and a loaf of bread and head out now. What do you say?"

Esther's ingenuity—or maybe manipulation—impressed Murray. Whatever it was, he had a feeling he and Jenny were both incapable of arguing with her at the moment.

Five minutes later, Murray was jogging alongside Jenny's bicycle as she pulled Esther on the trailer behind her.

Murray wasn't sure how far he'd run, but it was farther than he'd ever run before, he knew that much. Esther seemed confident they'd be able to make it to the two churches she's scouted on the map, but then again, she was riding in relative comfort on the bicycle trailer he'd built. Distances felt a little different to him as he ran alongside, and even for Jenny as she pedaled with a heavy load behind her.

But soon enough, a small wooden church came into view. Esther sat up tall on the trailer as they approached. "It's a Catholic church," she said.

Murray wondered what kind of religious education Esther had that she could decipher what kind of church it was before they'd even arrived, but then he saw the sign in front: St. John's Catholic Church.

Jenny parked the bicycle, and Esther used her crutches to step off the trailer. Her face was flushed even though she'd been sitting in the trailer the entire way.

"Are you sure you're feeling okay?" Murray asked. He kept his voice down, knowing that Esther wouldn't want Jenny to hear him ask. It would certainly worry her to know he saw something that made him feel the need to question her.

Esther waved Murray off, although her cough as she strode toward the church was full of phlegm.

They entered the tall front doors and faced a much larger church than the last one. Murray noticed a lack of enthusiasm on Esther's part, even though, according to her, this was one of the three most likely hiding places of her grandfather's treasure.

"You don't think it's here," Murray said to her.

Esther shook her head. "There's no cemetery. Our father told us that his father buried the treasure in a church with a cemetery. If there's no cemetery, this can't be it. But that's a good thing."

"Why?" Murray asked.

"These floors are stone. If our grandfather buried it here and then it was covered with a stone floor, we'd never be able to dig it up."

"Well, that was a waste of a trip," Jenny said, her words spreading through the cavernous church.

"Not at all," Esther said, followed by a rattling cough. "Now we have it narrowed down to two."

"Maybe," Jenny said. "Or two hundred. We don't really know, do we?"

Esther ignored her and turned on her heels. She lumbered out the door and down the steps, hobbling with her crutches and coughing as she went.

"She doesn't sound good," Jenny told Murray. "We should take her home. We can search for the other church tomorrow, or next week or something."

"Good luck convincing Esther of that," Murray said, and Jenny's half smile told him she'd had the same thought. Still, when they returned to the bicycle, they gave it a shot.

"Esther, this is ridiculous," Jenny said. "Look at you. If Mom and Dad knew we were out here with you in this condition, we'd be in so much trouble we wouldn't be allowed to leave the house for a month."

"Then I guess we'd better make the most of this time, hadn't we?" Esther said.

Jenny looked to Murray for help, but Murray just shrugged. "The second church is supposed to be close to this one, right? Let's have a look and then get her home to bed."

The church did end up being close, but their route was circuitous. They passed right by the tiny dirt road that led to the church and didn't circle back until they'd been running and riding for a good mile. By the time they figured it out and made it to the church, Murray wasn't sure he could run all the way back home. He'd probably end up walking, which meant he wouldn't get home until around midnight. And his mother would not approve of that.

But Esther seemed energized. A small cemetery was situated near the church, and it was definitely old. Esther lifted herself off the trailer and started toward the church entrance.

Halfway there, she stumbled. She managed to catch herself before she fell, but when Murray grabbed her arm for support, he was shocked by the flushed color of her face. She shivered, too, despite the warm temperatures. And as Murray held her arm, she coughed several times, as if trying to get something up from her lungs.

When she finally spat to the side, Murray saw red.

"Okay," he said. "We have to go. Right now. You're way too sick for this. I shouldn't have agreed to come here. I should have listened to Jenny, and we should have taken you back after the last church."

"No!" Esther said.

"Look what you just coughed up. It was blood, Esther. Everyone knows what that means." After a long, quiet moment, Murray whispered the word they all feared. "Consumption."

Jenny, standing a few yards back, gasped and put her hand over her mouth. Esther sensed her sister's panic and shook her head.

"Don't be ridiculous," she said. "It's just a little cold. And anyway, we've come all this way. Do you think we should just turn around rather than spend two minutes to see if it's here?"

Murray saw her logic. They were already here. And with Esther's health, who knew how long it would be until they could make it back.

"Two minutes," he said.

Esther resumed walking toward the church. Murray and Jenny followed several paces behind, as if their worry and concern about Esther might be mitigated by distance.

When they entered the church, Esther had already found the darkest corner and was on her knees searching for a sign of something buried. But it was another wood floor, and by the time Murray and Jenny arrived, Esther's demeanor had already deflated. It was as if the energy she'd had when they arrived gave way to the illness. She looked more fatigued than Murray had seen her.

"It's not here," she said.

Murray wanted to say something to console her, but before he could, Esther bowed her head and started coughing violently. Her body leaned backward and then forward as she became racked with cough after terrible cough. Murray and Jenny watched, horrified and helpless. Murray barely noticed that Jenny had grabbed his wrist and was holding on for dear life.

When Esther finally stopped coughing, she spat on the floor again, and again Murray noticed a dark shade of red on the wooden grains.

"Let's go," he said. "We have to get you home. Right now."

Murray couldn't believe it when Esther murmured, "No, we can't. I'm fine." But then she started to cry, as if even she knew the truth.

With Murray under one arm and Jenny under the other, they hauled her out of the church and set her on the bicycle trailer.

Jenny began pedaling and Murray ran alongside. He no longer worried about not being able to run the whole way home. With worry for his friend fueling his body, he felt like he could run forever.

An hour and a half later, the farmhouse finally came into view. Murray couldn't feel his legs. His lungs burned. But the thought of stopping had never entered his mind.

Beside him, Jenny pedaled with an expression of grim determination. No one had spoken a word the entire ride home. The only sounds had been the squeaking of the trailer tires, Murray's heavy breathing as he struggled to keep up, and Esther's frequent coughing spells.

When they reached the house, Jenny ran inside and called for her parents while Murray went to Esther and wrapped her arm around his shoulders. She felt heavier than he expected, and he practically dragged her inside. When her father saw her, his eyes bulged and he rushed toward Murray to help.

"Call the doctor," he said to his wife.

He and Murray led Esther down a hallway and into a bedroom. They gently set her on the bed just as she started coughing again.

"I'll get her shoes off. You get her some water," her father said.

Murray did so without thinking. His brain seemed to work on automatic as he went to the kitchen for a glass of water, returned to the bedroom, and set it on a bedside table.

Jenny and her parents were surrounding the bed while Murray stood just behind them. He wasn't sure if he should leave or stay. Was he welcomed here? Just last week he'd been reading in the oak grove because he wasn't allowed inside. But this time, he was a part of what was happening. More than that, he feared he was a reason for it.

After several minutes, Esther's coughing stopped and the anxiety in the room seemed to calm. Jenny looked at him for the first time and seemed startled, as if she had forgotten he was there. She walked around the bed and touched his elbow, leading him out of the bedroom.

"The doctor should be here soon," she said. "She's comfortable for now. There's nothing more we can do until he sees her."

"I should have listened to you," Murray said. He wiped at his eyes, a preventive measure. "We should have come home after the first church."

"We tried. You tried, too, remember? When Esther gets something in her head, she's very strong-willed." She took Murray's hands in hers. "It's not your fault. And besides, she's going to be okay."

Murray couldn't get a handle on his emotions. His new friend was in bed sick, maybe even dying for all he knew, and he was at least partially responsible for allowing it to happen. And then there was Jenny, her soft hands on his, her compassionate green eyes trying to comfort him when it was her sister who was sick. He had no idea what he was supposed to do or how he was supposed to feel.

"Can I wait here?" he finally asked. "Until the doctor sees her. I'd go crazy at home, wondering."

"Of course," Jenny said. "You're with us now. We're in this together."

Murray longed to hug her, but he restrained himself.

"My mother just got a telephone at our house," he said. "I should call her."

Jenny led him to their telephone, and he called his mother to explain the situation. His mother's concern was palpable even over the static-filled telephone line. When he hung up, Jenny was waiting for him.

"My parents say you shouldn't walk all the way home in the dark," she said. "They'll bring a blanket out, and you can sleep on the couch until morning."

"Thank you," Murray said. He called his mother back to let her know. Then, just as he was about to collapse in exhaustion onto the couch, a loud knock rang through the house. Murray, Jenny, and both of her parents rushed to the door.

The doctor had finally arrived.

They waited for what seemed to be forever, although Murray knew it was probably no more than a half hour before the doctor exited Esther's room, a grim expression on his face. Esther's parents, along with Jenny and Murray looked at him expectantly.

"Let's sit," the doctor said, and motioned to the couch Murray was to sleep on. Jenny and her parents sat on the couch, and the doctor took a chair opposite them. Murray, still not sure if he belonged, stood by the hallway.

"I'm afraid the worst is true," the doctor said. "Esther's consumption has returned."

Even though Murray had suspected as much, hearing the words from the doctor sent a cold chill down his back. There was no greater threat to life than consumption. No worse news they could have received. He was so scared for Esther that he wanted to cry. But he couldn't, not in front of Jenny and her parents.

"But how?" Esther's mother asked, bewildered. "Consumption is a city disease. No one gets it out in the country."

"It is certainly rare out here," the doctor said. "But not unheard of. Especially for someone prone to sickness, like Esther."

"What can we do?" Esther's father asked, full of determination. "How can she beat this?"

The doctor sighed, which Murray knew wasn't a good sign. "I've bled her some, and she'll need to rest. If she gets some strength back, exercise out of doors has helped some people with the illness. It's possible she'll bounce back, like she did last time."

"Some people?" Jenny said. "How many? What are Esther's chances of improving and getting back to normal?"

The doctor sighed again. "In my experience, those with consumption fall to the illness sooner or later. Even if it goes away—like it did for Esther recently—eventually, it comes back. Consumption is persistent, I'm afraid."

Murray couldn't handle hearing any more. He moved quickly down the hallway, excusing himself as he left the house and ran straight to the oak grove. There, he lay down in the place where he'd read the first time Esther had been sick.

He thought of the last few months. He thought of Esther when she first arrived at the top of the ditch. He thought of her at his birthday party, and joking with him and Jenny, and how excited she was when they'd planned their quest. And he thought of her now, seriously ill in her bed.

Finally, Murray let go and began to cry.

Murray didn't know how long he lay in the oak grove, crying. But other than a blanket of stars strewn across the sky, it was pitch dark when he heard tentative footsteps approach.

He sat up and wiped his eyes. But when Jenny sat next to him and let her tears flow, Murray did the same. They were in this together, he and Jenny. There was no reason to hide what he felt.

"How is she?" Murray asked.

Jenny stared straight ahead as she spoke. "Sleeping, on and off. But each time she wakes up, she only wants to talk about the stupid treasure."

"What?" Murray said. "Does she know what the doctor said?"

"Oh yes. She overheard the entire conversation. She knows everything."

"And she still wants to find your grandfather's buried treasure? It might not even exist, for all we know."

"I know. But I think Esther has known for a long time that her life will be a short one. For us, this is all shocking and new. But for her, the doctor only confirmed what she's always known."

"Maybe so," Murray said. "But I still don't get it. A shortened life is one thing, but she almost died tonight."

"I know." Jenny shook her head and threw her palms up, helpless. "Esther is who she is." After a moment of silence, she said, "She wants to see you."

Murray swallowed hard. He followed Jenny out of the oak grove and back into the farmhouse. Jenny ignored her parents, who were holding each other silently on the couch, and led Murray into Esther's room. As soon as they entered, Esther sat up. She looked remarkably better than she had just a few hours before.

"Oh good," she said. "I was hoping to get to talk to you two."

Murray didn't know how to respond. Esther had just received what sounded like a death sentence, and yet here she was, acting just like herself. "How are you feeling?" he asked.

Esther shrugged. "Better than a couple hours ago. I think we can go to the third church tomorrow. It has to be there."

"No way," Murray said. "Esther, are you crazy? We can't do this anymore. You could die."

"Didn't you hear the doctor?" Esther said. "I'm going to die anyway. Please don't let me die in this bed. Let me find the treasure. Let me discover what's worth more than gold. Come with me."

"I can't," Murray said. "I want to help you, Esther. I really do. But . . . I can't be a part of this anymore. Not now. Not until you get better."

"That's the thing, though, isn't it," Esther said. "What if I don't get better?"

"You did the right thing," Jenny said. "I told her the exact same thing."

Murray and Jenny sat on the couch. The room was lit by two flickering candles. Jenny's parents had gone to bed after Esther had stabilized. They all needed their rest for what was to come.

But Murray knew he wouldn't sleep much that night. Not in a strange place, not with Jenny so close to him, and not with all he had learned about Esther's illness.

"We'll help her get better," Jenny said. "Then we'll search the third church. And either way, that should be the end of it."

"What do you mean?" Murray said. "You think it's actually there?"

"Could be. Esther has spent a lot of time thinking about this—and researching it. And she seems convinced. But if it's not there, it probably doesn't even exist. If it's not in this last church, I think she'll give it up."

Murray wasn't sure he agreed, based on what he'd seen of Esther's determination. "We should go check. Just us. Tomorrow. We can tell Esther if it's there or not."

Jenny shook her head. "There is no possible way Esther will take our word for it if we tell her it's not there. She would have to see for herself. I can promise you that. And if we did find it? How terrible would it be for her to spend all that time and energy and effort trying to find it, and then as soon as she gets too sick to join us, we discover it for ourselves? It would be better if it didn't exist at all."

She was right, Murray knew. If he and Jenny found whatever was buried, the fact that Esther missed out on the highlight of the adventure would hurt her terribly. He could still see her expression when they'd returned from the hot-air balloon ride.

"Then we wait," Murray said. "We'll help her get better, like you said. And once she does, we'll continue where we left off."

They sat quietly for several moments before Murray felt Jenny looking at him. In the candlelight, her eyes looked almost transparent.

"Thank you for being here," Jenny said. "Thank you for being Esther's friend. Her whole life—" Jenny paused, then shook her head. "I know it's sad, but I think you're the best friend she's ever had."

"And she's mine," Murray said. "Even though I've only known her for a few months."

Jenny laid her head against Murray's shoulder. "I'm so tired," she said. He could almost feel her heartbeat next to him, could hear her breathing slow as she drifted off to sleep. He sat there, wide awake, for some time, enjoying the feeling of Jenny's head on his shoulder. Determined to hold the moment infinitely, to never let this night go. He would never forget how it felt to have this girl's head resting on his shoulder.

But an hour later, as the clock struck three, Murray lost the fight and slipped into a deep sleep.

Esther Brennan awoke to silence in the house.

She lay in her bed in her home, safe for the time being. Yet she felt terror. But it wasn't the terror of what she knew would come. Not the persistent cough that would never leave her. The fatigue and weight loss until she floated away. Esther knew what was coming for her. She knew all about consumption.

But that's not what terrified her. Her terror came from the realization that she might never leave this bed again. That her remaining time, however long or short that might be, would be a painful decline over which she had no control. Others would make decisions about what was best for her, because she was the sick one and they still saw her as a child.

But Esther didn't feel like a child. At thirteen years old, she had been through more than many adults. After a few wonderful early years that she barely remembered, she had contracted polio. Certainly she wasn't alone in that, but the partial paralysis of her legs that required her to walk with crutches made her an outcast. She had been an outcast at eight, she was an outcast at thirteen, and she would be an outcast for the rest of her life.

And she could handle that. After all, there were benefits to being an outcast. She didn't have to worry about trying to be popular or what other kids thought of her. She could delve into whatever interested her, rather than the newest thing the kids at school were into.

What were they going to do? Tell her she was strange? She already knew she was strange. Ironically, that's what made her free to be herself.

No, it wasn't the outcast part that bothered Esther. It was the thought of being powerless over her own life, her own decisions. Maybe everyone was right. Maybe she should lay in bed and hope for the best and accept whatever came.

But Esther Brennan wasn't built that way.

Esther lay as quietly as she could for several minutes. She counted the seconds, stifling the coughs that threatened to break through. When five minutes had passed without a sound, she slowly—very slowly—began moving her feet off the side of the bed.

Once she was sitting up with her feet touching the cold wooden floor, Esther evaluated how she was feeling. Better, she decided. Still a bit dizzy, and her lungs felt heavy and her head ached terribly. But at least she could move again. She could only guess how long that might last. If she was going to do this, she had to do it now.

So she eased herself up from the bed, grabbed her crutches, and found a candle and a box of matches from inside a drawer. She took the key, which was sitting on the bedside table, and crept down the hallway and into the kitchen, where she found a stack of neatly folded rags near the sink. She set the candle, matches, and key on one of them, bundled it up, and put it in a pocket sewn into her nightgown.

She continued slowly, trying to keep her crutches as quiet as possible while creeping toward the front door. In the living room, the sight of Jenny with her head on Murray's shoulder gave her a mix of contentment and longing. The two were meant to be together; she'd seen that the moment she saw them in the ditch together that first time. But it only increased the feeling of being an outcast.

The front door creaked when she opened it, and Esther froze in place, listening for any stirring from Murray, Jenny, or her parents.

She counted to one hundred, then slowly slipped out the door and closed it behind her.

The night was pure freedom.

The sky was clear, with stars shining so thickly she thought a million must have been added just for her, just for tonight. A breeze blew from the south, warming the air and keeping the chill away. Esther closed her eyes and took a deep breath, smelling the autumn leaves. Every experience was more potent in the dark.

Nothing could compare to this feeling. A hundred years of lying sick on a bed couldn't hold a candle to this one beautiful, immersive moment of bliss. It was worth it, she decided right then and there. No matter what, this moment was worth it.

The bicycle and trailer were still sitting near the front door. Esther couldn't remember much about what happened when they had arrived home, but she had a faint recollection of being carried inside. By whom, she couldn't say.

She set her crutches on the trailer. Then, in her nightgown, she pulled the bicycle from where it rested against the side of the house and swung her leg over it. A feeling of power swept over her. She controlled her destiny. She could decide what would happen. No one could tell her what she wasn't capable of. Tonight, Esther was in charge.

"Here goes nothing," she whispered into the night air, and pushed off from the ground.

It wasn't until her feet completed a few rotations that she realized she could, in fact, pedal. She had learned to ride as a young child, but ever since polio had taken away full use of her legs, she'd avoided bicycles. Her right leg in particular struggled, and the last thing she needed was another embarrassing incident of not being able to do what everyone else could.

But it turned out she could do it. Sure, one part in the rotation shot a bolt of pain up her leg, and she couldn't really push down with *her right foot. But the momentum from her left foot made up for it. The result was similar to her walking stride. Halting and jerky, but good enough to get around. Esther decided she liked the way she rode a bicycle.*

She hadn't grabbed the map, but she didn't need it. She had studied it enough to know exactly where the third church was. The third, and final, church. The treasure had to be there. Esther just knew it was. She could feel it in her bones.

It didn't take long for fatigue to set in. The excitement wore off after about a mile of riding, and the result was an evaporation of her energy. She realized once again that she was, in fact, very sick. At one point, she had to stop pedaling, lean over, and cough violently to bring up a mixture of phlegm and blood. But she wasn't going to let it stop her.

Although she knew her way, the distances felt much longer in the dark. Several times she second-guessed herself. Once, she nearly turned around, thinking she must have missed a turnoff, only to see the small dirt road just before she changed course.

When she guessed she had ridden four miles, meaning there would be about two more to go, Esther realized she had made a mistake in coming out here alone, at night, when she was so sick she could hardly coax her body to move. She realized the space between what she longed for and what her body was capable of.

She stopped the bicycle and looked to the sky. She gazed at the stars and wondered what she should do. Her entire body was protesting so adamantly. Every movement was an intense labor with so little reward. Her throat and head throbbed. Her lungs were filled with lava. She wondered how she could possibly get all the way back home.

But what if she did make it home? What waited for her there? A deathbed, she knew. Maybe not tonight or tomorrow or the next day, but soon. Everyone knew that was true. If she only had one night to live, then she might as well live it all the way.

Esther took a deep, shaking breath and pushed the bicycle forward into the dark.

The rest of the ride felt better. It felt like her body had put up one last protest and once she overcame it, she was able to tap into some reserve of energy her body had been saving.

The path became wooded. Tall maples mixed with elms, and birches cast shadows in the moonlight. The farther she rode, the more the woods thickened, full of twisting branches and swaying leaves. Esther was struck by the beauty of the forest. The river ran next to her, gurgling in the dark. When she saw the river double back on itself twice, she knew she was close.

The outline of a church building silhouetted by the moonlight nearly made Esther fall off the bicycle. She had expected it to be there—or at least she thought she had. But actually seeing it, actually being here, was something close to a religious experience.

She pulled the bicycle to a stop, hobbled to the trailer to grab her crutches, and looked around. To the right of the church building, a small cemetery glowed in the moonlight. Behind the church, a large hill seemed in the act of swallowing the church. Even from outside, Esther could tell that the back wall of the church was earthen. With trembling hands, she reached for the small door and pushed it open.

The church had been abandoned long ago from the looks of it. That fact caused a surge of adrenaline, giving Esther another shot of energy. The idea that the treasure could have been buried in a church where dozens or hundreds of people passed over it every week had always seemed a little far-fetched. Esther fully expected to find it in an abandoned church like this one, which could have hidden the case forever. A place where no one would have stumbled across a small pile of displaced earth. A place so old it still had a dirt floor.

Yes, Esther had always known the church would look exactly like this. Old, decrepit, halfway to falling down, almost hidden by the forest.

Beautiful.

Esther brushed cobwebs aside as she limped her way into the church. The sound of small animals scurrying away only made her more excited. She reached into her pocket, removed the kitchen rag, and unfolded it. She lit the candle with a match and squeezed the key in her palm.

The candlelight illuminated an eerie scene of drooping rafters, a collapsed wall, and what looked to be an old, wooden altar. In another context, it would have been terrifying. To Esther, it was perfect.

She put the key into the pocket of her nightgown, set one crutch aside so she could hold the candle, and limped farther into the dark recesses of the building. She knew the treasure would be in an alcove, to the side and out of the way of most foot traffic. So she hobbled to the side of the church and continued toward the front. Sure enough, she entered a small space that seemed like the perfect place to bury something.

The only problem was a large beam above the alcove had collapsed and was bending downward at a concerning angle. It looked as if it could fall to the ground at any moment. But Esther had come this far. She wasn't going to let a little danger deter her.

As she took a step toward the alcove, a wave of dizziness overtook her. She nearly fell to the ground and only kept her balance by dropping the candle and putting all her weight onto the one crutch she still had. Through this bout of lightheadedness, she realized the dropped candle could start a fire. That the entire church could burn down, and she'd never find the treasure.

When the dizziness passed and her vision cleared, she realized the dirt floor had snuffed the flame. But now it was pitch dark, and she couldn't see the ground to find the candle.

Esther stood still for a moment, contemplating what to do. She was about to drop to her hands and knees in search of the candle when a ray of moonlight filtered into the church and illuminated the alcove she was hoping to search. It was like a beacon calling her, and she followed the light, limping through the church with her single crutch until she ducked below the wooden beam and into the alcove.

As the clouds outside the church shifted, moonlight lit the area so clearly it was almost like day. And there, right in the moonbeam, was a disturbance in the floor—a small bulge in the dirt, as if a hole had been dug and something had been placed inside, taking up the space where the dirt had been and creating a bump.

Esther dropped to her knees, ignoring the clatter of her crutch, ignoring the weight of her lungs, ignoring the dizziness threatening to overtake her, ignoring the sweat dripping from her brow and the chills running over her skin and the throbbing in her temples.

She hadn't thought to bring a shovel. Of all the things she had prepared for, how could she have forgotten a shovel? What did she think she would do when she found it? Dig it out with her hands? It was a ridiculous oversight.

But she was here, and using her hands was her only option, so Esther first set the key on the ground near her knees, then used the side of her hand to brush away any loose dirt. Once she couldn't move any more dirt using that method, she used her fingertips to dig into the hard dirt floor. If a case was buried there, she was determined to find it.

✳   ✳   ✳

With the sound of a rooster crowing, Murray startled awake. The first thing he realized was that Jenny's head was no longer resting on his shoulder. She was curled up on the opposite side of the couch, breathing softly and looking like an angel.

Feeling suddenly self-conscious about being so near Jenny as she slept, Murray eased up from the couch. He wore the same clothes and the same shoes as the day before. As the rooster crowed again, Jenny began to stir, and Murray walked down the hallway toward Esther's room.

The door was open, which struck Murray as strange until he realized Esther's parents had probably checked on her in the middle of the night and left the door open so they could hear if she were to cry out. But as he peeked his head around the doorframe, a pile of blankets on the bed seemed clumped in a strange way. Murray wasn't sure how they could be covering Esther's whole body. Surely she was larger than the blankets.

Murray entered the room and approached the bed. With every step, he became more and more certain that Esther couldn't be under the blankets, but it didn't concern him. Even as he reached the bed and moved the blankets aside to verify that the bed was, indeed, empty, Murray wasn't worried. Surely Esther had left her bed before Murray woke up and was in the kitchen getting a drink of water, or maybe in the outhouse. Nothing else would make sense at all.

But as he returned to the living room to see Jenny sitting up on the couch, a delayed panic hit him with full force. He stopped in his tracks and stared at Jenny, suddenly unsure how to tell her what he'd just seen.

Jenny bolted from the couch. "What is it, Murray?" Then, because only one explanation could have caused the fear in Murray's eyes, she said, "Where's Esther?"

Murray shook his head. "I don't know. She's not in her bed."

Jenny was speaking before Murray even finished. "What do you mean she's not in her bed. Where is she then?"

Murray looked toward the kitchen, but the silence made it obvious she wasn't there. "The outhouse maybe?" he said.

Jenny burst past him and out the front door, and he followed her outside. She ran around to the outhouse, knocked on the door, opened it, then slammed it shut again. When she returned to Murray, her eyes were wide with terror.

"She went looking for it," she said. "She went to the church."

"No," Murray said. "She wouldn't do that. She was so sick. Far too sick to do something like that."

Jenny looked around. "Where's the bicycle? We left the bicycle and trailer right here," she said, pointing to the side of the farmhouse. "Where is it?"

"I can't believe it," Murray said. He covered his mouth with his hands. He felt as though he might vomit. "When did she leave? And why isn't she back?"

"We have to go find her," Jenny said.

"What? No," Murray said. "We have to wake up your parents and have them call the police."

Fear colored Jenny's eyes, but her voice was level and composed. "No. It's barely even morning and we're way outside town. Who knows how long it would take for them to get here. And then we'd have to explain everything and convince them to look for the church." She touched Murray's hand, sending shivers up his arm. "We need to go get her, Murray. And we need to do it now."

"We don't have the bicycle. And we don't know where the church is, if she's even there."

Jenny sprinted inside and returned a moment later with the map Esther had used to mark where the three churches were located. She gazed briefly toward the pasture. "Our horse threw a shoe," she said. "We'll have to run." She didn't wait for Murray's reply.

Fueled by fear, Murray hurried to catch up.

As they ran toward the church, a cold wind blew through their hair. It pushed against them one moment, then swirled and propelled them the next.

The wind was uncontrolled, it was free, it was alive.

Every mile or so, they stopped to consult the map, but only for a moment. There was no time to rest. The distance didn't matter. Murray didn't even notice the miles go by, and the look of raw determination never left Jenny's face. Fear and adrenaline propelled them as they ran through the wind.

An hour after they had left the farmhouse, hills rose up in the distance. The road they were on led straight into them. Off to their right, a river snaked silently in the faint light of dawn.

"Esther River," Murray said. "That must be it."

"Look for the place where the river doubles back twice," Jenny said. "If we find that bend, we'll find the church."

Over the next twenty minutes, neither of them spoke, but Murray felt Jenny pick up her pace several times as they ran toward the hills.

"There it is," Jenny said sometime later, and she pointed to their right.

Murray squinted into the woods. About a hundred feet away, the sparkle of early morning sunlight on water twisted into the shape of an S, or, with slightly sharpened edges, an E.

"Oh, my gosh," Jenny said. She was gazing straight ahead. Murray turned and saw it too. A small structure of some sort. A building, although from this distance it was impossible to tell what it was, but it appeared to be very near the hillside.

With each stride forward, the outline became clearer. Soon, Murray realized it was a church, and he saw what appeared to be a small cemetery to its right. But he didn't say anything and neither did Jenny.

Finally, they reached the entrance to the church, both sweating and breathing hard. It had probably been six miles, although Murray hardly remembered any of the run. It was like time was lost to him; his brain was so focused on Esther that it couldn't register the past hour.

But when Jenny pushed the rotting door of the church open, Murray's entire being was present in the moment.

"Esther?" Jenny said tentatively as she poked her head through the doorway. Her voice was swallowed by the empty space.

When there was no response, she opened the door wide to let daylight in. Before stepping inside, Murray looked to his right and felt his stomach drop. Leaning against the wooden building, the front tire of a bicycle poked out from around the corner. At the same time Murray noticed the tire, Jenny said Esther's name again, only this time it came in the form of a shriek.

Murray rushed into the church behind Jenny and saw the terrible scene that would haunt him for the rest of his days. Esther lay on the dirt floor, the brass key in her open palm, unconscious.

Jenny rushed to her and put her finger to Esther's neck. After a pause, she said, "I can't feel her heartbeat. She's barely breathing. We have to get her out of here."

"The bicycle's on the side of the church," Murray said. "I'll bring it to the front."

Murray bent toward Esther and took the key from her hand, feeling an intense responsibility to keep it safe. His mind raced as he ran out of the church, grabbed the bicycle, and rode it to the front of the building. He kept seeing Esther's pale face every time he blinked his eyes, so he forced them wide open no matter how much they dried out.

He ran the few steps back into the church, where Jenny was already trying to lift Esther from the dirt floor. Murray ducked under one of Esther's arms and together, he and Jenny dragged her out and set her as gently as possible onto the trailer. Jenny hopped on next to her, sat cross-legged, and put Esther's head in her lap.

"Ride fast, Murray," she said. "Please, ride as fast as you can."

Murray met Jenny's eyes for the briefest of moments. "I promise," he said.

He didn't know why he said that. He didn't even know what he was promising. That he would ride his fastest? That Esther would be okay? That he would never leave Jenny for the rest of her life?

Murray didn't know. All he knew was that his friend needed him to ride fast. So Murray rode as fast as his legs would allow.

Murray rode as fast as the wind.

Murray paced outside the farmhouse while Jenny, her parents, and the doctor stayed with Esther in her bedroom. He didn't know what was going on, and the uncertainty was driving him crazy.

He had kept his promise to Jenny. He had pedaled with every ounce of strength he had the entire way, never letting up, never slowing down. Not until he pulled the bicycle into the Brennans' driveway and skidded to a stop at the front door.

His legs were too wobbly to stand, much less help carry Esther inside. Fortunately, her parents were outside, worrying and wondering. When they saw the bicycle speed toward the house, they jumped into action. Esther's father lifted her from Jenny's lap and rushed her inside, with her mother trailing behind in desperate tears. While Murray leaned a hand against the bicycle seat for support, Jenny had walked up to him and kissed his cheek. Then she had turned and gone inside while Murray stood paralyzed by overwhelming emotions.

That was an hour before. At least. And he hadn't heard a thing since. He wanted so badly to go inside, to see if Esther was okay. But it wasn't his place.

But he couldn't go home either. Not without knowing if Esther was dead or alive. So he waited.

He was sitting on the ground, leaning his back against the farmhouse, when the front door opened and Jenny came out. Murray could tell she'd been crying. He longed to make her pain go away. But he knew the things happening here were well beyond his power to control.

. "Is she . . ." Murray said, but he couldn't get himself to finish the question.

Jenny's brow crinkled, as if she didn't know how to answer the question. "She's alive," she finally said. "But Murray . . . she's not . . . the doctor says . . . she probably won't make it through the day."

Murray's head was shaking back and forth, although he wasn't conscious of making it happen. It was as if his body was saying what he couldn't seem to vocalize. No. No, no, no, no, no. It couldn't be. Esther couldn't possibly die. She was too strong, too vibrant, too real. The idea that she could cease to exist simply made no sense. No sense whatsoever.

"She was conscious for a few minutes," Jenny said. "She tried to talk, but she couldn't. But it was so strange." Jenny's look of confusion deepened. "If I didn't know better, I would have said she was smiling. Then she lost consciousness again. That was thirty minutes ago."

Jenny looked into the distance, as if enjoying the view of the farmland, the oak grove, the horizon. "You can come see her. My parents said it's okay. They said to tell you they appreciate all you did to try to help, but they won't be able to tell you that. They're . . . well, they're hurting right now. Like all of us."

Murray stood to join Jenny, but before they walked into the house, he took her hands in his. He looked into her ocean-green eyes and felt a connection to her that no force in the universe could shake. Murray knew, in that moment, that he would never leave Jenny's side. Not ever. Not for anything. They were bound together by tragedy and love and forces deeper than Murray could possibly articulate.

"Let's go say goodbye," Jenny said. Then she turned and walked silently into the farmhouse, still holding his hand.

Jenny had been right. Esther looked as if she was smiling. She lay on her bed, eyes closed, her chest barely rising and falling. Murray saw an empty bottle labeled MORPHINE on the bedside table and realized the truth—they were keeping Esther comfortable until she died.

Her parents had left the room, giving Murray a chance to spend a last moment with Esther. He covered Esther's hand with his own, something he'd never done when she'd been conscious. He squeezed her hand gently, hoping she could feel it, that she could know how sorry he was. And how much he loved her. She was his dear friend, and he would never, ever forget her.

Murray didn't know what to say, and he didn't know what to do. He wanted to curl up and lay next to her, he wanted to read to her and tell her jokes. He wanted his friend back.

But he knew that wasn't going to happen. And as he heard Esther's parents' footsteps creaking the floorboards outside the bedroom, Murray knew it was time to go. He squeezed Esther's hand once more, then turned and walked from the room.

The final moments were for family.

Hours later, Esther succumbed to her illness. Murray held Jenny's hand as they sat in the oak grove, looking at the house that still held Esther's body. While Jenny wept quietly, Murray found that he couldn't cry. It was strange, but he could barely even feel.

Shouldn't he be feeling the excruciating combination of loss and grief and guilt? Surely those terrible emotions were inside him, just waiting to explode. But in this moment, all he could do was stare at the old farmhouse, hold Jenny's hand, and scrutinize this perplexing emptiness.

He still held the key. He opened his hand now and looked at it, hoping to feel a connection to Esther. But he felt nothing.

"I think we should bury that key," Jenny said, sniffling as she stared at it with him.

"Bury it? Why?" Murray said.

"I don't know." Jenny's voice was gravelly from crying. Her eyes were red and swollen when she looked at Murray. "It just feels right. On one hand, I know how important it was to Esther, and we should remember that. On the other hand, I never want to see it again. It seems like a way to both honor and dispose of it."

"Where?" Murray asked.

Jenny stood and reached for his hand. "Follow me."

They stopped by the barn to grab a small gardening shovel, then began walking. They walked in silence, each deep within their own thoughts. Their own regrets. They walked for a long time, Murray following Jenny's lead. Finally, Murray realized where they were going.

"Why here?" he asked.

"Esther cared about you more than you know," Jenny said. "She would want it to be in a place where you were together. Where all three of us were together. And this is where it all started."

Murray took her hand as they walked across the schoolyard, all the way to the ditch on the far side. They stood side by side, looking down at the place where he had first met both Esther and Jenny.

Wordlessly, they climbed into the bottom of the ditch. Jenny sat for a moment, as if reliving their times together. Then she shifted onto her knees and began to dig.

The hole she dug was less than a foot deep, but it would be more than enough to keep the key safe from time and disturbance. When she looked up, Murray pulled the key from his pocket and set it in her palm.

Jenny turned it back and forth, as if studying all sides of it, all aspects. Her eyes were illuminated in a shimmering sadness as she reached to the bottom of the hole she'd dug and gently pressed the key into the dirt, making a small indentation.

"I don't know whether to love this key or hate it," she said.

"Let's go with love," Murray said. "Remember how happy she was, how excited she got anytime she talked about this stupid key?"

Jenny laughed once, loudly. It seemed out of place. *Like everything about this*, Murray thought. Out of place. Nothing was like it was supposed to be.

But there was nothing to be done, other than cover the key with dirt in a ritual of honor and anger, celebration and sadness. So that's what Jenny and Murray did.

Afterward, they sat in the ditch for a long time, neither one able to comprehend the idea of a world without Esther.

CHAPTER 11

1996

Having lived for nearly one hundred years, I've come to believe that all of life can be beautiful. Sure, there are things like sunsets and newborn babies, or lightning in the distance on a summer evening and home runs at Wrigley Field. Those are what I think of as "easy beautiful." But then there's "hard beautiful," and it's a real thing, too.

You see, sometimes life throws curveballs at you and things don't go the way you want. Maybe a spouse leaves or a loved one dies. It's hard to think of those things as having any beauty, and that's the truth. Especially when you're in the middle of them. But if you look deeper, you'll see it.

You'll see that having things turn out different than what you expect—even different than what you want—opens doors you never would have considered if your original plan had worked out. Maybe the loss of a job leads to finding your true passion. I once knew a fella who lost his leg in the ravages of war, but it turned out the lass that took care of him in the hospital became his wife. Years later, he told me he was grateful he'd lost the leg because a less severe injury wouldn't have landed him in the bed where he met the love of his life. His wife was more important to him than his leg had ever been.

Even the worst things we experience—the death of someone we love—has an element of beauty, if you look hard enough. After you lose someone, how much more potent is the memory of your time together? How much more raw is the love you feel for them after they're gone?

Don't get me wrong. I'd give just about anything to have Esther back, and to have my boys, too. But something about the loss makes them even more special, even though they only live in my memory now.

And I think that's beautiful.

Jenny spent most of my story staring at the key, a sad look on her face. But I realize now that I don't need to protect her from that. It's okay if seeing that key makes Jenny sad. It should. Maybe sadness isn't something to be afraid of, not something to be pushed away and avoided at all costs. Sadness is a universal human experience. It's part of what makes us alive. Sadness is something to be felt.

As if she's thinking the same thing, Jenny looks up from the key and straight into my eyes. "Thank you, Murray," she says. "Thank you for telling me. For reminding me. I do miss Esther so. But I can't miss someone I don't remember, can I? You brought her back for me, in my mind."

Her gratitude is touching, and it sure means a lot to me that she can express it. It seems like she's been fading a bit as the day wears on. This morning, I wasn't so sure I was making the right decision in taking her to Aspen Leaves tomorrow morning. Even though we both agreed it was the best move, I had second thoughts when she seemed so aware this morning.

But I know I don't have a choice. Her decline throughout the day has made that clear. And without Deb's help, I couldn't care for Jenny even if she wasn't getting worse.

"I don't understand," Brooke says, bringing me back from my thoughts.

She's sitting cross-legged down in the ditch, right where Jenny and I used to read, looking more angry than confused.

"How's that?" I say.

"I said, I don't get it."

And now there's no mistaking the anger in her voice. Or her eyes, for that matter. She's glaring at me like I did something terrible, but I don't know what it could possibly be. I just told a story, that's all.

"You're telling me Esther died trying to find that treasure, and you guys just buried the key and never looked back?" Her withering stare makes me look away. I'm afraid of what she might say. "Wouldn't you feel some obligation to fulfill the quest that meant so much to her that she was willing to die for it?" Brooke says.

"I mean, I watch you two together and I think I might be starting to understand at least a little bit about what love is, but then . . ." She shakes her head and seems to get more and more angry with every word. "This thing was her passion, she risked her life for it. She lost her life trying to find it. And you didn't even care about it. How is that showing love?"

"You don't understand," I say. "It was too hard. Too painful. We couldn't deal with it. We were too young."

"Well, you're not young now, are you? But you still never planned to find it."

I'm about to give a strong retort, more because I'm feeling attacked than because I think I'm right. But Jenny puts a hand on my forearm just before I let Brooke hear it.

"She's right, Murray," Jenny says. "And you're right, too. We were too young to face it, and that's understandable. But at some point, it was no longer understandable. And that point was a long time ago. We need to find the treasure, Murray. We need to finish the quest. For Esther's sake."

Now, I can understand what Jenny's saying—and Brooke for that matter, too. But it's getting late, the sun is getting low. Jenny hasn't been as sharp the second part of the day. Continuing this quest would be irresponsible. At the very least we should wait until tomorrow and see how Jenny's feeling.

But tomorrow Jenny needs to go to the memory care center. If she doesn't show up, if we give up that spot, who knows when we might be able to get her in there. Who knows what might happen with a nearly hundred-year-old man trying to care full-time for his nearly hundred-year-old wife with advanced Alzheimer's. And Deb, our helper, is on an airplane somewhere.

So tonight is our only chance. We waited eighty-six years to do this. And maybe Brooke is right, maybe it was eighty-six years too long.

But we still have time. And the truth is, I think we have a chance to find the treasure, if it really exists. Because the truth is, I think I have a pretty good idea where to look for it. And I think I've known for a very long time.

Brooke pulls the old Ford into the Fox River Forest Preserve and slows to a crawl. We all scan the area as we make our way deeper into the woods. If I'm not mistaken, somewhere in here is the modern-day location of what was an old, abandoned church back in 1910. The third church. The one where we found Esther all those years ago. And if it was abandoned eighty-six years ago, it's probably no more than ruins now.

I'm surprised by the flicker of excitement I feel. It starts in my chest and pulses up into my throat every time I imagine what it would be like to find the treasure. I've always associated that treasure with tragedy. All my thoughts about it have been polluted by fear. But not now. Now that I've made the decision to search for it—to actually try to find it—a beautiful, pure excitement spreads through my entire aging body. In this moment, I don't feel so old.

This is what Esther was talking about. This is why it meant so much to her. What I feel is only a spark, only a glimpse of the passion she felt, but it's enough to make me understand.

And that's new for me, this ability to understand why Esther was so motivated, so determined. It's something I could never comprehend before. I always wondered, how could she put herself at risk like that? Even knowing she was unlikely to live a long life, how could she be so careless? So reckless?

It was for this spark. The one I feel now. This feeling of possibility and adventure. This feeling that I'm alive.

I strain my eyes to follow the river through the trees. If we can find the bend where the river doubles back on itself twice—creating an E for Esther—we might have a chance to find the ruins.

Sitting next to me, Jenny stiffens. She gets a crinkle in her brow. And I feel my heart sink. Not now—that's all I can think, over and over. This can't be happening now. She's done so well today, and we're finally on the cusp of something we've put off for eighty-six years. It's a journey we're on together—a quest. She can't disappear on me now.

"Where are we?" Jenny asks. Her voice isn't her own.

I try to remember what Doc Keaton's pamphlet said about situations like this. How can I keep Jenny here, with me? How can I keep her calm and feeling secure? "We're going to finish our quest, love," I say.

"There's the river again," Brooke says. I don't think she's picked up on Jenny's change in manner. She's focused on the task at hand. "It keeps going in and out of view. But it's right over there. Do you see it?"

"I catch a glimpse once in a while," I say.

Then, seemingly out of the blue, Jenny grabs at the door handle. "I want to go home," she says. "Where am I? I want to go home."

Before I have a chance to soothe her, she unlocks the door and opens it. Thankfully, Brooke sees what's happening and stops the car so Jenny doesn't get hurt. But Jenny manages to exit and starts walking alone into the woods.

"Wait," I say. "Sweetheart . . ."

But she doesn't listen. I get out of the car and follow as quickly as I can, cursing the throbbing in my knee the whole way. Brooke stands near the driver's side door, but doesn't seem to know what to do. Jenny stops near a tree. When I reach her, she's staring at the trunk.

"It's okay," I say. I hope my words will calm her, maybe reassure her a bit. I can only imagine the disorientation she's feeling, and the fear that results from it.

I take a chance and put my hand gently on her shoulder. She doesn't stiffen, which I take to be a good sign. I just stand with her, and I'll stand with her as long as she needs me to, knee pain or not. It's just my presence, nothing special, but it seems to calm her.

There's a tightening in my chest as I stand here with my wife. A feeling of loss. That spark I felt just moments ago is still there, trying to burst into a flame. It's excitement, anticipation, and something deeper—something more meaningful. Connection, I realize. Connection to my fellow adventurers. That's what it is. A feeling that we're a tribe, we're one unit, we're together.

It saddens me to realize this feeling was available the whole time, for eighty-six years, and yet I put it off, I avoided it. I waited too long. Because now, with Jenny standing in the woods, disoriented and confused, it's obvious we can't continue. As much as it pains me to admit, I know this is the end of our quest.

After a minute in which the only sound is the chirping of a robin, I say, "Let's go home, love."

To my great relief, she turns to follow me. Wordlessly, I lead Jenny back to the car. Brooke helps her into the back seat and closes the door. I thank her, and expect her to head straight to the driver's seat to take us home. Instead, she squares her shoulders to me.

"We still need to find the treasure," she says.

I manage to suppress my anger, and chalk up her lack of understanding to immaturity. "There are more important things to deal with right now," I say. "Esther is long gone, but Jenny's still here. We need to do what's best for her now."

"I understand, but this isn't just about Esther."

"How's that?"

"It's about Jenny. You know how you had your little side plan? To take her around to places but not search for the treasure?"

"Sure, I do."

"Well, Jenny had a side plan, too. She took me aside, just like you. And she told me it was really important that we find the treasure. She told me not to let you quit. Not until you found it. Even if she was struggling."

I look through the car window at my wife, calm but with a blank look on her face. "Why would she say that? Did she know I wasn't planning to look for it?"

"I don't know. All I know is that she was really adamant. She said I needed to make sure we came here today, to the forest preserve. And we needed to find the treasure."

"When did she say all this? This was today?"

I realize it had to be today. I just met Brooke this morning.

"When you were in the bathroom this morning," she says. "At my house. Or, what used to be my house."

I can't figure it. Jenny was very clear-headed at the time. Why would she say those things to Brooke?

Brooke gives me a serious look. "Jenny knew this might happen, and she made me promise to continue anyway. It sounded really important to her."

I look to the river in the distance and try to figure out what I'm supposed to do. What was Jenny up to? How could she expect me to allow this to continue, even if I didn't think it was best for her?

"Mr. McBride?" Brooke's voice is tentative, like she's afraid to say what she must. "I think I might know where it is."

"Where the treasure is?"

"Not necessarily the treasure. But the church."

"You do? How?"

"Jacob and I used to come here. Like I said, we wandered all over. There's a little building, not far from here. I guess it's not really even a building, but it used to be. We used to go hang out in there. A lot of kids do," she adds, as if trying to excuse her behavior.

I don't care about what Brooke and her boyfriend were up to, but if she's saying she knows where the church is, and that Jenny planned for us to find it for some reason, then maybe I should have her take us there.

I look at Jenny again through the window. "I'll try one thing. If it doesn't work, we need to take her home. No matter what she said."

I open the door and lean over as far as I'm able. "Sweetheart, we can go home if you'd like," I say. "Right now. We'll get you home. But do you remember the quest?" I know it's a direct question, but I'm taking a chance here. I pull the key from my pocket and show it to her. "Do you remember that we're looking for the buried treasure that can be opened with this key? With something worth more than gold inside? Do you remember that, my love?"

As Jenny stares at it, her eyes soften. The confusion bordering on anger turns to embarrassment. But with me, she never needs to feel embarrassed, not for anything.

"Brooke thinks she might know how to find the church where we found Esther that morning long ago. Do you remember?" Jenny nods slowly. "The day she died."

"That's right. And Jenny, I think Esther was in the right place. Only she never found it because she became too sick. I think she lost consciousness before she could find it, see? But I think it was there. I think Esther knew it, she was sure of it. That's why it was worth it to her to sneak out in the middle of the night. She knew what might happen, but she did it anyway. That's how sure she was that it was in that church. And it's been abandoned ever since. So I think there's a chance it could still be there." Despite everything, the possibility that the treasure could be so close is exhilarating.

Jenny's shoulders loosen, and the crease in her eyebrows go smooth. "We should go look," she says.

"You're okay with doing that?" I ask. "You feel well enough?"

Jenny puts her hand on mine. "I'll try to stay with you, Murray. I'll try my hardest to stay with you."

Brooke drives faster than I expected her to, but I guess she understands how fragile this situation is. How tenuous Jenny's grasp on the moment is. And besides, she knows where she's going.

After just a few minutes, I see it. The river bend. The sun, low on the horizon, shimmers across the water as it doubles back on itself twice, creating a perfect S. Or, with slightly sharper edges, a perfect E.

Brooke pulls the car off the road and onto a gravel shoulder. She points to some hills right near the river. "There," she says. "See it? It looks like it's nothing but a bunch of fallen logs, but there's an old building of some sort buried in there."

I squint in the direction she's pointing and sure enough, there it is. Ruins. Real ruins. With logs that were obviously cut to size and a roof that has fallen in on itself. It's pushed right up against a hill, so close it looks like the hill must have been the back wall at one point. What else could it be but the church?

And then the clincher. Just off to the side of the pile of logs, a few small headstones pop out of the ground, gray and weathered by time, forgotten.

"Take the shovel," Brooke says. She hands it to me, then all of us make our way out of the car. Brooke looks toward the ruins, then back to me and Jenny. "I'll be here if you need anything, okay?"

At first, I'm surprised she's not going to join us. She has seemed so excited about this quest and was so adamant that we finish it. But then I realize the truth—it's not that she doesn't want to come with us. It's that she wants to give this moment to Jenny and me. Just the two of us.

I nod to Brooke, then take Jenny's hand. Together, we begin to make our way alone into the woods.

We get to within about thirty feet of what was once a church when Jenny stops dead in her tracks.

"Murray," she says. "It's Esther."

I can't figure out what she means. Does Jenny see Esther? Or does she think she does? It's like she's seeing back in time. Back into her memory. Into a place where her brain still functioned like it used to. When the world made more sense to her.

Maybe she's seeing an apparition, or maybe she's just jolted by the memory of what happened the last time we were here, so long ago. I don't doubt that either one is possible.

Either way, Jenny takes a deep breath and leads me the last few steps, and we duck into the ruins.

*   *   *

It's dark inside, despite the fact that the sun hasn't finished setting. It's cramped and hidden, almost like a cave made of fallen wood.

It had been a small church to begin with, even before it collapsed. Just a single room made of wood, a dirt floor, and an altar of some sort near the front. A place for prayer, nothing more. No trappings, no decorations, no pretentiousness. This was a house of God.

Still is, if you ask me. I believe God made this earth, every bit of it. Sure, mankind has built things on it. But every single thing humans have made has come from what God put here first. So the collapsed wooden walls, the moss growing on the roof, the knee-high weeds covering most of the dirt floor—they're all part of this house of God.

It feels sacred here. Maybe it's just the knowledge of what happened so long ago. Esther. My new best friend, who I read to in a ditch in the schoolyard. Here's where our adventure came to an end.

And yet, here I am. With Esther's sister, the love of my life.

"I feel her here," Jenny says, squeezing my hand. "I feel her here so strongly. Oh, Murray, she was here." She looks at me with hope that borders on pleading. "She was happy when she was here, wasn't she?"

I nod hard, as certain as I've ever been. "She was on her quest," I say. "It's exactly what she wanted to do, and this is exactly where she wanted to be. So yes, I think she was happy."

And I believe that. I'm not just saying it for Jenny's benefit. Sure, Esther was sick. So sick she would die the very next day. But Esther was happy here. She was at peace.

I remember where Esther used to say to look—in the corners, off in the alcoves. With the roof and walls collapsed around us, there's not much room to maneuver, and we need to be careful not to knock into anything that might be load bearing. Sure, the roof has already come down, along with most of the walls, but there are still plenty of logs and beams and slabs of wood balancing precariously.

There's a crumpled beer can at my feet. It looks like it's been here for a hundred years, which probably isn't too far from the truth. It's a brand I've never heard of, or maybe it's just that it's so dark in here.

Evening is coming on fast. I look into the darkness and wait for my eyes to adjust, but ninety-eight-year-old eyes take whatever time they decide they want to take. Next to me, Jenny doesn't seem to be seeing much better. She squeezes my hand and leans into me.

There's one place in the church letting in more light than any other. Off to the side, a large beam looks to have fallen and wedged itself into the ground. When that log fell, that must have been when the whole thing came down. Now, it props up the rest of the ruins. It also put a hole in the wall, allowing a soft ray of evening sunlight to shine in.

Jenny and I go to it, carefully picking our way through weeds and beer cans and pieces of an old pew. It feels like the beam of sunlight is leading the way.

When we get there, my eyes slowly adjust, and I see this corner of the church more clearly. It's an alcove of some sort, just the sort of place Esther used to tell us to look for. The sort of place she thought the treasure would be buried. And with the rest of the church inaccessible and the sunbeam lighting our way . . . I don't know if it's Esther or fate or God, but every fiber of my being feels that we're in the right place. This is where Esther and Jenny's grandfather buried the treasure worth more than gold after losing his wife, shortly after childbirth. If the legend is true.

"Murray, look." Jenny points to my shoe, or at least that's what I think at first. Slowly, I realize she's pointing next to my shoe, at a small patch of dirt slightly different in color than that around it. And the biggest sign of them all, it's slightly raised, with a small mound—just a little bump—protruding from the flat ground.

"It can't be," I say, even though I think it must be.

I drop to my knees faster than I should and thump down hard. An intense pain shoots up my thighs and into my lower back, but it barely registers. I put the shovel into the earth and push the blade down.

The dirt gives easily and the shovel slides smoothly into the soil. It sticks a bit when I try to pry up the scoop of dirt, then it releases all at once, flicking a shower of old soil into my face. Jenny's soft giggle behind me sounds like the wood thrush in the weeping willow outside our home.

I wipe my eyes with my sleeve and continue digging, more carefully now. I make the hole wide enough for the case I've had in my mind's eye. Something like an old fishing tackle box, gray and rusted, with a locking latch at the side.

I'm envisioning that case, imagining sliding the key in and unlocking it, when I push my shovel down into the earth again . . . and it clinks against something hard.

It could be a rock, of course. But the soil here is so thick and black and soft that I don't think that's what I've hit. I lean over the hole, stretch my hand down deep, and use the shovel to brush away the black dirt that hides whatever is in the hole.

Jenny gasps and touches my shoulder. I simply stare in wonder. It was real. That's all I can think, over and over again. It was real. Esther was right. A small, metal case sits in the dirt just beneath where I kneel.

There really is a buried treasure.

But that's not all. There's an inscription on the top of the case. Letters scratched into the metal, as if by a rock or something with a sharp edge. I tilt my head to the side to see it better, then reach down and brush the remaining dirt aside so the letters become clear.

Jenny's breath catches behind me, but I barely hear it. Shock can do funny things to a person. In my case, my ears start ringing and my eyesight blurs. But not before I see exactly what Jenny sees. The letters carved into the top of the case spell a word.

Esther.

CHAPTER 12

1910

*S*he tore at the ground with her fingertips, breaking her finger-
nails and rubbing the skin raw. But once she broke through the
top crusty layer of dirt, the soil became soft, deep black, and thick.
Esther was able to slide her hand in, using it like a shovel to scoop
large amounts of soil out of the ground.

It didn't take long. It wasn't buried deep. And when she touched
the top of a metal case, she knew exactly what it was.

A treasure worth more than gold.

Esther didn't even try to control her breathing or her heart
rate. She frantically dug and tossed and shoved and pulled until,
finally, she had a small metal case lifted by the handle. She held it
up before her in the moonlight.

The adrenaline rush gave way to a peaceful, quiet moment
as Esther stared at the metal case. She tilted her head to the side,
examining decades of dirt now plastered against the old, gray
metal. Her head swooned and she fought a bout of dizziness.
When her vision swerved, she set the case on the ground beside
her and closed her eyes.

It didn't help. The dizziness continued. And then a cough burst
out of her without warning, followed by a torrent of hacking, gut-
tural sounds that produced a concerning amount of phlegm. Esther
turned away from the metal case and spit the phlegm away. But
then she returned, immediately, to the case. She knew she didn't
have much time.

With shaking hands, Esther took the key from the dirt floor, oriented it to the lock on the case, and tried to slide it in. The keyhole was blocked, packed tight with years of dirt. So Esther used the tip of the key to chip away at the keyhole, hoping to reopen the space.

It took several minutes, but eventually she managed to clean the keyhole of dirt. This time when she tried to slip the key into the hole, it fit perfectly.

Her heart jumped despite a throbbing in her head. She turned the key in the lock, which creaked and scratched with the rotation. When she put pressure on the lid, it swung open on its hinge.

Esther tilted the case until moonlight shone into it, revealing its contents. There was no genie in a bottle, no diamonds. When Esther reached into the case, she came out with two sheets of paper, folded in half, aged, and yellowed at the corners. She wiped her nose with her sleeve and stared at the papers as she unfolded them. Even though she knew she didn't have much time, even though she felt feverish and achy, she wouldn't rush. She wanted to savor this moment.

The first piece of paper was a note, written in looping cursive. The second appeared to be some sort of legal document. Esther forced herself to read the legal document first.

It was disappointing, as expected. On the top, the words "Land Title" were scrawled in official-looking print, and the text contained a list of building descriptions. Esther realized the list of buildings—the farmhouse, the tractor barn, the hayloft—matched the buildings on her family's farm. It listed the acreage and boundaries. It was nothing more than an old homestead claim for their property.

She set the document back into the case, hoping the other piece of paper, what appeared to be a note, would somehow contain something worth more than gold. A land title document certainly didn't.

Esther took a deep, rattling breath, and turned her attention to the note. With flowing, cursive script, it looked nothing like the legal document, thankfully. Esther adjusted the paper into the shifting moonlight, and read:

My dearest son Sean,

Only five days ago, you entered the world. In a few days more, I fear you will lose your mother. An infection, they say, will prevent me from seeing you grow. It will prevent you from ever knowing your own mother.

But in our brief time together, you have revealed to me something more valuable than one hundred years of life. Something worth more than gold. You have taught me this simple, life-altering truth about love:

Love is something we give.

I know this because of what I feel for you—an infant unable to consciously decide to receive and reciprocate my love. But that can't stop it. It can't be thwarted or denied. Because love—true and absolute love—is a thing that is given.

You may ask why this is so important—how could this simple understanding be worth more than gold?

Because of the power it has to change your life.

If love is what is given, you have complete control over how much love you have in your life. Because at any time— no matter the situation—you can choose to give it. If you want more love in your life, simply give more away. We have an infinite supply inside of us that can never run dry.

*I have so much more love to give you. But know
this—in the short time I was with you, I gave with all my
heart. I gave a love so pure and true that it revealed to me
a fundamental truth about the very nature of love. And
that is worth more than anything in the world. That is worth
more than gold.*

*With all the love I can give to you,
Mother*

Esther realized her hand was covering her heart as she finished reading the note. "So beautiful," she whispered to herself. She looked into the old rafters of the ruined church, imagining her grandmother as she wrote those words. What a wise woman she had been. What a staggering truth she had revealed.

We each control the amount of love we have in our lives. Because at any time, no matter what's going on, we can choose to give it.

Esther felt a smile creep over her face. She felt powerful, more powerful than she had ever felt before. Nothing could stop her if she decided to give her love. Not her crutches, not her illness. Nothing. She was free. She was in control. For the first time in her life, she had the power.

But how should she give her love? Who should she give it to?

An idea sprang to mind and Esther rifled through her pocket until she found her notepad and pencil. There in the moonlight, with her hands still shaking, her brow still sweating, and her head still throbbing, Esther wrote a letter of her own:

Dear Jenny and Murray,

*Surprise! I found the treasure! If you're reading this, you
have as well. Wasn't the adventure amazing? Wasn't the*

quest unforgettable? Wasn't the discovery exhilarating?
Those were the things I wanted to give you. That's why I put
this back and told you to find it for yourself. Because I love
you, and I wanted to give you that experience. Read the
letter. You'll understand. It really does contain something
worth more than gold.

Esther

Feeling satisfied, Esther folded her letter and set it inside the metal case, along with the legal document and the letter from her grandmother. As she latched it shut and locked it with the key, a small rock caught her attention.

How many times had she scratched her name into the wood in some hidden corner of their barn and hayloft? It always felt good to leave a little mark, to etch a little bit of herself into the surroundings, maybe to be discovered, maybe to be her own little secret. The uncertainty felt like possibility. It felt like a little bit of immortality.

So Esther took the rock and scratched her name deeply into the top of the case. Then she returned the case to the hole in the ground and slid all the dirt back on top of it. Now it would be there for Jenny and Murray to discover.

Esther giggled, imagining the excitement her sister and best friend would feel when they found it. But as she finished covering the case with dirt, a drop of blood slapped against the soil. When Esther wiped at her nose, the back of her hand came away with a streak of dark red.

The dizziness returned, this time stronger than before. As she stood, a violent cough exploded from her chest. It heaved her body so dramatically that she almost dropped the key, but she squeezed it into her palm just in time.

Fatigue overtook her, and she slid to the ground. As she lost consciousness on the dirt floor of the abandoned church, Esther smiled to herself. She had found it. She had discovered something worth more than gold.

And her final act had been to give her sister and her best friend an adventure, a source of excitement and happiness.

Her final act had been to give her love.

CHAPTER 13

1996

I stare at the open case, and the contents it has held secret. I take a deep, shaking breath.

"No wonder," I say. "You . . ."

I turn to Jenny, to ask her about what I've just found, but when I see her eyes, I know. The confusion is back, along with the fear. The cruel, cruel disease that's eating away at her brain has no soul, no conscience. It doesn't care what's happening. It only destroys, indiscriminately.

I put the key back in my pocket, grab the metal case, and stand ever so slowly. Jenny says nothing as I lead her toward the exit. She doesn't even look at the case.

As soon as we step outside, sunlight nearly blinds me. It was so dark inside that I didn't expect it to be bright out here. But the sun is on the horizon, shining right on us. We use the light to step carefully back toward the car.

Brooke is waiting for us. Her eyes widen with excitement when she sees the small metal case I'm carrying.

"Are you serious right now?" Brooke says.

But as soon as she sees Jenny, her excitement melts away. Brooke turns quiet and looks like she might cry. She sees exactly what I saw.

Although Jenny was there in body when I was reading the letters, she wasn't really there at all. She told me she would try to stay with me, and I know she did. She tried with everything she had. And today has been a wonderful day. People assume dementia is only a story of tragedy, but those people should have seen the beautiful day I had with the love of my life. There's been nothing tragic about it. This day has been a thing of beauty. Still, all things come to an end. That's true whether someone is living with dementia or not. And as we come to the end of this day, this blasted disease has finally won out. It was, of course, inevitable. "Take us home, please," I say to Brooke. "My love needs to rest."

The ride back toward Lemon Grove is strange.

I'm in a strange car. I hold a strange case that I never really believed existed. I'm with my wife, who I love more than life itself, but who sees me as a stranger.

Strange. The whole thing just feels so darned strange.

I knew things couldn't go on the same forever, never changing. All things change, constantly. It's simply the way the universe operates. It's the way our lives work.

Still, on those days when Jenny was declining, I was able to convince myself that she would be okay. That she wouldn't forget me, couldn't possibly.

Or maybe it's more accurate to say I couldn't allow myself to see the obvious truth—that Jenny will decline, and she will die. And I'll have to watch, helpless to stop it.

Jenny cries silently next to me. There's fear in her eyes. For me, that's the worst part. Confusion is terrible, and when she's frustrated it's hard to watch. But when the love of my life is afraid of me, well, that's a whole different level of hurt.

I bring out the key again and hold it in my hand for her to see. It worked last time. It brought her back. But she just crinkles her brow and looks at the key and the metal case without any understanding. Another tear slips down her beautiful cheek.

I hate what I must do. Hate it more than I've ever hated anything in my life. But the truth is, I can't take care of Jenny anymore, not even for the night. Reality is like Jenny's disease—it simply is what it is, whether I accept it or not.

"Brooke," I say. Even while I'm saying the words, my mind is racing with ways to avoid saying them, trying desperately to figure out if I should simply stop talking. But I don't stop. I say, "Can you please take us to Aspen Leaves Memory Care?"

Brooke looks back at me in the rearview mirror. There's no surprise in her expression, and I take that to mean I've made the right decision. With a sad smile, she nods and turns the car to the east.

Doc Keaton and I have talked about this. We have a plan.

Today has been magical, absolutely magical. Jenny and I went on a quest—I can hardly believe it. Almost two hundred years between us, and we went on a quest today. A treasure hunt. And we even found the treasure. Jenny hasn't enjoyed herself this much in months, maybe years.

But there have been two sides to this day, and as the last of the sunlight fades on the horizon, I can't ignore the other side. Over and over throughout the day, Jenny has disappeared into herself. Her mind has betrayed her. The confusion, the frustration, and mostly the fear. That's what I'm not able to solve. The best thing I can do for Jenny is get her into a safe, comfortable environment with people who are trained to care for her.

I have Brooke pull up to the first pay phone she sees. I dial the number Doc Keaton gave me for this situation, not knowing who the number will call. When Doc Keaton himself answers, I realize it's his home telephone.

"Hi, Doc," I say. When he asks how I'm doing, I say, "It's time."

There's a long silence on the other end of the line. That's the thing about Doc Keaton—he cares. We aren't just names and symptoms listed on a piece of paper, or even an interesting puzzle to be solved. When he hears me say it's time, his voice changes. I can tell he's holding back tears because I hear the same thing in my voice.

"You're doing the right thing," he finally says. "The hard thing, I know. But the right thing. Remember that, Murray. And remember that you'll be with her."

I can't think of anything to say to that. It should help, I know, to realize I'm doing right by Jenny. But it doesn't ease the aching in my chest one bit.

"I'll call ahead to Aspen Leaves," Doc Keaton says. "They'll be waiting for you. They'll have the room ready for Jenny."

"Thanks, Doc," I say. And because anything else I say will come out as nothing more than a cry, I hang up the phone and limp back to the waiting car.

I carry the metal case at my side as we walk through the automatic doors at the entrance to Aspen Leaves. I hold it by the handle, almost like a lunch pail, and hold Jenny's elbow with my other hand. Brooke is helping guide her other elbow like the new friend she is.

Jenny is quiet. It feels like she's given up, although I know that's not true. To give up you have to make that decision; Jenny isn't capable of that right now. It's more accurate to simply say she's calm. She's not fighting what's happening to her.

Doc Keaton was true to his word. They are ready for her. Not only that, the good doctor himself is here waiting for us. He must have left his home the moment he hung up the telephone.

He greets Jenny with a hug, which Jenny accepts with neither protest nor interest. "I'll lead you to your room," he says. "It's comfortable. I think you'll like it."

His presence is a godsend. A place as new and strange as this nursing home has all the characteristics of something that would set Jenny off, but she remains calm and silent as she follows Doc Keaton down the hallway.

The admission process is quick and painless, thanks to Doc Keaton. A nurse helps Jenny settle into a room with a bed by the window. She lays down on it and within moments she falls fast asleep.

Doc Keaton makes his way over to me and squeezes my shoulder. "She loves you," he says. "No matter what she might do or say, Jenny loves you. You know that, right?"

I wipe a tear from the corner of my eye and nod slowly. I don't want to think about why Doc thinks he needs to remind me of that.

"I'll leave you alone with her now, but I'm a phone call away if you need me. If you need anything, I'll be here in ten minutes. Okay, Murray? You understand?"

I mumble a "thank you." Doc Keaton pats my shoulder a few times, then leaves the room. I overhear him talking to a nurse in the hallway, asking them to take good care of us because we're some of his favorites.

He's a good man, Doc Keaton.

I hear his footsteps squeak down the hallway, and then he's gone. Brooke stands in the corner quietly, fidgeting with her hands like she isn't sure if she should be here. I motion to a chair in the corner and she sits.

"I don't know what to say," Brooke says as she watches Jenny sleep. "I just met her today, but I feel like I've known her forever." She laughs a little, but it's quiet. "Probably because I told her things I haven't told anyone else."

"She has that effect on people," I say. I move closer to the bed and cover Jenny's hand with mine, careful not to wake her. "She's always had a way of making everyone feel special. Trust me, I know. I've felt special for eighty years. Much more special than an old man like me deserves."

"I don't know about that," Brooke says. "You're pretty great, too."

I shake my head. "I'm just a man. But together . . . together we're great."

A frantic-sounding pair of footsteps in the hallway increases in volume as they get closer. Then Helen bursts around the corner and into the room, breathing heavily from running. She stops just past the threshold and takes in the scene before her.

"Brooke called me," she says to me, like she needs to explain her presence here. "Is everything okay?"

"As much as can be expected," I say. "Jenny just needed more care than I can give, so we came straight here."

Helen gazes at Jenny with a look of deep sympathy, but when she turns to Brooke, tension returns to her shoulders. It's the eggshells again. She knows how angry and scathing her daughter can be. She knows the trials Brooke has been through with her boyfriend and the lousy car and losing their home. And in her eyes, I see guilt that she has no business feeling. She's done her best, that much I'm sure of. She shouldn't have to add the accusations of her daughter to her list of worries.

For Brooke's part, she's staring at Jenny like she's trying to decipher a puzzle. Then, without a word, she slowly stands up, walks straight to her mother, and wraps her arms around her.

"I love you, Mom," she says. She keeps her mother pulled tightly in the hug while she talks, like she's worried she won't be able to continue if she has to make eye contact. "I don't blame you for anything that's happened. I know you've done everything you can. And I appreciate your optimism. I understand that it's for me." Finally, she pulls back and looks straight at her mother. "We'll get through this together. Because you're my mom, and I love you."

Through shimmering eyes, Helen looks at me like she's trying to figure out where this new, affectionate daughter came from. Like she thinks I've performed some sort of magic. And it does feel a little like a magic trick, how far Brooke has come.

But I had nothing to do with it. I was nothing more than a spectator. A member of the audience. The magician that made it happen was the lady now sleeping in bed—my beautiful, wise, sweet-hearted wife.

"My Murray," Jenny says from the bed a few minutes later. They're the two most beautiful words in the language.

Jenny sits up in bed and her eyes flick to Brooke and Helen, but there's no recognition there. She smiles sweetly toward them, but I can tell it's a smile of politeness, not familiarity. How strange it must feel to Brooke and Helen to be forgotten.

"Murray," Jenny says. "I've been thinking. Do you remember that buried treasure Esther talked about? We should go find that. Why didn't we ever find it?"

I swallow hard, unsure if showing Jenny the case will be helpful or harmful right now. I decide to give it a shot.

"Actually," I say. "I was thinking the same thing. I hope it's okay, but I already took the liberty of locating it and digging it up." I lift the case onto the bed next to Jenny and she gasps.

"This is it? This is the case?"

"It is. And what's more, it contains something worth more than gold, just like Esther said it would." I smile at Jenny, unsure of how much she remembers. "But of course," I say, "you already knew that, didn't you?"

I reach into the case and pull out the contents one by one. The legal deed to the homestead. The letter written by Jenny's

grandmother. The short note from Esther. And one more letter . . .
from Jenny to me.

"You've been keeping a secret," I say.

Jenny's coy smile makes me laugh out loud. Brooke gasps and
rushes forward to look at the note. It's simple and to the point:

My Dearest Murray,

*The enclosed letter contains a treasure worth more than
gold—an absolute truth about the nature of love. Read it if
you'd like, but for me it was nothing new. I already knew all
there is to know about love, because I learned it from you.*

*I discovered the treasure worth more than gold. Now
it's your turn.*

With all my love,
Jenny

I wave her note in the air between us. "No wonder you pushed
so hard for me to look for the treasure forty years ago. You had
gone and found it yourself, and then you did exactly what Esther
did and returned it to the earth." I chuckle in awe at this truly
amazing woman. "No wonder you told Brooke to make sure we
find it today. No wonder . . ."

I don't know how much Jenny understands or how much she
remembers, but she has a little grin on her beautiful lips.

"Will you read them to me again?" she says. "The notes from
my grandmother, and from Esther?"

"Of course," I say. I read the letter Jenny's grandmother wrote.
Then I read Esther's short note, which brings a tear to Jenny's eyes,
although the soft smile never leaves. "And this here's the note you
wrote," I say, holding it up in front of her.

"There's another page?" Jenny says, and she points at the paper still in the case.

"Just a legal document that was in there with it," I say. "The title for your family's land, near as I can tell. Looks like you still own 160 acres and all the buildings on it."

Jenny's eyes flick to the girl standing in the corner along with her mother. Our new friends. The friends Jenny doesn't remember. Or so I think.

"Brooke and Helen should have it," Jenny says.

The room is silent for several long seconds. It's an uncomfortable silence as Brooke, Helen, and I all try to figure out how to respond. Truth be told, it would make all the sense in the world to give Brooke and her mother this home. They have no home. Jenny and I only have one living relative, Chance, who already has more money than he knows what to do with. What an amazing, life-changing gift that would be.

But I can't help wondering if Jenny is capable of making that kind of decision right now. Two minutes ago, she didn't remember who Brooke and Helen were, and now she wants to hand over all the land that has been in her family for generations? I can't help but wonder if she'd be doing this if her mind was clear. Helen and Brooke's silence tells me they're thinking something similar.

And then this cursed disease that has caused Jenny so much confusion and pain and anxiety . . . this wretched sickness that has changed our lives so completely and will surely take Jenny's life . . . that very same disease provides us with a little miracle.

Jenny's gaze turns inward. She's confused, I can see. She can't remember what just happened, even though it just happened. Even though all the evidence is right in front of her. She simply can't remember.

And then she sees the case next to her on the bed. She sees the letter from her grandmother, the note from Esther, the one she wrote to me, and the legal document. The crinkle in her brow deepens.

I take her hand. "It's the buried treasure Esther talked about all those years ago, love." I don't ask if she remembers. I can tell she can't. So for the second time, I read the letter from her grandmother and the note from Esther. I show her the note in her own handwriting. And I explain again about the land title and how all the land and the buildings on it still belong to her. Then we all wait, holding our breath, to see what my wife says next.

Jenny looks straight at Brooke and Helen. "You have need for that old farmhouse more than we do. You two should have it. As your new home."

If I wasn't sure of Jenny's wishes the first time, there's no denying it now. That act of generosity? The decision, on the spot, to give what she has to someone who needs it more? That's just Jenny. And whether her memory is working right or not, my Jenny's still here with us.

Helen sees me nod my approval and clutches her chest like she can't believe what's happening. "You're not serious," she says, looking from me to Jenny and back again.

Brooke's eyes are wide, too, like she's terrified of misunderstanding. "You mean we have a home?"

"A big home," I say. "With more bedrooms than you can shake a stick at. And land as well, although the barns aren't in very good shape." I take the document and hold it out to Brooke. "You can keep this safe until we have a chance to transfer everything over to you and your mother."

Brooke accepts it tentatively, like she's not sure it's real. Then she squeezes me in a hug so tight I can barely breathe. With tears in her eyes, she goes to Jenny, leans down, and hugs her, too.

"Thank you," she says. "I can't thank you enough."

Jenny seems confused about being hugged. "Thank me for what?" she asks.

Brooke kisses her cheek and says, "Thank you for showing me that love is real after all."

Hours later, Brooke and Helen have left to spend the night in a homeless shelter. I offered our house for the one night since Chance and Olivia don't move in until the morning, but Helen refused. She didn't want to take the risk that Chance and Olivia might show up before she and Brooke left in the morning and besides, she said, what we'd already given was more than enough. They have a home, thanks to an act of love from a virtual stranger, who is also a good friend.

So now, as the day turns into night, it's just Jenny and me, in this strange room that isn't our home. Darkness has descended on what has been a beautiful, wondrous day. A day that gave us one last adventure, one last chance to feel fully alive.

I think back on that wish I made at my birthday party all those years ago. That very first wish—that Jenny Brennan might someday love me. Even the wild imagination of a thirteen-year-old boy could never have dreamed of what the next eighty-six years would hold. My wish has come true over and over, day after day after day. I know without a doubt that I truly am the luckiest man to have ever walked God's green earth.

The soft yellow light coming from the lamp beside Jenny's bed makes the room look like a sepia photograph from years ago.

Everything feels blurred around the edges. The vibrant color of the day has drained away.

There's a blanket that covers the room. I've felt it before, when my boys were sick. It's an essence of some sort, although I don't know how to describe it. A presence, I'd call it. It seeps into everything, forcing us into this moment. There is nothing else but here and now.

But then, when Jenny speaks, I realize that's only true for me. Jenny is somewhere else.

"Murray," she says. "We're out of garlic. I was going to make soup tonight. We need garlic."

No, my love, I think. *You're not thinking straight. You won't be making soup tonight. Not tonight, and not ever again.*

"Oh, you're right," I say. "I'll make sure to run out and get some. Don't you worry, love."

"The boys are coming over tonight with their wives, so I need to make sure everything is right. They don't visit as often as I'd like. I must get it right."

The boys are dead, love. Dead and buried. They won't be coming over for supper.

"I'm sure they'll love your soup, sweetheart. They always have."

"Where am I? Why isn't there anyone here to help me?"

You're in a nursing home, sweetie. Things will make sense again soon. Your confusion will be gone.

"I'm here. I'll help you. Would you like me to fluff your pillow?"

"I can't lie down now. The boys are coming. I have to get up and start dinner."

Stop this! Come back to me! Don't do this!

"I think the soup is ready, love. And I'll go get some bread. The boys won't be here for another hour. You have time to rest."

"Who are you? Do I know you?"

Do you know me? I'm your husband! I've been your partner through thick and thin for as long as I can remember. You're the love of my life, and I'm yours. No one has ever known a love like ours. I'm Murray!

"I'm Murray."

"Murray? Murray McBride?"

Yes, Murray McBride! And you're Jenny McBride. And two shall become one.

"That's right. I'm Murray McBride."

"It's nice to meet you, Murray McBride. I think you and I are going to be friends."

I lay my head on Jenny's chest and hold her hand for all it's worth. "That's right," I say. "We are. You can rest easy now, love, because you and I are going to be the very best of friends."

ONE MONTH LATER

There's a nice, comfortable bench I like to sit in. It's in the grassy courtyard at the hospital. It's completely enclosed in here, which suits me just fine. All the hubbub of the world can go on outside, but in this courtyard I can watch the pigeons strut and the squirrels play, all while the sun shines down and warms my skin.

Jenny is resting comfortably up in her room. Aspen Leaves was everything Doc Keaton said it would be, but after only a few weeks there she developed an infection. Her medical team made the decision to move her over here to the hospital. They said it's likely she'll stay here even after the infection clears, in their hospice care unit. It wasn't the original plan, but then again, how often does life go exactly as planned?

So I split my time now. I go home to sleep at night; I spend most waking hours by Jenny's side, and I'll continue to do that until . . . well, I don't allow myself to go beyond that. I'll continue to be by her side, and that's that.

But today I'm having a little excursion. My field trip is what Jenny called it in one of her clearer moments. She still has those. Very briefly, and only every other day or so.

That's why I'm outside now, rather than at Jenny's side. Because I'm waiting for my ride to arrive for my field trip. In the meantime, I watch the birds and animals and wonder why more people don't take advantage of this beautiful space.

Just as I think that, a group of three people walks by, but it looks like they're just passing through, making their way from one building to another. It's a nice-looking young mother with two kids walking behind her. One of the kids wears a baseball cap and

Little League jersey and the other kid pulls an oxygen tank, just like Jenny's using now.

"Come on, Jason, we're going to be late for your treatment," the mother says. The boy seems to ignore her. He seems fascinated by some sort of bug on the ground. Finally, the other kid grabs his arm and drags him toward his mother.

"Fine, Tiegan," the boy says. "I'm coming. Geez."

Since I'm watching the group walk into the hospital, I don't notice Brooke and Helen until they're standing right next to me. "Well, hello," I say.

I stand and extend my hand toward Brooke because it's been a while since I've seen her and her mother. But she ignores it and leans in for a hug. I pat her back lightly and oblige Helen with an embrace as well. Never have been big on hugs and all that, but I guess they're friends now. After all we've been through together.

"Are you ready?" Helen says.

I glance up at the third floor, where Jenny's currently sleeping. "Ready as I'll ever be," I say. "You'll have me back for dinner, right? Jenny's expecting me."

The truth is, I'm not sure Jenny would notice if I wasn't there, but that makes no difference to me. Love is about what you give, and I plan to give that woman all the love I have, right until the last.

"No problem," Helen says. "We're parked this way."

She leads me to the same old Ford—still without a second gear, it turns out—and drives us out of town and toward their new farmhouse. Just before we turn onto the gravel driveway, something catches my eye and I press my nose right up against the window.

"Did you see that?" I say. "Oh my Good Lord and Savior. It was beautiful! Astonishing!"

"What? What is it?" Brooke asks. She's a bit startled at my excitement.

I turn in my seat as much as I can, craning my neck to watch it drive away. "A minivan!"

"You have got to be kidding me," Brooke says. "All that for a minivan?"

"Yeah," Helen says. "He's got a thing about minivans." The two of them have a nice little laugh together.

I watch the minivan slide down the road, all smooth and sleek. I keep envisioning the engineering marvel even after it's out of sight. Those really are something, minivans.

Soon, we get to the long gravel driveway, so I force my focus onto the farmhouse. Even from a distance, I can see they've done wonderful things with it.

"Will you look at that," I say. "You've got it shining like a new penny."

And it's true. When we arrive, I step out of the car and take it all in. There are windows now, although they look used, and the sills have a fresh coat of paint. The old stones seem to have been washed clean, and daisies grow in a little garden just outside the front door.

"It's nothing special, since we don't have any money to fix it up," Helen says. "But with a few rags, a little bit of paint the hardware store was going to throw out, and some elbow grease, I'd say we've made it livable."

"The plumbing still works?" I ask. I remember Jenny's family putting that in shortly after we were married, and it barely worked then.

"It's a bit temperamental, but we'll make do," Helen says. "The bigger scare was just after we moved in when we realized there were probably back-taxes to pay. Of course, we had no idea how we'd come up with money for that. Did you know about that?"

"Know about what?"

"The taxes. Jenny never told you?"

"I'm afraid I don't follow. Jenny was supposed to tell me something about taxes?"

Helen and Brooke exchange a look. "Apparently, when Jenny found the treasure all those years ago, she started paying the taxes on the property. It's completely up to date. We don't owe anything. It turns out, we now own this free and clear. Thanks to you and Jenny, we have a home."

"Although—" Brooke says. But before she can say more, her mother shushes her.

They communicate in silence for a few moments while I wait for someone to explain what all the silent communication is about.

"Although what?" I finally say.

"Well," Helen says. She wrings her hands like they're dishrags. "It's just that . . ."

"My aunt in Iowa is sick," Brooke says. "If we sold this place, we could buy a small house near her and help take care of her."

"We wouldn't do that," Helen says quickly. "To sell such an amazing, thoughtful gift. I wouldn't dream of it."

"Why not?" I say. "It's yours now. You can do what you want with it."

"But," Helen says. "Well . . . really? I mean, you wouldn't consider that . . . thoughtless of us? Or ungrateful?"

"Why would I consider it ungrateful? Jenny and I gave you this property because we wanted to help you. If the best way to help is to sell it and use the money to be near family, then that's what you should do."

"You wouldn't mind?" Helen says. "Truly?"

"Only thing I mind is losing my friends. But that's how life goes, as they say. Things change." I feel a little something in my eyes, so I pretend to scratch at them. "Just don't ask me to help move you out, because I'm not interested."

I try to be stern when I say that last part, but Helen doesn't buy it. She comes right up to me and gives me another hug.

"Yes, well," I say, because I'm not big on getting all mushy. "Let's see the inside, shall we?"

The two of them share a little smile, laughing at the old man. But to tell the truth, it doesn't bother me a bit. These here are my friends, even if they do move away. And if my wife has taught me anything, it's that sometimes friends like to give friends a bit of a hard time, maybe even laugh at each other. It's just another way to show love.

There are still a few signs of construction laying around—a hammer left on the table and a can of paint on the counter—but it feels as cozy as any home I've been in. And right there on the dining room table, I see the old copy of *Little Women*.

Brooke sees me looking at it and picks it up. She flips through the pages, as if she's enjoying the scent of the old paper. "We're almost done," she says. "Just a few chapters to go."

"We?" I say.

Brooke's cheeks go a bit red. "I asked my mom to read it to me. Each night, just before bed, we curl up by the fireplace and she reads a chapter or two."

"Well, how do you like that?" I say. "That's wonderful to hear. A good, close relationship with your mother? Now that's worth something in my book."

Brooke gives her mother a sweet smile, one I couldn't imagine coming from the kid I met just one month ago. "I agree," she says. "I might even say it's a treasure worth more than gold."

The End

ACKNOWLEDGMENTS

When I started writing this story, it had been more than two years since I had written a word of fiction. Maybe that's why it was so difficult to write. And maybe that's why I feel like I had more help with this book than any of my others.

I rely heavily on my "tribe." The feedback they provide guides each subsequent draft. It's enormously beneficial to me as an author, but it asks a lot of those who help. So the least I can do is acknowledge their generosity:

David Sharp: You've been steadfast and reliable through several of my books. It doesn't hurt that you're one of the better writers I know and always willing to share your genius ideas with me. If only you could write my books for me, I'm convinced they would be much better.

Sheala Henke: Like David, you've been with me since my original writers' group, which met at a Northern Colorado Writers' Conference more years ago than I care to admit. Like clockwork, I can always rely on you to go through my pages before our next meeting and provide beneficial feedback. Your beautiful, lyrical style is a nice balance to my "A-to-B" method of writing.

Ronda Simmons: You round out my current critique group. For several years, your encouragement and support have been a buoy in times of frustration. Thank you for loving Murray (almost) as much as I do.

Mary Ellen Bramwell: You were a surprise star on this project. When Black Rose Writing sent you my manuscript for editing, I didn't expect much. Boy, was I wrong. If it weren't for your attention to detail and your useful guidance, this story would never have come together. I'm grateful for your honesty and skill. And I apologize for all the times I didn't take your advice on commas. I know I have a problem.

Kim Catanzarite: I found you on Reedsy a few manuscripts ago and have never looked back. You bring a level of professionalism to your editing that I undoubtedly need.

I also received help from my family.

To my wife, Anne: It's difficult to show you my early drafts because I want so desperately to impress you. (You remember how Murray still wants to impress Jenny after eighty years together? This is where it comes from.) But without your keen eye and gentle honesty, my stories would be so scattered as to be unreadable.

My daughter Lily: You contributed much to this story. In addition to your consultation on the *Little Women* aspect, we talked through ideas in coffee shops, and you gave me endless encouragement.

My daughter Maya: Thank you for inspiring me to be my best self. Book sales and reviews from strangers are wonderful, but when you proudly put my books on the bookshelf in your dorm room, it made me feel like a real author.

To my sister, Julie: This is way overdue. Although you haven't been a part of any of my published books, it was you who suffered through years and years of terribly written manuscripts as I tried to learn the craft of writing fiction. I can't imagine how difficult it must have been to slog through those early works . . . and then somehow give constructive feedback while still finding encouraging things to say. But doing so was a gift (which you gave for free). Without that gift, I never would have had anything published. I guess this thank-you is better late than never.

Cyndy Luzinski, with Dementia Together: You've been an excellent resource about the realities of dementia. Any failures or inaccuracies in this story were entirely despite your help. I really did try to make it "not just another tragedy."

Tim Kathka: You generously met me at a coffee shop to tell me about your beautiful wife, Lela. You told me you wanted to help people provide better care for their loved ones living with dementia. I think Lela would be very proud of what you're doing. I wish I could have met her. And I'm glad the movie star's sister was too young for you!

My original publisher, Reagan Rothe at Black Rose Writing: You deserve a huge thank-you for bringing Murray McBride into the world. When everyone else said no, you said yes. And the investments you've made in giving him a wider audience have truly changed my life. I'll be forever grateful.

To the team at Union Square & Co, I could write for hours and never succeed in expressing my gratitude.

Barbara Berger, executive editor: The day I received your email will go down as one of the most exciting and transformative of my life. You have made my dreams for Murray come true—for readers to be able to walk into a bookstore and find him on the shelves. Your professional guidance is appreciated more than I could possibly say. You've been my partner on this project and I hope we get a chance to do it all again.

To the rest of the team at Union Square & Co. that worked on this project, I didn't have as much contact with you, but I appreciate your contributions every bit as much.

Alison Skrabek, project editor. Patrick Sullivan, cover designer and art director. Erik Jacobsen, cover design production. Richard Hazelton, interior designer. Kevin Ullrich, creative operations director. Sandy Norman, production manager. Hayley Joswiak, copyeditor. You all are my unsung heroes and heroines. Thank you for your diligence and professionalism. I wish I knew how to give you the recognition you deserve.

And finally, thanks as always to you, the reader. It still surprises me that there are people out there who enjoy and connect with the stories I write. I'm grateful you decided to pick this one up. I hope you enjoyed it.

BOOK CLUB QUESTIONS FOR DISCUSSION

1. Living with dementia is a main theme of this story. Have you known anyone who has had dementia? What was that experience like? Did the story seem accurate?

2. This is the first Murray McBride story with multiple time frames woven throughout the story. Did that structure work for you? Did the two storylines connect in a meaningful way?

3. What did you think of the friendship between Murray, Jenny, and Esther? Did you ever have a similar friendship? How did their age make their search for the buried treasure more poignant?

4. A theme of the story is that love is something that is given. Do you agree with that? Can love still be real if there is no one to receive it? Or if it is rejected? What did you think about the sense of control Esther felt from that realization?

5. Esther risked her life in her attempt to find the buried treasure. Did this make sense, considering her situation? Why or why not?

6. What did you think about the ways Murray tried to help Jenny as she struggled with dementia? Was there more he should have done, or less?

7. When we first met Brooke, she was disillusioned with love. By the end of the story, she was more optimistic. Have you ever experienced any of the feelings she had? What caused them, and how did those experiences change the way you think about relationships?

8. When Brooke hears about Esther's death, she gets angry with Murray and Jenny for never finishing the quest. Does this response make sense? What obligation do we have to the wishes of those we love after they're gone?

9. At the end of the story, Brooke says that she and her mother read *Little Women* to each other. Have you ever read to another person? Why is it such an intimate, relationship-building thing?

10. Throughout this three-book series, Murray has had three wishes: that Jason's five wishes come true (*The Five Wishes of Mr. Murray McBride*), that Jason finds meaning by finding another to help (*The Final Wish of Mr. Murray McBride*), and that Jenny might someday love him (*The First Wish of Mr. Murray McBride*). Which of these was most emotionally powerful? Which was most meaningful to you?

Please check out books one and two
of the Murray McBride trilogy for your next great read!

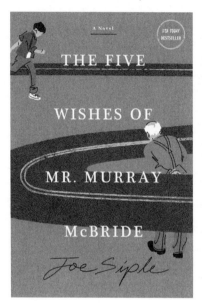 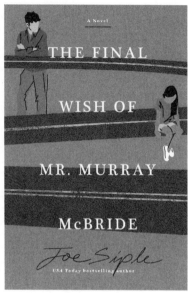

PRAISE FOR *THE FIVE WISHES OF MR. MURRAY McBRIDE*:

2018 Maxy Award "Book of the Year"
"A sick young boy and an elderly man looking for
something to live for form a deep bond in this debut
novel. . . . A sweet . . . tale of human connection."
—*Kirkus Reviews*

"An emotional story that will leave readers meditating
on the life-saving magic of kindness."
—*IndieReader*